Home of the Shadicans

Heroes of Balyita

Home of the Shadicans

JOSIAH MASTRIANO

RESOURCE *Publications* · Eugene, Oregon

HOME OF THE SHADICANS

Resource Publications
An Imprint of Wipf and Stock Publishers
199 W. 8th Ave., Suite 3
Eugene, OR 97401

www.wipfandstock.com

PAPERBACK ISBN: 978-1-7252-6561-5
HARDCOVER ISBN: 978-1-7252-6545-5
EBOOK ISBN: 978-1-7252-6562-2

Manufactured in the U.S.A.   05/22/20

Contents

Take note, dear reader, of the indexes provided for your convenience. I believe to tell this story correctly that I must use odd terms along with a plethora of characters. Feel free to refer to the provided indexes regularly if you are confused by any term or if you lose track of which character is whom.

Also take note that the year of each chapter is including in the heading, and is indicated by the abbreviation B.Y. This abbreviation stands for "Balyita Year," and then is followed by what year the events of the chapter take place.

Introduction

"Every story begins somewhere."
—Dusty

"Let me tell you a story.

A story filled with battles, adventure, friendship, and love. A story of good versus evil. And a story I was a part of.

This is a map of the Northern Kingdoms of Balyita (pronounced: Ball-Yita). Since the fall of creation, all of Balyita has been consumed with great turmoil, wars, and evil. Wars fought for land, money, dominion, or simply to oppress those who are different. Some humans have even tried to exterminate my kind, but to no avail. Abada is strong and loving; He provided a leader for us in that dark hour, and not only that, but also a safe haven for us to take shelter in. But, I digress. That is not the story you are here for today.

However, as you will soon see, we are not the only ones that evil has prompted men to try and annihilate. The denac are always trying to crush any beacon of light by swaying weak and selfish men to do their bidding. The biggest of the lights the denac wish to crush is the Aceic Order. For over a millennia, the Aceic Order has existed in the Northern Kingdoms as a unique entity; an organization that cares for the good of all creation and not selfish gain; keeping all of the surrounding King-doms in check. The Aceic Order has done so with Abada's help, and with the ability they have to control various elements. The ability to control a component of Balyita is a rare gift; only a tiny fraction of human kind receive it, and even fewer ever realize that they have the gift. Having the

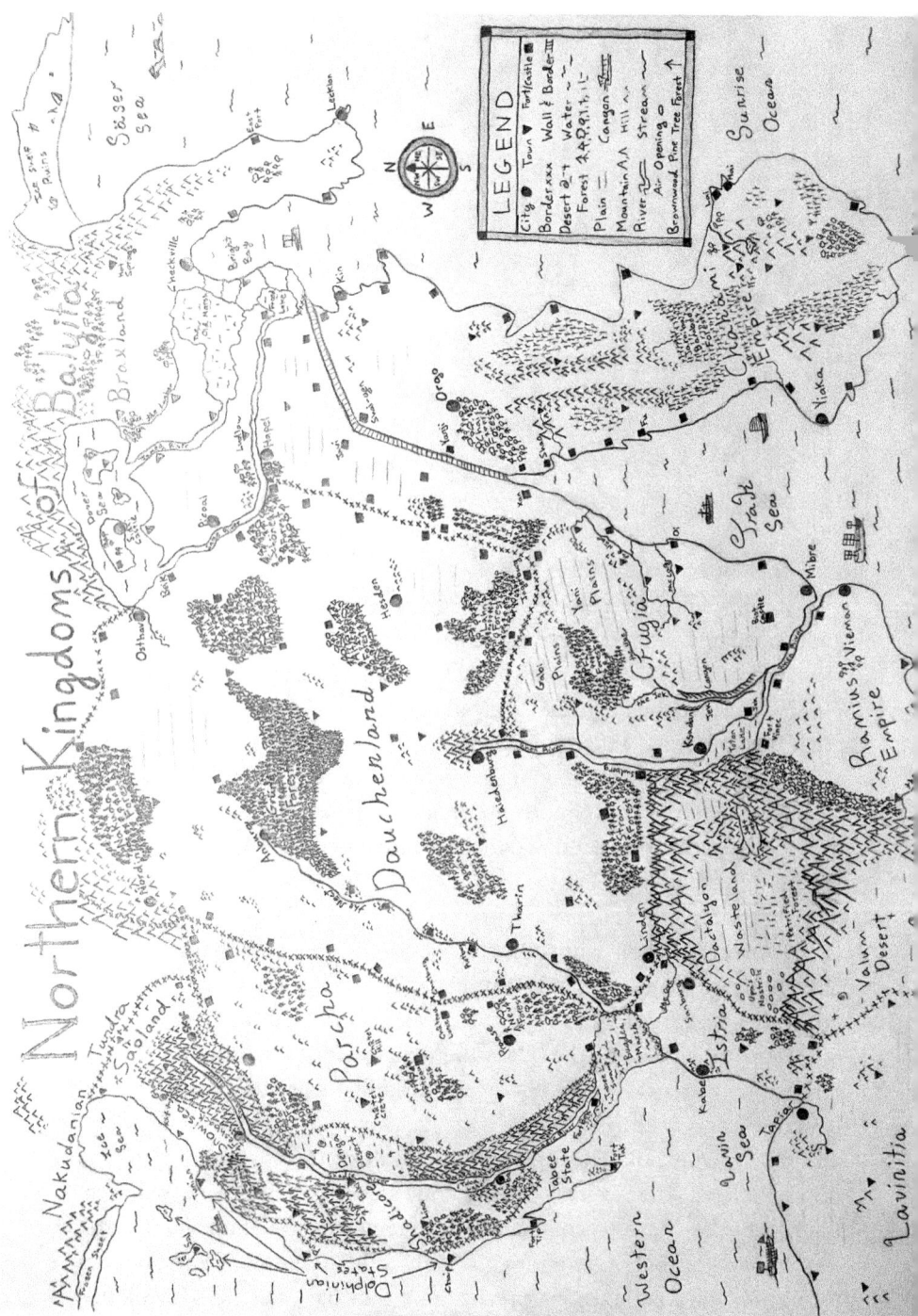

ability to control an element is the foremost requirement for being offered the privilege of joining the Aceic Order. Any man or woman gifted with this special skill will have at least one ability; whether that be the ability to control fire, sound, rock, crystals that lie beneath Balyita's surface, or something else. My tribe is also gifted in a similar way; every one of us is given the honor of carrying the ability to control and direct light, though few of us master it these days. Sometimes we are gifted with the ability to control something beyond light, but this is a rare occurrence. The ability to control light has saved my tribe many times in years past by allowing us to hide from those who sought to exterminate us. Because we are different and nearly half the size of the humans, they often enjoy trying to subjugate or destroy us. So as you can see, even though the Aceic Order has tried to be a light to the nations, evil is still rampant.

Balyita is now in its fourth millennia, and is far from utopia. An evil presence looms over the Aceic Order's headquarters in Haiedenburg; Dauchenland's capitol. Dauchenland is the largest of the Northern Kingdoms. Dauchenland's ruler, King Lustan, otherwise known as the "King of Gold," has become terribly ill. With no heir of his own, the king's nephew Kafahr stands ready to take the throne. Most of the people are overjoyed at the idea of Kafahr coming to the throne; as Kafahr promises prosperity and to take care of the common folk, something Lustan has never done. However, members of the Aceic Order's council are concerned; Kafahr has convinced the commoners that the Aces have failed the people by allowing taxation and oppression to reign. While it was true the Aceic Order had become frail over the last fifty years, Kafahr's claims were greatly exaggerated. The Order had tried several espionage and sabotage missions to put a halt to various evil actions that king Lustan had engaged in; but with little success. The Aceic Order could only do so much to fight oppression without an all-out war, and this action was out of the question. A surprising decline had been occurring in the recruitment of new element controllers in the last forty years, resulting in a weakening of the Aceic Order's numbers. Rumors had been circulated through Dauchenland that figures resembling ghosts had been killing ace children. While it was true that many children who could control elements turned up dead or missing shortly after discovering their new ability, and even though this often happened under suspicious circumstances, the Aceic Order could find no solid evidence to support the rumors. And with King Lustan being so consumed in riches and gold, he could hardly be bothered to draw his attention to conspiracy theories. However, the Aceic Council's head member, Maskima, couldn't help but wonder in the back of his mind if Kafahr and his now deceased father, Kusan, were somehow behind these disappearances."

Chapter 1

A Nail in the Coffin
B.Y. 4005

"One should know when to fight, and when to run."
—Shadican Proverb

Ottokar awoke with a start to the sound of bells ringing in the distance. His stone room in the tower was still dark. Ottokar laid in bed for a moment with his sleeping cloak wrapped tightly around him, and then he groggily got up and walked over to his window in the cool, stony room. He hated the cold. As he arrived at the window, a gust of icy early autumn wind greeted him. He had had enough of this miserable weather. Being a fire ace, he used his hand to create a small fire ball for warmth. The weak ball of fire hovered just above his hand; close enough to begin warming him, but not enough to burn him. He felt better almost instantly.

"Finally, now I'm warm enough to think" he muttered to himself.

He then gazed out of the window of the Aceic Order's tower. The nearly full moon was still shimmering in the night along with the twinkling stars, forming beautiful constellations Ottokar knew all too well. After gazing at the position of the moon for a moment, he guessed that it was still several hours until dawn. He then directed his attention down the mountain toward Haiedenburg. Even from this distance, the city looked enormous; which is what one would expect from the center of the largest empire in the known world. It was mostly dark, but Ottokar could see miniscule flickers of fire in the city from the lamp posts lighting the streets. Beyond that, he could make out little.

Ottokar then remembered the reason he had stirred from his sleep; the bells. The ringing was coming from Haiedenburg. The whole time he had been awake, they had not ceased ringing.

"They have to be the bells from the King's Church down in Haiedenburg." Ottokar thought aloud.

Those were indeed the only bells loud enough to be heard up in the mountains where Ottokar was. If the bells were ringing for this long at this hour of the night it could only mean one of four things: either Haiedenburg had an enemy advancing towards its gates, the city was on fire, a member of royalty had been born, or a member of royalty had died. Ottokar immediately knew that it was the last of these options; King Lustan was dead.

Suddenly Ottokar was wide awake. He extinguished the fire ball that was in front of him. As he thought about the dangerously uncertain future, he felt a shiver run down his spine.

Ottokar heard a knock at his wooden door, and heard the hinges creek behind him. He turned and saw the Aceic Head, Maskima, stick his head through the half open door.

"Good, you're awake." Maskima said, and entered the room. His silver hair and beard shimmered in the dark night.

"How could I not be, sir?" Ottokar replied to his mentor.

In an attempt to lighten the concern they both felt, Maskima retorted, "That's fair, those bells are so loud I'll bet the four corners of the empire can hear it."

Ottokar gave a half smile to his friend who was now standing next to him at the window. Even Maskima, who had deep wrinkles on his face from smiling so much in his life, was somber.

Maskima kept himself in good shape for being the oldest member of the Aceic Order; he was quite a formidable opponent on the battlefield. Ottokar, who was now thirty-eight years of old, had looked up to Maskima ever since he joined the Aceic Order at the age of; which was the usual age an Aceic soldier began his or her training.

"I don't know what this means for us." Maskima said, as he gazed off towards the city.

"Me either."

Maskima started stroking his long beard as he looked off towards Haiedenburg.

"Sir, I know this is not the best time, but I would like to be able to go home for a couple hours and make arrangements to get my wife, Retta, and son, Maxstrom, to safety. I thought I would have more time to get them out of Dauchenland than this. . ."

Maskima stopped stroking his beard and turned to look at Ottokar.

"Of course. If we do not take care of our own families, why are we even bothering to protect this world? Take the time you need, but don't delay. I have a feeling that this is going to be a long day."

"Yes sir, thank you. I also will need to make some arrangements for that young fire ace I am supposed to meet next week."

"Oh, right, I forgot you were bringing Barz in earlier than we usually do. We most certainly need to keep that quiet; now more than ever."

There was another creek at the door. Ottokar and Maskima both turned and saw a child's figure in the doorway.

"Dad, what's going on?" Maxstrom inquired as he groggily rubbed his eyes.

"Oh hey, Max, glad you're up. The king just died."

"Oh." Maxstrom responded. Maxstrom, who was only eight years old, was unsure of what to make of this news.

Ottokar walked over to Maxstrom, kneeled to his height, and put his hand on Maxstrom's shoulder.

"Tell you what, Max. We are going to have to cut your stay at the tower short this time. I need to take you back into Haiedenburg and drop you off with mom."

"But I thought I could stay for the rest of your duty station! I was looking forward to more hand-to-hand combat lessons tomorrow." Maxstrom complained.

"That was the plan, but plans change. I am sorry, Max. Now go get your things."

"Okay." Maxstrom responded dejectedly and walked to the stairs.

Ottokar stood up and walked back over to the window. Maskima's gaze toward Haiedenburg had not faltered for the duration of Ottokar and Maxstrom's conversation.

"Did you not have the heart to tell him he's going to be leaving Dauchenland?" Maskima inquired.

"No. He'll figure it out soon enough."

"How old is your son, Ottokar?"

"He turned eight this past summer."

"And was there some story to how he got his name? I can't remember."

"There is. It was prophesied before he was born that he would be able to control water, like you can, but of course we kept that quiet because of all the ace children that were disappearing and ending up dead."

"Ah, right, now I remember. And that's why you named him Maxstrom?"

"Aye, even though we've only seen him successfully control fire. He just hasn't figured out how to control water yet."

"So you think he's a double ace?"

4

"We do. But in the meantime, I've already begun to show him some tricks to hone his fire ability. One thing at a time; no need to push him too hard."

"That's wonderful! I am sure he'll make a fine Aceic soldier, if he so chooses."

Ottokar simply nodded to his friend's reply. He could detect the uncertainty in Maskima's voice. He seemed worried about the future, and rightfully so. The Aceic Order had grown so weak and ineffective over the last half decade that the people of the Northern Kingdoms felt that Aces had failed them, especially the people of Dauchenland. Beyond that, with all the anti-Aceic propaganda that had been spreading, all Kafahr had to do was look at the Aces wrong and the people would undoubtedly rise up against the Aceic Council. And what were the Aces supposed to do if the people they were assigned to protect turned against them?

"How is your son doing, Maskima?" Ottokar inquired, realizing he was being rude.

"Matakar is doing alright. He's stationed near the southern border of Dauchenland in the small town of Sudberg."

"That is not too far away; just past the Strom Forest. But I've heard there is good deal of unrest in the south."

"Indeed. He's already had to deal with several protests against his presence." Maskima informed, crossing his arms.

"I'm ready, dad." A voice from behind them declared.

Ottokar turned to see Maxstrom in the doorway with his backpack on.

"Alright, can you head down to the stables and get our horses ready?"

"Sure." Maxstrom responded as he let out a yawn. "Are you sure we couldn't stay until morning?"

"I'm sure; we have to go now. Go ahead down, I'll be there shortly."

Maxstrom turned and walked down the steps.

"I should probably head down to the Citadel soon and make sure of what's really going on." Maskima muttered to himself.

"Well I will see you down there then!" Ottokar responded as he grabbed his bag, which was always packed, and walked to the door.

"Citizens of Haiedenburg, your King is dead!" Kafahr cried passionately from the podium at the gate to the citadel. "And as the only living relative of the former king, I stand to be crowned!"

A cheer went up from the enormous audience flooding the streets. A hoard of people had gathered to hear the news, even at this early hour.

"Although my uncle will be missed, his policies and greed will not! Good people of Haiedenburg, and all of Dauchenland, this day marks the beginning of your freedom!"

Again the audience cheered.

"The wealth that was wrongfully stolen from you will be returned! I will have the useless gold lining of the Citadel stripped, and it will be returned to those whom it was stolen from! Not only that, but you can be sure that recompense will fall on those who stood silent in this former era of oppression!

"Do not forgot, oh Dauchenland, how I stopped the king from turning you into his slaves to dig holes in the middle of your farm fields in a futile search for gold! And do not forget the time I boldly opposed my uncle when he wished to enact a muster of children to bolster his army! And certainly do not forget the time I, and only I, stepped in to stop my foolish uncle from declaring war on Crugia, our ally for over seven hundred years! My uncle was consumed with a quest to own all the gold he could, regardless of who that hurt, and who he had to take the gold from. But that will not be my agenda as king! I will be here for you, the people! Here to return your wealth to you, here to give you better living conditions, and here to end the oppression of lords on their servants!"

The audience went wild. Cries of "Thank you!" and "About time!" were heard throughout the crowd.

"Oh, and I will be lowering Lustan's insanely high tax as well."

More applause ensued.

"My coronation will be at noon. Although I would love for all of my people, the people of Dauchenland, to attend; the Citadel is unfortunately only so large. One would think if it was big enough to fit my uncle's ego for the last fifty years, then it should certainly be large enough to fit all the of the Northern Kingdoms inside—but alas, this is not the case."

Laughter erupted from the audience.

"So, my good people. Until then, I beseech you to return to your homes, and I declare tomorrow a national holiday; only food locations are to remain open for celebration. I fare thee well until the morrow!"

Maskima, using his ability to control sound, had amplified Kafahr's speech from outside the city so he could listen in. He was still riding on the path leading from the Aceic Tower in the mountains down to Haiedenburg, and he wanted to be sure that he didn't missing anything.

"You can be sure that recompense will fall on those who stood silent in this former era of oppression" Maskima said aloud to himself, quoting from Kafahr's speech. "Why do I feel like that was directed at the Aceic Order?"

Maskima continued riding down the steep path towards Haiedenburg. It was a clear night, and he looked down towards the bridge he would have to cross to enter Haiedenburg. He could just barely make out Ottokar and Maxstrom crossing the bridge and approaching the gatehouse with its iconic twin white towers.

"Good luck, my student." Maskima whispered, even though he knew Ottokar wouldn't hear.

As Maskima neared the end of the steep and windy decline from the mountain, he heard some rustling from the bushes near the base of the path. As he approached, the rustling stopped. The foliage was fairly dense, and he wondered if the noise could be from a deer. He stopped for a moment and gazed into the bushes, trying to see if he could identify the creature. All of the sudden he heard a high pitched metallic sound and felt a stinging pain in his left shoulder. He fell off of his horse and cracked his right wrist onto the ground. He cried out in pain, and his horse bolted.

Maskima quickly recovered his senses, and saw two figures with dark cloaks and with white ghostly masks step out from the foliage. They both held some odd looking sticks with metal tubes at the end.

"The ghosts" Maskima thought to himself. Several of the disappearances of ace children, children who could control elements, that he had investigated over the last couple years had included reports of children being kidnapped or killed by pale ghosts covered in black cloaks.

One of the ghosts pointed his stick at Maskima, and he saw that the metallic tube was hollow. Maskima realized that the weapon the ghosts were holding launched some kind of projectile, which also explained the pain he felt; he had been shot. As the ghost got ready to fire the weapon, Maskima knew that unless he acted now, this moment would be his last. He clenched his left fist and shot a high pitched sound blast at the ghosts. Immediately both of them threw their weapons down and clenched their heads, trying to block out the sound. Maskima then used his ability to control water to collect some of the moisture from the damp air, threw it at the weapon that was just aimed at him, froze the water around the weapon, and then pulled it to his hand. After quickly melting the ice, he aimed the stick at one of the ghosts and fired the weapon. There was another loud metallic sound, and the ghost collapsed to the ground, limp.

"Glad to see you can die." Maskima declared with a smirk.

The remaining ghost made no reply. Maskima then aimed the gun at the second ghost and pulled the trigger; but nothing happened. The weapon apparently only shot one projectile at a time, so Maskima tossed it aside.

Both Maskima and the ghost stared at each other, and then began circling one another. Maskima rapidly clenched his left fist and launched a concentrated sound blast. But this time, the ghost was ready. He immediately threw himself into a cartwheel and dodged the focused blast. Now standing on the higher ground, the ghost jumped towards Maskima, feet first. Maskima saw the dropkick coming, but could only put both of his hands in front of his face to shield against the strike. He went flying back, and hit the rocky ground with a thud. Maskima cried in pain, both from the injury to his back and from the kick to his broken right wrist. The ghost was immediately back on his feet, and jumped towards Maskima again. Maskima had to act quickly. He clenched his fist and launched another sound blast. Because the ghost was in the air, he could not dodge this attack, and the sound blast threw him to the side; the ghost collapsed next to Maskima.

8

Maskima looked up and saw that the sound attack he had just launched had knocked some of the rocks on the path above loose, and now several small boulders were falling towards both him and the ghost. Maskima rolled to his left to avoid the avalanche; and just in time, because one of the boulders impacted right where Maskima had been laying. The ghost, just recovering from being disoriented by the sound blast, tried to stand up and evade the impending doom. But it was too late, because another smaller rock, about the size of a fist, came flying down and hit the ghost in the side of the head. The ghost fell to the ground, motionless. After the small avalanche had passed, Maskima ran over to see if the ghost was alive so he could question him. He rolled the ghost over onto his back, pulled back the hood, and then realized that the ghostly white face was actually a mask. Maskima ripped off the mask and checked to see if the 'ghost' had a pulse, but there was none. He then looked at the face of the man to see if he recognized him, but he did not.

Just then Maskima heard his name yelled from above. He whirled around and aimed his fist at the noise, ready to launch a sound blast at any impending threat. But to his relief, it was two of his fellow council members, Javon and Alenard, descending from the Aceic tower in the mountains.

"I must say, I am quite glad to see both of you." Maskima declared as they both ran down the path.

"Are you alright?" Javon yelled as he neared Maskima.

"Well, I'm not dead."

"You're bleeding!" Alenard said as they both arrived to Maskima's location. "And that wrist doesn't look too good either."

"What happened? Who were these cloaked figures?" Javon asked.

"I was attacked; ambushed. I think that these are some of the ghosts we have been hearing reports about."

"You mean in the kidnapping of gifted children?" Alenard questioned. "That would actually make sense. . ."

Javon pulled out his short sword, tore off a piece of his cloak, and then started to wrap it around Maskima's shoulder to stop the bleeding.

"I think there might be something in there." Maskima informed.

"What?" Javon questioned, halting his work.

"Those sticks with the metal tubes? They launch some sort of projectile, and I got hit by one of them. It sounded like it was powered by a spring or something."

Alenard walked over to one of the sticks and picked it up. After looking at it for a minute, he set it down and went over to one of the dead ghosts, and searched him.

"Aha!" Alenard exclaimed.

"What? What did you find?" Maskima inquired.

Alenard pulled a large pouch off of the belt of the ghost and brought it over. "I think you got shot with one of these."

Maskima took the pouch with his left hand and opened it. Inside were oddly shaped metallic and rock cylinders that came to a point. They were just a little larger than the width of Maskima's thumb, and twice as long.

"They look like some type of large and heavy dart. Huh, it also seems like some of these are made of stone. Javon, could you see if the one in my shoulder is too, and if so, pull it out?"

"I can try." Javon said, who could control stone. He then stood up in front of Maskima, who was sitting on the ground, and placed his right hand a couple of inches away from Maskima's left shoulder. He then clenched his hand into a fist and pulled his arm back slightly. Maskima gave a brief cry of pain.

"Well from what I'm feeling, it is definitely made of rock." Maskima muttered under his breath.

Javon, not wanting to cause Maskima harm, asked "Should I pull it out slowly or quickly?"

"Please, do it quickly. Just give it a strong. . . AH!"

"Got it!" Javon replied. He took the stone dart, suspended it in midair to inspect it for a moment, and then tossed it aside.

"Maybe a little warning next time?" Maskima retorted, clenching his shoulder in pain.

"Sorry, I thought you wanted it out quickly." Javon stated as he started bandaging up Maskima's wound.

"What are we going to do about your wrist?" Alenard questioned. "Should we go back up to the tower or into Haiedenburg for medical treatment?"

"Let's go into Haiedenburg. But not to any medical centers; I don't want to cause a scene."

"Sounds good, sir." Javon replied. "Well, that bandage should hold until we can get you properly looked at."

"Thanks lads. Could you both lend me a hand up? I am not as young as I once was, and fighting these goons took it out of me."

"You don't say." Alenard declared. "You are quite ancient."

Maskima gave Alenard a stern glare.

"You know, I'm only in my sixties." Maskima retorted.

"If you keep up those snarky comments, you'll be lucky to be to make it to Maskima's age, Alenard." Javon interjected.

"I'd be lucky to make it to Maskima's old age at all."

The trio all let out a good chuckle at this response. Alenard and Javon then helped Maskima to his feet, and crossed the bridge into Haiedenburg.

"I don't think you understand. I do not travel across countries. That isn't my job. To do trading with Shadicore we go to Parchan trading posts near the border. I don't go there myself. Besides, Shadicore doesn't even do much trading with us; most of their goods don't sell here in Dauchenland. On top of all of that, there's that legend of the sand monster to reckon with, so I'd have to hire some protection to cross the desert." Aliofi declared as he looked up at Ottokar from his slouched posture.

"Believe me, I am well aware. That's why I'm willing to pay you whatever you ask."

"Ottokar, have you not been listening to anything I said?"

Ottokar was getting quite frustrated at this point. "Listen, Aliofi. We have been friends a long time. I need you to do this for me. Not just for me, for my family. With everything happening now. . . I don't know how everything is going to turn out. And I want my family to be safe. Besides that, you should leave as well, for your own safety. Just for a little while. Even if you don't normally trade with Shadicore."

"I understand that, and I am glad you are concerned with my safety. But Ottokar, a trip like that could cause some serious problems in my trading business."

"That's why I'm telling you to name your price."

Aliofi looked down at the ground for a moment, revealing the small balled spot on top of his head. He furrowed his thick eyebrows, a common mark that he was deep in thought. After a moment, he looked up at Ottokar.

"I suppose I owe you one for saving my life in that fire a few years back. Just get me what you can for payment."

Ottokar reached into his bag and pulled out a small sack. "I hope this will do."

Aliofi took the bag slowly, and untied the string at the top. He looked inside, and his goateed chin dropped.

"That is four hundred and sixty gold pieces." Ottokar declared. "It should be more than enough to compensate you for your trouble."

"Ottokar, I. . . I cannot take all of this. I would feel like I'm robbing you. And I'm almost afraid to ask how you got gold pieces, you know, with King Lustan and all."

"Do not worry about that. All you need to know is that I came by it honestly. And since Lustan is no longer with us, you should be able to use it with no trouble. Just take it; on the condition you leave today, and as soon as you can."

Aliofi, with his mouth still hanging half open, looked up at Ottokar, and after a moment said "Okay, fine. I should be ready to leave at dusk."

"Perfect. I will have my family here."

There was a knock at the door of the bakery. Alenard tensed with concern as they hid in the back room.

"It's too soon for Javon to be back." Alenard whispered as he tried to hear who was at the door.

"Keep in mind Alenard, we are in an established business that opens at dawn. And it is dawn. That's why Bacham hid us in the back room." Maskima responded calmly.

Alenard was not comforted by Maskima's words, and listened carefully as Bacham went to the door.

"Bacham, where is he?" A gruff, yet faint voice at the door questioned.

"He's in the back." Bacham responded.

"I think he just sold us out!" Alenard whispered, looking at Maskima in shock.

Maskima looked at Alenard with a raised eyebrow.

"Relax, it's just Putkan."

Alenard groaned and ran his fingers through his short, brown hair.

"So not only are we in fear that some assassins dressed like ghosts might find us at any second, but now I have to deal with Putkan's abrasive personality too?"

"Alenard, you should be more empathetic towards Putkan. You know what happened to his wife." Maskima replied sternly.

"Look I get that, but that was almost a year ago. Now he just uses that as an excuse to be an abrasive, angry jerk."

"Put a cork in it." Maskima responded in a hushed tone. He then looked up at the doorway as the drapery was pushed aside, and Putkan's stoic face become visible.

"Putkan! Glad you found me." Maskima welcomed.

"Javon told me what happened. We have to do something." Putkan declared in a matter-of-fact tone as he pushed the curtain aside and walked boldly into the room.

"Putkan, settle down. We don't have solid proof Kafahr is behind this."

"But we do. Have you not heard every speech he gave the last ten years? And what about these fliers that keep popping up all around the city?" Putkan responded in exasperation as he waved a piece of paper in Maskima's face.

Maskima leaned in to read the flier. He had to squint to make out the words.

"Down with the Aceic Order. They have allowed corruption to reign." Maskima looked up at his companion. "Putkan, there is no evidence that Kafahr is behind this."

"You can't be serious, Maskima. We all know he wants us gone! Who else could print all of these in such a short time period? And now, suddenly when Lustan dies, these assassins come out of nowhere and get enough nerve to attack the Head of the Aceic Order? It isn't a coincidence."

"I never said it was a coincidence. But Putkan, you know what will happen if we go after Kafahr without proof. We have to have a solid reason to try to overthrow his rule. And even then, I fear that the people would still side with him."

"Well then, let's just assassinate him."

"That kind of talk will get us into serious trouble." Maskima responded in a hushed tone as he gave Putkan an angry look.

Putkan scowled at Maskima's reply, and crossed his arms. He then looked over to the other side of the room and almost sneered when he saw Alenard.

"I didn't even notice you. Quiet as a rat, as always."

"I couldn't help but notice you. Your arrogant ignorance is more obnoxious than Javon's awful singing." Alenard responded, crossing his arms in return.

At this insult, all of the veins on Putkan's face stuck out with anger and he struck a fighting pose.

"Hey! No. Not right now. I know both of you have your problems, but right now is not the time to work them out, especially if 'working it out' means you're going to fight. We need to unite to face this looming threat. And besides, if you both start tearing up this place trying to kill each other, all of Haiedenburg will know exactly where we are, and have all the more reason to hate us. Can you both just be decent to each other until this crisis passes?"

Putkan thought for a moment about Maskima's request, and then relaxed his pose. But suddenly, the curtain, which was to Putkan's back, was gently moved aside. Putkan instinctively reacted, and throat punched the unsuspecting Javon. In response, Javon could only stumble back and fall onto the cold stone floor, gasping for breath.

"Oh. I'm sorry, Javon."

"Nice going, Putkan." Alenard declared sarcastically, as he leaned against the wall. His arms were still crossed.

Putkan squinted angrily at Alenard.

"We'll settle this later, you rat."

"It's. Quite alright. I'm more offended you guys don't like my singing." Javon responded as he got back on his feet. "I thought I had waited until it was safe to enter. Guess I was wrong. Oh, and I brought you medical supplies, Maskima."

"Thank you, Javon. Bacham had some bandages available, so I'm actually good."

"Oh. So I showed my face in the streets, got my singing insulted, and took a throat punch for nothing?" Javon responded in a dejected tone as he looked off to the side.

"If you're that upset, you can change my bandages for me then." Maskima replied, almost chuckling at Javon's childlike behavior.

Javon looked up, and then walked over to Maskima. He began preparing the new bandages and disinfecting agent.

"So what is our next move?" Alenard asked Maskima.

"Well I sent out an order about a month ago that when the king died, I wanted all of the Aces to return to Haiedenburg. So while Kafahr is sending messengers out to the four corners of the kingdom and proclaiming that he is now to be crowned king, he is also giving my Aces instructions."

"But then Kafahr will think we're up to something." Alenard declared. "Not likely. It has happened several times in the past that most of the Aceic Order has gathered to one city to pay respect to a new king. So if things go well, then Kafahr feels respected. If things go ill, then we are ready in full force; even though our full force isn't much these days."

"Smart thinking." Alenard said. "So. . . dare we go to the coronation?"

"If we don't go, Kafahr will pretend to be insulted and use that against us. So unfortunately, I think that means that we should all go, since all of us are on the council."

"You mean I have to go listen to that raspy voiced buffoon Kafahr give a speech, but Ottokar gets a free pass?" Putkan chimed in with frustration.

"Ow!" Maskima yelled. Javon had just poured some of the disinfectant into his shoulder wound.

"Sorry." Javon responded.

"You know, I already disinfected that." Alenard interjected.

"It can't hurt to do it twice!" Javon retorted.

"Yes. . . it can." Maskima grunted, still in pain. "Look Putkan, Ottokar wanted to make arrangements to get his family out of the city, so I let him. I told him to come back as soon as he could; and I trust he will find us when he is done. He is our espionage and intelligence expert, after all."

Suddenly, they heard the bakery door open. The room immediately fell silent; everyone wanted to see if they could hear anything. Bachman said something in a quiet voice, and something was whispered in response, but none of them could make out the voice. There was silence for a moment, and then they heard footsteps approaching. Putkan pulled his fists to his chin and used his ability to create some electricity in front of his knuckles, preparing to zap whoever was about to enter the room. The curtain was pushed back. To everyone's relief, they saw it was Ottokar.

Ottokar looked up and did a double take when he saw Putkan ready to hit him in the face with electricity.

"No. I'm not a threat." Ottokar declared with a stern look.

Putkan breathed a sigh of relief and then turned off his electricity. Ottokar then quickly stepped into the room and pulled the curtain back over the entrance. He had changed into his armor, which consisted of spaced metallic plates filled in by tough leather. Ottokar's armor also had a massive left shoulder guard. But his armor did not have a helmet, as was common for an Aceic troop's armor design.

"I'm glad you decided to show up, Ottokar. I was worried that you'd get to miss out on Kafahr's speech." Putkan declared. He was clearly relieved that another ace would have to put up with Kafahr.

"We're going to the coronation?" Ottokar asked, and then saw Javon bandaging Maskima's shoulder. "Are you alright? What happened?"

"Long story short; I ran into some assassins. Those ghosts we heard about aren't made up, but they aren't actual ghosts either. But aye, I figured that even though it might be dangerous for us to go, it would be worse if we didn't, because then Kafahr could use that against us."

Ottokar quizzically looked at Maskima for a moment as he tried to process Maskima's overly shortened summary.

"I suppose that makes sense."

The curtain moved aside, allowing another figure to enter the room, and all five of the Aces jumped into fighting poses, ready to launch their respective element attack.

Bacham, who was the one who had entered, saw that he had startled everyone and apologized.

"Sorry about that fellas. I figured you all would want some fresh bread."

All of the Aces relaxed. Bacham then looked over at Ottokar with surprise, who had just extinguished a blue fire ball; his signature opening move.

"That's quite impressive, Ottokar. I didn't realize you could create blue fire."

"Yes; it takes a good deal of strength, but blue fire is actually quite a powerful tool. Thank you for the bread, Bacham. You are very kind to us." Ottokar responded.

"Ah, it is the least that I can do." Bachman said as he handed out some freshly baked rolls to the Aces. "Everyone seems to blame you for what's been happening in Dauchenland the last fifty years, but I know you did the best you could. Folks just seem to like to have their ears tickled and blame others for their problems, regardless of who the blame truly belongs to."

"Truly spoken, Bachman. If only the people of Dauchenland saw things the way you did; then I think all of these problems we have would not exist." Alenard responded, trying to subtly put back the stone he had pulled from the floor with his ability.

Bachman smiled at this compliment, gave a nod, and then left the room.

"We should probably get cleaned up and make our way to the Citadel. Being late would be worse than not going at all. Are you able to move, Maskima?" Ottokar questioned.

"It's my shoulder, not my hip, Ottokar. I can walk."

"I think what Ottokar meant is that an old man like yourself should be careful." Alenard chimed in with a smirk as he stroked his small, jawline beard.

Maskima simply glared at Alenard.

"The sun just rose, and the coronation is at noon. We have plenty of time to get there." Putkan declared resolutely.

"No, I agree with Ottokar; we need to be there early. Besides, as the Head Ace of Haiedenburg, I have a responsibility to inform Kafahr of the assassination attempt on my life. It is my duty to inform the king, or in this case, the soon to be king, of any impending threats or problems."

As Alenard and Putkan went over to the water basin to use the water to wash their faces off, Ottokar quietly approached Maskima.

"Maskima. . . are you sure it's such a good idea to bring Putkan to this? He can be. . . well. . . you know. Unstable, emotionally? Especially after the murder of his wife. . ."

"I know, Ottokar. I didn't even want him to be on the Aceic Council after what happened. But he still is. . . so he has to be with us. If he isn't, Kafahr will take it as an insult."

"I think that is a risk worth taking."

"I do not, my friend. I respect your judgement and I understand your concern. But I need you to trust me on this."

Ottokar reluctantly nodded his head. "Well, after all, you are the Aceic Order's head council member, so I do have to follow your orders."

Maskima chuckled.

"Oh, I almost forgot. I need a few minutes to write and send a letter to Saoland, and then I still need to mail the letter to Barz's parents about when and how to bring him." Ottokar added.

"Saoland? That's a ways away. Does that have something to do with that other ace child we found?"

"Unfortunately, it does. I heard from my friend there. The ghosts, or assassins, got to the poor kid. Rayduan wasn't able to stop them."

"These ghosts! They have killed or kidnapped too many of these children. Well, write your letter quickly and get to the courtyard soon. I am going to go inform Kafahr about what happened to me." Maskima declared as he slowly stood up and began walking towards the door.

"I hope you are not seriously harmed!" Kafahr declared, as his servants trimmed his hair to be his usual bowl cut style. Kafahr wanted to look clean and kingly for the impending coronation.

"Certainly not, my lord. It takes more than just a couple of thugs to take me off my feet."

"From what you're telling me, it doesn't sound like these individuals were mere thugs. It sounds like the work of assassins." Kafahr declared as he stroked his thin moustache with a skeptical, yet amused look on his face.

"That is a possibility. On top of that, these men were in suits that matched the description of the things responsible for the disappearance of many of the gifted children throughout the Northern Kingdoms."

"I thought the disappearances were simply coincidental, and that you had no solid evidence to say otherwise?"

"That was true until today, sir. I do not know who these people are, or even how many of them there are, but I believe that they are indeed responsible. We need to bring them to justice."

"I could not agree more, Maskima! And the advanced technology they possess that you described disturbs me. I will be assigning you a protective detail for the time being."

"No, sir. That will not be necessary. My job is to protect the people of Dauchenland, and I would be strongly opposed to any such action." Maskima responded as he unconsciously clenched his fist.

Kafahr stood up, and started having his servants dress him in his armor.

"No Maskima, I insist. Take several of my guard with you. They will keep you safe." Kafahr declared with a faint smirk.

"My lord, and I mean this with all due respect; but if I must sprint out of this hall to avoid having your guard follow me, I will. Having your men protect me would proclaim weakness to the people around me."

"Hmm, as you wish, I suppose. Well, I presume you will be at the coronation?" Kafahr muttered in disappointment.

"Of course. I wouldn't miss it. The Aces look forward to the good you plan to do for the people."

"I'm glad you do. The people deserve better than the last fifty years of torment they have had to endure. And justice must be served to those who sat silent in this time of need." Kafahr said, as he looked down his nose at Maskima.

"I hope you realize that the Aceic Order did all they could to prevent the evil and oppression in this time."

"Oh of course, of course." Kafahr said, waving his hand towards Maskima. "I know that, but the real question is not what I know, but rather what the people believe."

"My lord, I know we have not had a good relationship since your mother passed. . ."

"You mean since you let her die when I was seven?" Kafahr shot back as he furrowed his eyebrows.

"Kafahr. I did everything I could."

"So you have said. So you have said. But my father, Kusan, told a different story."

"I am sorry."

"Do you really think that matters?" Kafahr yelled angrily.

Maskima had been aware of Kafahr's subtly aggressive attitude throughout most of the conversation, but at this remark, he figured it was time to go.

"Well, I wish you the best in the ceremony my future king, and look forward to working with you." Maskima said, and then turned to started walking away.

"Today will mark a new era for the people of Dauchenland; it will be life changing. I will finally take my father's work to the next level!" Kafahr hollered with a sly grin.

Maskima paused for a brief moment. There was something concerning in Kafahr's tone. He turned to look at Kafahr for a moment, and saw an evil smirk resting on Kafahr's face. Maskima then spun around and briskly walked out of the room.

"Why do we have to be so close?" Putkan grumbled. "I want to be further away so I can slip out when Kafahr starts to ramble his lies."

"Putkan, please, shut up. Do you want anyone to overhear you saying that? Do you realize what kind of trouble that could get us into?" Maskima scolded sternly.

Alenard leaned over to Ottokar and whispered, "Believe it or not, Putkan doesn't need to do much to seem smart. All he needs to do is just not talk."

At this Ottokar burst out laughing, and had to quickly compose himself.

"What? What's so funny, Ottokar?" Putkan questioned.

"Nothing." Both Ottokar and Alenard replied at the same time.

"You both need to get control over yourselves. You look like a bunch of school girls! People are staring." Javon whispered in a serious tone.

Trumpets began to blow, announcing the arrival of Kafahr. He entered from outside the citadel, as was the usual practice for the coronation of a Dauchenland king. This action was meant to symbolize that the king was still one of the people, and that he had a responsibility to them. He was greeted with thunderous applause and cheers from the packed citadel.

Kafahr then went around the palace fountain, and proceeded up the steps towards the King's Palace. His armor glistened in the bright, autumn day, and his robe fluttered in the wind. Silence had fallen on the audience, and the only sound that was heard was Kafahr's metal boots clinking against the stone steps as he ascended toward the palace.

A priest welcomed Kafahr as he reached the top, with the five provincial representatives of Dauchenland behind him. The priest then turned to the audience, and asked in a loud voice:

"In front of all of these witnesses, do you declare that you will fulfill the rule of King to the best of your ability? Caring for the interests of all people; not only the high and powerful, but also the low and weak? Do you agree to protect Dauchenland from invaders, both foreign and domestic, even if it means giving your life?"

"I affirm all of this!" Kafahr yelled.

"Then I command you to kneel, facing these people you intend to govern." Kafahr did so, and the priest stepped forward, gesturing for an aide with a sword to come forward. The aide handed the sword to the priest, and the priest drew it.

"With this sword, I bestow upon thee the title of Head Knight of Dauchenland."

The priest then tapped both of Kafahr's shoulders, and then handed the sword back to the aide. He then signaled a second aide to come forward with the crown and scepter.

"And with this crown, I declare you King of Dauchenland! Rise, King Kafahr."

The audience burst into applause.

"And now, King, and Head Knight of Dauchenland, I give you this scepter; which symbolizes your power to govern. May you rule well, judge wisely, and live a long life!"

The audience erupted into even more applause and cheering, and many started chanting "All hail King Kafahr! All hail King Kafahr!"

Kafahr stood before the people, and motioned for them to be silent.

"My people. Long have you waited for the day when a new king, a king that cared for each and every one of you, would stand before you at this very spot! You have been groaning under turmoil and oppression for fifty years. But I say no longer! I am your savior, and from this day forward, you have been saved by me!"

Everyone ruptured into more applause and wild cheering. Javon looked over at Alenard and Ottokar and whispered "This sounds like borderline blasphemy."

"And now, I am officially shutting down Lustan's gold venture. There will be no more digging of gold in this land as long as I am king! Each miner will be allowed to return to his home, and given fair recompense for his wasted time and effort. And of course it is of no surprise to you that the Aceic Order was silent, and allowed oppression to rule, during this time."

Maskima whispered to himself, "But that's not true. . ."

"It is clear that the Aceic Order is drawing to an end. Maskima himself has told me that there are less and less gifted children being recruited each year; and as a result the Aceic Order is weak and frail. Even if they still wanted to care for the people, they would no longer be able to!"

Yells of agreement came from the audience, while the Aceic Council received angry looks from the crowd.

"And so, it is because of this weakness that my father began training a new, elite group for you! An order of highly trained guards; here to protect and defend Dauchenland. I give you, the Purman Order!"

Thunderous applause broke out, and the palace doors swung wide open. Out walked two dozen figures dressed in black cloaks with white masks, headed by a figure with no mask. This person was carrying a large metal plate on his back, and had several pouches on his belt.

"No. . . the ghosts." Maskima whispered.

"That's who attacked you? Let's do something then. Now! We have the proof!" Putkan said to Maskima.

"No!" Maskima exclaimed, putting a hand on Putkan's chest to stop him. "Putkan, we can't. No one would believe us."

"This new Purman Order is equipped with a weapon that I like to call dart guns. These dart guns launch small projectiles, and are a fair match to any ace's ability. On top of that, these soldiers are trained in evasive combat techniques, which will enable them to maneuver themselves better than the Aceic Order ever could. Heading this order is my loyal servant, Hiffa. Hiffa is a double ace who refused to join the Aceic Order because of their failure to serve the people. He controls metal, and also has the rare gift of being able to control the acidic sap from the ayoxium flower."

Hiffa straitened his posture to be seen as more bold than before, and brushed his hands against his acid pouches to be sure they were still there.

"I've never heard of this ace. . ." Maskima whispered to himself in suspicion.

Suddenly, Putkan saw it. He saw a small dagger at the waist of the Purman Order guard nearest him. The design was unique, but he had seen it once before. It was the same style of weapon that had found in his wife's neck. As he looked at the other ghosts in disbelief, he saw that several had the same dagger; it seemed to be a mark of their higher rank.

"Maskima, look at the daggers." Putkan said in a daze, hardly able to speak.

"What?" Maskima asked, taken aback by Putkan's subdued tone.

"The daggers. On the ghosts."

"Oh. Oh! Putkan. Listen. That's more than enough proof to bring Kafahr down. I can handle this. Don't do anything rash."

"But they took her from me." Putkan declared in shock, staring blankly into the distance.

"Putkan, calm down. Listen, let's go. We can leave."

"No. This needs to end, now!" Putkan screamed, suddenly snapping with emotion and rage. He jumped out of the crowd and started running up the steps towards Kafahr and the Purman Order soldiers.

"No! Putkan! Stop!" Maskima yelled, running after him. Maskima jumped in front of Putkan just in time. "What are you doing?"

"What is the meaning of all this?" Kafahr yelled down to the two aces. He had put his hand up to halt his Purman Order soldiers, who had all aimed their dart guns at Maskima and Putkan. "Maskima, there had better be a good explanation for this interruption."

"You! You were the one that murdered my wife!" Putkan yelled, tears streaming down his face.

"What? That is preposterous!"

"You are a liar!" Putkan yelled. "You're the one that had my wife killed! And you're the one behind the gifted children disappearing, and you are the one responsible for the attack on Maskima!"

The audience let out a gasp.

"I will forgive you these grievous insults and accusations, and chalk it up to your emotional distress. You are clearly not in your right mind. But you need to leave. Now. I am going to show you mercy, even though I should have you executed on the spot for disrespecting your king!"

"Putkan," Maskima whispered, "we need to leave, and do this another way. I can tell that the crowd is siding with Kafahr."

Putkan began to look around, and saw faces glaring at him. He then looked up at Kafahr, and saw that Kafahr was slowly approaching.

"Putkan," Kafahr spoke calmly, "You are confused. And that is okay. But now, you need to go home and recover your senses."

Kafahr then came within a foot's distance of Putkan, and whispered so only Putkan and Maskima could hear "Don't worry Putkan, I had my assassins do it quickly." He then looked right into Putkan's eyes and smirked.

Putkan couldn't take it anymore. He pulled his fist back and shot a lightning blast at Kafahr's face. Kafahr threw himself backwards to avoid the attack, and the bolt hit one of the Purman Order soldiers behind Kafahr, knocking him to the ground.

Kafahr then quickly drew his sword and swung at Putkan and Maskima. Maskima saw the attack coming, and grabbed Putkan as he threw himself clear of the blade. Kafahr was enraged that his attack had failed and yelled to the Purman Order soldiers behind him "A member of the Aceic Council has attacked me! We are at war with the Aces! Kill them all!"

The bystanders immediately started running for the Citadel gate to escape the impending fight. Ottokar, Alenard, and Javon, who had only half followed Maskima and Putkan up the stairs, instantly sprung into a fighting pose to protect Putkan.

The Purman soldiers also lost no time, and quickly jumped into action. They started running to encircle the group and began to unload their guns toward the aces. Hiffa barked orders to his troops as he ripped pieces of metal off of the plate he was carrying and started launching it at the Aces. Javon and Alenard quickly slammed their feet into the ground to knock the stone foundation below the steps loose, and then created a stone wall out of the ground to protect them and their friends. But they could only react so fast; before they could protect Maskima, he took a projectile to the neck, and fell halfway down the steps, lying limp. Putkan took several shots, one to the arm, one to the side, and one to the knee. He collapsed to the ground and cried in pain as the wall went up around him. Ottokar bolted over to Maskima to see if he was still alive, but he was dead.

An eerie silence fell over the palace; and the only thing that could be heard was the metallic sound of the guns being reloaded.

Alenard and Javon knocked a few small holes in their wall so they could see the Purman soldiers, and then began to throw the smalls pieces of rubble over the wall at the their enemy.

"Gah! These soldiers are trained well! I can't get a clean hit on them." Alenard yelled.

"Maskima is dead, and Putkan is badly injured. We need to get out of here!" Ottokar bellowed.

"Well in case you didn't notice, we're kind of surrounded right now." Alenard retorted. "Any ideas on how to do that brilliant plan of yours?"

"We got one coming over the wall!" Javon shouted.

Ottokar immediately dropped to the ground and kicked a huge blue fire blast towards the Purman soldier. Apparently the Purman soldier was wearing a fireproof cloak, as the blast did not burn him. However, the blast did throw him into the edge of the wall and gave Alenard enough time to peg the soldier in the face with a rock. The soldier fell motionless to the ground.

"We can beat these guys after all!" Javon cried excitedly. "There's another one coming over!"

This time, the soldier had his gun ready, and shot at Ottokar. But Ottokar immediately rolled out of the way. The dart ricocheted off the ground, and hit Putkan in the head. Javon ripped off a chunk of the wall, and threw it at the soldier, who received the hit and fell into the midst of the aces. Although dazed, he attempted to stand up. Alenard reacted quickly and pulled a small stone up from underneath the Purman soldier, and hit him in the jaw. The soldier's head snapped back and he fell against the back of the wall.

Ottokar looked over at Putkan, and instantly saw that he was dead. He then heard a sizzling sound, and saw that acid was beginning to eat through the wall on the side Hiffa had been; it was moments away from crumbling and exposing their flank.

"We have to move! If we stay here we're all going to die. Javon, Alenard, we need to make a run for the gate."

Alenard looked in that direction.

"But it's closed! One of the Purman soldiers must have shut it."

"Then I want you both to take the walls and throw them at it. We need to get out of here! Now!" Ottokar yelled as a dart came flying through one of the small holes in the wall and glanced Ottokar's giant left shoulder guard.

After seeing the accuracy of the Purman soldiers, Alenard and Javon didn't hesitate. They quickly loosening the walls from the ground, picked them up using their abilities, and threw them full force at the closed metal gate. The trio then took off running after the flying walls as fast as they could. The impact threw the gate to the ground, opening a path to their freedom.

The three aces ran with all their might as a slew of darts followed them. Javon pulled up a thin wall behind them as they ran out the gate to cover their retreat.

"Unacceptable!" Kafahr screamed at his men. "I had you trained to be the best, and you let them escape! Find them, now! And kill them!"

"Where is dad? I thought we were supposed to be leaving soon! It's almost dark." Maxstrom inquired as he looked out the window of their house in Haiedenburg.

"I know Max. If he's not here soon we'll just need to leave without him. Maybe he's already at the caravan waiting for us."

Retta heard a horse galloping down the street.

"Kafahr has issued a curfew because of the Aces on the loose!" The rider cried as he ran down the street. "You must be in your homes from dusk to dawn!"

"That's not good. We need to leave, now."

Retta looked at her son and said "Now look Maxstrom. If anyone asks, I want you to pretend that you can't control any elements; just for today. We're going on a stealth mission."

"Alright, mom." Maxstrom replied.

"Good, now let's go." Retta responded as she grabbed her son's hand.

Retta and Max quickly ran down the labyrinth of cobblestone streets to the trading center of Haiedenburg.

"There you are! Where's Ottokar? We need to leave!" Aliofi declared.

"I don't know."

"If we don't leave right now, I'm not sure we'll get out of the city before the gates close."

"Then I guess we don't have a choice." Retta replied, looking behind her.

"I'm going to hide you both in these fruit buckets until we get clear of the city. Get in and I'll cover you with apples."

Retta quickly put Maxstrom in one of the baskets.

All of the sudden, a questioning voice came from the entrance behind them.

"Excuse me, what do you think you're doing?"

Retta turned and saw that it was a Dauchenland guard.

"Oh, I'm uhh. . ." Retta stammered.

They couldn't afford any more delays, and the guard was on the ground right next to her. Retta, who was standing in the wagon, decided to kick the guard in the face as hard as she could. The guard fell back, clenching his nose.

"I need help in here!" The guard yelled through his hands.

Retta jumped off the wagon and hit him in the face again, knocking him out. She then looked at Aliofi, who was watching her in shock.

"Get your caravan out of here, now! I'll stay behind and hold them off. Get Maxstrom to safety!" She ordered.

"But. But Retta. . ."

"Do it, now!"

Aliofi quickly grabbed a sack of apples, dumped them over Maxstrom, and yelled the command for his three wagon caravan to move out. Just as the wagons rolled around the corner and onto the cobblestone street, two more guards ran into the loading dock.

It took the caravan two weeks to make it out of Dauchenland. Even though Dauchenland had many paved roads throughout the kingdom, new rules and regulations established by Kafahr, because of the war with the Aceic Order, slowed the caravan's travel with various security checks. But Aliofi did a great job of hiding Maxstrom in plain sight. The caravan headed west and passed through Tharin, crossed the Nect, and then went north to Chatburg. From there, the caravan crossed the border into Parcha and passed through Chateau Lance.

Once they made it out of Dauchenland, the caravan had to travel just over a week through Parcha, heading through Chatel Mill, Chatel Crete, and then finally across the Denga Desert. After crossing the desert, the caravan reached the Shadic River. Since Aliofi hadn't been to Shadicore in quite some time, he had miscalculated their path across the desert. As a result, they were not near any Shadican towns, and due to a limitation in supplies for their trip back, Aliofi had to drop Maxstrom off where they were.

"Well, Maxstrom, here we are. We'll help you cross the river, but we dare not go any further, otherwise the Shadicans would probably deem us a threat and execute us all. Ottokar told me to tell you that he is friends with the head chief, named Tapito. Remember that, and tell that to the first Shadican you see, and you should be taken care of." Aliofi said as he looked at the young boy standing next to him.

"When are mom and dad going to come?" Maxstrom asked.

"My guess is that your parents are going to come and take you home once it's safe to go back to Dauchenland. So until then, you need to stay here with the Shadicans."

"Sir?" Dega, one of Aliofi's trade companions inquired.

"Aye?"

"Can I speak with you in private for a moment?"

Dega walked over to a spot behind one of the wagons, and Aliofi followed him.

"Are you really sure this is a good idea?"

"What do you mean, Dega?"

"Handing a child over to those katlicans; alone! They may be small, but those cat-like creatures are vicious. The Parchans fear them, and from the stories I've heard, that fear is for good reason."

"Dega. This is what Ottokar paid me to do. He knows the chief of the Shadican tribe. Besides, I've traded with the Shadicans before, in my youth. They're decent enough when you show them respect."

Dega frowned. "I dislike all of this."

"I know, but Ottokar wouldn't send his only son to them if he didn't know what he was doing. Besides, we made it through the desert without running into any sand monsters, so that has to be a good sign, right?" Aliofi question.

Dega shrugged.

Aliofi let out a breath, and then turned to walk back to where Maxstrom was standing. Maxstrom was looking back over the desert they had just crossed.

Aliofi looked at Maxstrom with a sad expression. He then went over to two of his servants, and had them unload a canoe from one of the wagons. He then helped them put in Maxstrom's sleeping supplies along with food and water for a few days. Aliofi then instructed his servants to row Maxstrom across the river, drop him and his supplies off, and then quickly return.

Even though the servants were strong, it took them a while to row across the river due to its width. When they finally reached the other side, they quickly dropped Maxstrom off with his supplies as instructed, and returned back across the river. Maxstrom stayed on the beach and watched them go, saw Aliofi load the canoe back into his wagon, and then head back across Denga Desert. Eventually, he couldn't see them at all anymore.

It was starting to get dark, and Maxstrom didn't know what to do. He was a little scared of the dark. And now he was alone. But there was nowhere to go; so he just sat on the beach and burst into tears.

Meanwhile, unbeknownst to Maxstrom, several of the cat-like Shadicans were watching him from the shadowy forest.

"He's still here. And he's been here for almost two hours."

"We should leave. It's probably another trap."

"If it's a trap, it's a very convincing one."

"Chief. . . please don't tell me you're actually falling for this."

"Akbu, you're here to guard me, right?"

"Yes. . ."

"Good. So then if I decide to go out and offer this innocent child a hand, you'll keep me safe."

"Yes, but with all due respect chief, I'm more here to guard you against making dumb choices than to protect you while you're actually doing them."

"Wait! I think he hears us. He's looking into the woods."

"Look at that fire ball. He can control fire! He's an ace!"

"Aces normally aren't that young. . ."

"Akbu, an ace is simply anyone that can control an element. It has nothing to do with age. You're getting an ace and the Aceic Order's soldiers confused."

Maxstrom thought he could hear whispers in the breeze, but he couldn't make out what they were saying. It seemed to be coming from the forest, so Maxstrom walked closer, even though he was terrified.

"Hello?" Maxstrom called through a faltering voice. "Anyone out there?"

He was greeted with silence.

"If you're a Shadican, I'm Ottokar's son, and my father is a friend of Tapito, the Shadican chief."

More silence.

"Hello?"

Chapter 2

Forging a Hero

B.Y. 4013

"Everything is better with a friend."
—Shacbu

Shacbu, a Shadican, licked her right arm and then brushed the fur on her cat-like forehead back. She then drew her two swords, gripping them tightly in her four fingers, and struck a fighting pose by swinging her dual swords to opposite sides. The small spot of red colored fur that she had above her left eyebrow shimmered in the sunlight, and she glared at Maxstrom with her unwavering green katlican eyes. Being a predominately black furred katlican of almost three and a half feet in height, Shacbu was a member of the Shadican tribe, one of four tribes in the katlican homeland.

"It's no special abilities, right? You can't use light to hide in plain sight, Akbu, and I can't use fire or water?" Maxstrom, now sixteen years old and slightly over six feet tall, asked the two Shadicans that were ready to fight in front of him. He was standing confidently with his Shadican made sword, and the white robe he was wearing made him stand out in comparison to his black-furred Shadican duel mates. Adding to this distinction was the fact that his opponents were only about half his height, as all katlicans were.

"Yeah, that's right. But I don't need to hide from you to beat you, so that won't be a problem for me." Akbu said, his blue eyes shining with

eagerness. Akbu then ran his katlican paw through the fur on his head, making his Mohawk stand taller than usual.

Practice fights occurred often amongst the Shadicans, but this one was unique, because it was a human against two Shadicans, and not just any two Shadicans. Akbu was in charge of the elite Shadican guard as well as the best Shadicans with a sword in Shadicore. And Shacbu had recently been selected to be the next heir to the high chief; if, and only if she could meet the combat standards of the Shadican nation's council, which was elected primarily to oversee the selection and ascension of a new chief. The council had little power over the nation as a whole beyond this decision.

"Let's see you try," Maxstrom responded to Akbu, pulling his sword closer to his chest.

Akbu also pulled his single sword close to his chest, and then pointed it straight at Maxstrom. He then looked over at Shacbu. Shacbu, who had been watching Akbu, twitched her tail, which affirmed that she was ready to attack. Both sprung forward and began sprinting towards Maxstrom.

Maxstrom swung his sword low to the ground with all his might as Akbu and Shacbu came into range. Both the Shadicans saw this coming, and immediately implemented their agility training. Shacbu jumped over the blade and Akbu rolled under it; both kept moving towards Maxstrom.

However, instead of just dodging the strike, Shacbu used the opportunity to lunge towards Maxstrom's face. Maxstrom instantly saw the move. He moved his head to the left to avoid her oncoming swords and used the longer reach of his left hand to lightly grab her arms and throw her to the side. She flew to the ground and directed her focus towards performing a graceful recovery; she stuck both of her swords into the ground, flipped over them, and then removed her swords from the ground. She quickly snapped her head back to be sure Maxstrom wasn't pursuing her.

While all of this was going on, Akbu took a swing at Maxstrom's leg. Maxstrom jumped to the right to avoid it, but only mostly missed the blade. His reward was a light cut on his left calf through his white robe.

Akbu saw the blood and smirked "I told you I didn't need to hide from you to beat you."

As Akbu said this, Shacbu jumped towards Maxstrom from behind, swords ready. He saw this attack just in time, and Maxstrom used the flat of his sword to hit her out of the way. She was out.

"See, I thought we were going for strikes with the flat of the sword. Like that! Not drawing blood or ruining clothing!" Maxstrom retorted, looking at Akbu with a grumpy look.

"I never agreed to those rules. Just no elements. Right, Shacbu?"

"Sure, whatever." Shacbu said as she retracted her claws, which had given her a better grip on her swords. She then brushed the dirt off of her fur. This match wasn't the only time she'd been beaten quickly in the ring. She felt humiliated; again.

Maxstrom pulled his sword to the left and started sprinting towards Akbu. Akbu stood perfectly still, and waited for Maxstrom to swing. Once Maxstrom's blade was in motion, Akbu started running towards Maxstrom. He slid under Maxstrom's blade, and tried to swing at his legs again. But Maxstrom wasn't about to fall for the same trick twice; in fact he expected Akbu to try another leg strike. Maxstrom responded by jumping into the air and throwing himself into a roll, pulling his legs and whole body out of Akbu's reach. He quickly recovered, and turned to face Akbu.

"I have to be honest with you. That was actually half impressive."

"Gee, thanks Akbu. Don't compliment me too much now, wouldn't want it to go to my head or anything." Maxstrom responded in a sarcastic tone.

Akbu gave a laugh at this response, and then took off running towards Maxstrom. Suddenly, Maxstrom had an idea. Maxstrom dropped down into a squat, cutting his height in half, and swung his sword. This caught Akbu by surprise, and out of instinct Akbu jumped up. But this was exactly what Maxstrom was expecting. He easily redirected the direction of his sword up, and smacked Akbu to the side with the flat of his sword. Akbu, now soaring in midair, let go of his sword, and put himself into a roll to absorb the impact.

"Well, that was fully impressive Maxstrom." Akbu said, dusting off his fur and fixing his Mohawk. "I like how you changed the battlefield on me so quickly."

"I'm sorry, did you just give me a compliment? Did you hit your head in that roll, Akbu?"

Akbu smirked as he reached down to pick up his sword. "Don't get used to it, kid. I was going easy on you."

"You always say that." Maxstrom responded as he furrowed his eyebrows.

Akbu, still smiling, sheathed his sword and walked over to Maxstrom.

"Good fight" Akbu said, sticking out his small, cat-like hand.

"You're not going to dig your claws into me when I shake it or anything, are you?" Maxstrom asked as he hesitantly pulled his right hand back slightly.

"Nah, I like to have fun, but I do think I'm an honorable loser."

Maxstrom and Akbu both shook their respective hand and paw.

"You've come a long way in eight years kid. Just remember, no matter how much you know, there is always more to learn."

"Good job, Max." Niba, Akbu's wife, declared as she gave Akbu an affectionate hug. "Not many can say they've beaten my Akbu."

"Hey I did let him win you know." Akbu retorted. "I'm still technically undefeated."

Niba simply rolled her eyes at this statement.

"Max! Max! That was amazing. You were awesome! Totally the best." Dusty, Maxstrom's best friend and housemate, yelled as he came running up to them. He was a young adult Shadican, and his bright green eyes glowed with enthusiasm.

"Hey, thanks! To be completely honest, Akbu had me worried there for a minute or two."

Akbu smiled and pointed his finger at Maxstrom. "Ha! See, I knew I could get in your head. Well, I'll leave you two to hang out." Akbu said as he walked away with his arm around his wife.

"Max, could we go do some sword training? I just got out of my boring farming class. I had to sit still for a whole hour and listen to Sheni lecture us on seasonal rain!"

"Oh that sounds miserable Dusty. You'd think being part of the night watch would make her a bit more interesting, but I guess not. We can do some training for a few minutes; but I've been doing sword training most of the day, so I want a short break."

"Okay, I won't keep you long then, don't worry. I wish I could train with swords all day. Or go to light school and learn how to control light! That would be awesome."

"Dusty!" A voice called from behind Maxstrom. It was Meeka, Dusty's mom.

"Oh, hey mom." Dusty responded.

"Dusty, why is your fur so dirty? Did you do a roll at some point?" She questioned, her yellow eyes showing motherly concern.

"Oh, uh, I rolled as I ran away from Sheni."

"You need to keep your soft fur clean! It attracts dirt a lot easier than the average Shadican's fur." Meeka mumbled as she brushed the dirt off of Dusty and furrowed her pink nose. Pink noses were incredibly rare amongst the Shadicans; most of their noses were black, like their fur.

"Mom. Mom! I'm an adult now. I can do it." Dusty responded as he resisted.

"Oh, I suppose so." Meeka replied in a sad tone. "Just make sure to take your farming classes seriously, alright?"

"But they're so boring!"

"I know you don't enjoy them, but it's for the best. Farming is a good livelihood. Besides, our family has been farming for generations, and we really want you to continue it. That's why we're paying for your schooling."

Dusty sighed. "I still don't like those classes."

Meeka looked at her son with a sad look. Then she looked over and noticed Maxstrom.

Hello Max. How's your new house mate doing?"

"Dusty is great!"

"Glad to hear it. I assume you'll both be at the festival tonight?" Meeka inquired.

"Of course; we wouldn't miss it!" Maxstrom responded with a smile.

34

Maxstrom blinked his eyes several times; he was a little tired, and he realized he had been staring into the center of the gigantic bonfire for about a minute now. It was night, and the Shadicans were having a big feast, the Feast of Heaven.

Tapito, the Shadican head chief, gave a nod to Akbu, and he stood. Akbu was not only in charge of the Shadican Elite Guard, but he was also the people's spiritual leader. As such, he facilitated spiritual feasts. In keeping with his job description, he addressed the Shadicans: "Today we celebrate Abada's mercy to us and thank Him for allowing us to enter His new creation, even though we don't deserve it. Praise Abada, the God who is the creator of all!"

The Shadicans let out a wild cheer, and many took a large sip from their wooden cups which housed their root beer. This root beer was a strong brew of tree roots, such as birch root and others like it, mixed with honey. None of the katlican species drink actual beer; in fact, the entire species hates the taste of alcohol entirely.

"And as a result, we feast on fish!" Tapito yelled excitedly, her sunken yellow eyes bright with excitement. She had a small spot of white fur at the base of her neck, and was missing a piece of her right ear. Even though Tapito was an older Shadican, she still had plenty of energy, especially when it came to feasts.

Again the Shadicans let out a loud cheer.

"These Shadicans do have some strange beliefs." Maxstrom thought to himself. "I don't see why they would think they don't deserve heaven. I mean, assuming there is a heaven, I figure we would all deserve to go. And especially these Shadicans; they are kind creatures."

"I'd also like to propose a toast," Tapito said. "Eight years ago this coming fall, I was with Akbu and a few other members of the guard checking out our defensive posts on the Shadic River. While on this excursion, I ran into a young boy on the beach. And even though most of my advisors were concerned it might be a trap, I decided to offer a loving paw to this boy. Now, Maxstrom might as well be a Shadican; because he's family."

"Family!" The Shadicans echoed.

"Thank you all!" Maxstrom replied as he stood. "I'm so glad you've taken me in and that you decided not to throw me back into the river; even though that's probably what Akbu wanted to do."

"Alright, who told?" Akbu yelled in response.

The Shadicans erupted into laughter.

"And now we feast!" Tapito declared, cutting the verbal banter short.

The Shadican chefs, who had been slow roasting hundreds of fish, pulled the metal racks away from the massive bonfire, and immediately the Shadican crowd went wild trying to get themselves a fish.

Maxstrom simply sat back and watched the frenzy. Even though he thought some of the beliefs that the Shadicans held were a bit peculiar, he did enjoy their feasts, both because of the good food, and because of the celebratory atmosphere. Music created by flutes and drums filled the air, and most of the Shadicans that weren't eating were dancing. As he was watching the festive atmosphere, he happened to glance over to the side, and saw something odd. Talican and Nandu, two of Tapito's lower rank-ing advisors, were in the shadows whispering about something. He saw them both quickly glance in Tapito's direction as if they were talking about her. They both quickly looked at each other again and resumed talking in hushed tones. Maxstrom, being a curious person, decided to try to find out what they were saying. But just as he was about to get up and sneak over, he heard someone say his name.

"Max! Want some root beer?" Dusty asked as he walked over to Max-strom, holding an extra cup.

"Oh, totally! Thanks."

"Of course, I figured you couldn't say no to some freshly made Shadi-can root beer. So I'm still not for sure on whether or not I should use one or two swords. What do you think?" Dusty questioned as he sat down next to his housemate.

Maxstrom looked over towards the suspicious scene he wanted to investigate, and saw both Talican and Nandu nod at each other and then head in separate directions. Since Maxstrom's chance to figure out what was going on had passed, he directed his attention to Dusty's question.

"Well personally, I've seen you use both, and I think you look more confident with one sword. But go with whatever you feel is most comfort-able; I'm not you."

"Sounds good, I do think I feel more comfortable with one sword."

"Hey Dusty?" Maxstrom asked, wanting to get his friend's opinion on the scene he had witnessed with Talican and Nandu.

"Yeah?"

Maxstrom paused for a moment and thought about what he was go-ing to say. Dusty was a good Shadican and kind-hearted. But Maxstrom had seen his friend get paranoid over nothing before, and didn't want to put him through that again. So instead of talking about that odd scene, he directed the conversation to another strange scene around the fire.

"You see Shacbu all the way over there?" Maxstrom asked as he gestured in her direction. "She looks kinda dejected."

"Oh what, Shacbu? I didn't notice her at all." Dusty declared in an odd tone as he pulled his arms close to his side.

Maxstrom gave his friend a confused look.

"I'm wondering if she's taking that sparring match earlier today a little too seriously." Maxstrom declared in a reflective tone.

"Maybe. She does feel a lot of pressure since she's been selected as the next head chief. That's not an easy task since you have to be the best. If she doesn't meet the Shadican council's standards, they can reject her as the next ruler. And no Shadican who's been refused the position of head chief has ever been looked at the same."

"Exactly. Hey, do you want to come with me and talk with her?"

"Oh. Um. No. No, I'm good."

"Dusty. . . why not? You're usually extremely social."

"Um, because, uh. She's uh. A girl?"

"But I've seen you talk to girls before."

Dusty looked up at Maxstrom with a sheepish look on his face.

"Ohh, I was wondering if that's what it was." Maxstrom said with a smirk.

"Max. Max! You can't tell anyone. You know how embarrassing that would be? Especially since she's going to be the next chief?"

"Hey relax man, your secret is safe with me. But when I go over there to talk with her, I'll be sure to let her know that you're willing to do sword training with her."

"You better not!"

"Hey she might need a partner! You never know." Maxstrom declared as he got up and started to walk towards Shacbu.

"Max. . ."

"I'll be back in a few." Maxstrom hollered over his shoulder as he walked towards Shacbu.

"Max!"

Maxstrom walked around the bonfire. Shacbu was sitting alone. She was a little distance from the fire, and was quietly eating her fish.

"Hey Shacbu?"

She did a quick jump, and looked up at Maxstrom with a surprised look on her face.

"You doing alright?" Maxstrom asked.

"Yeah. Fine."

"You sure? You seemed to be a little grumpy about the match today. You used to be such a good sport." Maxstrom pointed out as he took a seat next to Shacbu.

"Yeah I just, I have a lot on my mind."

"Does it have anything to do with the announcement that you're the candidate for high chief?"

"Maybe a little. . ."

"Do you want to talk about it?"

"Not really. . . it just feels. . . like everyone is expecting everything of me now. And if I don't become the best fighter and meet the council's expectations then no one will ever look at me the same again, and I will have to live a life of shame. And on top of all that, I still haven't been able to master light and go invisible yet."

"Hey. Listen. I know it seems like the weight of the world is on your shoulders right now; but it's not as bad as you think. Regardless of whether or not you pass the test when the time comes, I'll still be your friend. And I'm pretty sure Dusty will be too."

Shacbu smiled while looking at the ground. "Yeah. . ."

"Besides, the average Shadican lifespan is what, forty? Tapito is only thirty; so you have at least ten years to become a master at fighting, and to learn how to master light. You've got plenty of time."

"Hey, that's actually a good point." Shacbu admitted in a relieved tone.

Maxstrom smiled at his friend. "If you ever get nervous again, use that as motivation towards training and improving. Both Dusty and I would be more than happy to train with you if you need it."

"Thanks." Shacbu replied.

Maxstrom looked up towards the bonfire, and saw a small commotion where he had been siting. He squinted his eyes, and saw Lubu trying to pull Dusty off of his seat. Lubu was a year younger than Dusty, and a known trouble maker; he had tried to bully Dusty several times before.

"Well, I think Dusty is having another run in with Lubu over there, so I'm going to head over and break it up. You good?"

"Yeah, thanks. I'll come over and join you both in a few minutes."

"Alright" Maxstrom said as he got up. Just then, Maxstrom looked up towards the bonfire, and saw Lubu push Dusty. Dusty lost his balance, and fell into the fire pit. Maxstrom immediately bolted for the fire. He looked for a source of water nearby, but saw nothing. He took a mental note, and knew that he'd have to control the fire to save his friend.

When he got there, he couldn't believe his eyes. Dusty was laying in the fire pit facing the center of the fire, but had his arms crossed forcefully over his face. Instead of the flame engulfing him, it was curving away from him, giving Dusty a berth of at least three feet. All the surrounding Shadicans stood dumbfounded at this sight. The music quickly died down as more and more Shadicans noticed the scene that was unfolding.

"Dusty, can you hear me bud?" Maxstrom inquired in a surprised tone.

"Yeah." Dusty replied with his eyes closed. He had winced as he had fallen into the pit, and still hadn't opened his eyes.

"Um, bud. Are you the one pushing that fire back?"

"I think so. Does it normally really strain your muscles to control fire?"

"Yeah, especially if I haven't practiced in a while."

"Then yes. I am. But. I don't know how much longer I can do this for. So could you help? Please?"

"I got you bud," Maxstrom said as he pushed his hands in the direction of the fire. The fire instantly moved back another foot from Dusty, and Dusty, who had now opened his eyes, quickly stood up and jumped out of the fire pit.

"Well what do you know Dusty, you can control fire too!" Maxstrom said, hardly believing the words coming out of his mouth.

"Lubu assured me it was an accident. Although he is a troublemaker, he is not the type to try and kill someone. Regardless, he will be required to fulfill some community service hours because of the incident." Tapito declared as she sat cross legged on her mat. It was the day after the feast, and Tapito had requested to see both Dusty and Maxstrom early in the morning in her treehouse. All of the Shadicans in Shavi, the Shadican capital, live in wooden treehouses built in the huge, durable Brownwood pine trees in a section of the Kachuna Forest. Large celebrations, such as the festival that had occurred the night before, along with other activities such as duels, usually took place on the forest floor.

"Good, he needs to learn to not be so mean." Dusty responded as he crossed his arms.

"So how common is this exactly?" Maxstrom asked Tapito.

"What, finding a Shadican that can control fire?" Tapito inquired.

Maxstrom nodded.

"Rare. Very rare. Most Shadicans can only control light, which many don't even bother mastering these days. So much unused potential. And most of the Shadicans that can control light are at the border."

"So, am I. . . in trouble?" Dusty inquired sheepishly.

"Quite the contrary. I'm well aware that you abhor your farming lessons, and just about everything else that doesn't involve a sword or some type of combat training." Tapito stated.

"I wouldn't say abhor. Just really, really, really hate."

"Dusty, that's literally exactly the same as abhorring something." Maxstrom interjected.

"No it's not!" Dusty yelled defensively

"Ahem!" Tapito coughed.

Akbu, who was off to the side, simply rolled his eyes.

Tapito continued, "Seeing as that is the case, I think that your path is to become a warrior, not a farmer, as your family initially thought was best. And in light of this new discovery, your family agrees with my decision to have you cease your farming lessons, and have you start training to master fire, light, and other combative arts."

"Yes! Yes!" Dusty yelled aloud as he stood to his feet started jumping up and down with joy. He then suddenly realized what he was doing, and rapidly sat back down. "I mean. Ahem. I'm. Sorry to hear that?"

Tapito then looked over at her secretary, Shenabu. Shenabu, the sister of Shacbu, was responsible for recording what was said in Tapito's meetings. She was sitting in the corner with furrowed eyebrows as she tried to figure out how exactly to express the emotion she had just witnessed Dusty display. Tapito waited for Shenabu to catch up before returning her gaze to Dusty.

"And seeing as you have no objections to this, I want to send you both to Duba in the south. There's an old friend of mine down that way that has amazing mastery over fire and light. In fact, he's actually the only one I know of that has the gift to control fire besides you two, at least in this corner of the world."

40

"But chief, what if my parents finally come looking for me while I'm down in Duba?" Maxstrom inquired.

"Shortly after you arrived here, your parents confirmed what Aliofi told you by sending word that they would come and get you when it's safe. Since then, they've been in hiding somewhere in Dauchenland preparing to overthrow the government, and we haven't heard anything from them in almost eight years." Tapito glanced off to the side as she delivered this statement, and then quickly returned her gaze to Maxstrom to finish her thought. "And from what I hear at our trading posts, Kafahr is still the ruler of Dauchenland. So I doubt your parents will be coming to get you anytime soon."

"But. . ." Maxstrom interjected.

"Max, I know you've not wanted to leave Shavi to train with your special abilities because you've been waiting for your parents. And I know you've been experimenting on your own and that you've been able to figure out a variety of neat tricks. In fact, I've heard that you're a natural with both fire and water. But that does not change the fact that it's been eight years since you arrived here. Your excuse to wait in Shavi has lasted too long. And you've already mastered the sword, as well as hand-to-hand combat; so there is nothing more for you to learn here. I would be failing in my duties to take care of you if I did not make sure you received professional training in all areas I was able to provide in as the Shadican head chief."

"But I. . ."

"It's not up for discussion." Tapito declared, suddenly becoming stern. "You both leave tomorrow morning."

Maxstrom's face displayed his frustration, but he knew Tapito wasn't going to change her mind.

"Alright, chief." He said, almost begrudgingly.

"I'm excited, but I'm not." Dusty declared as both he and Maxstrom walked back to their treehouse across one of the many rope bridges in Shavi.

"Why are you not?" Maxstrom asked.

"Well, one reason is because I'm going to have to leave home, and that's scary."

"And another reason probably has to do with a certain someone, right?" Maxstrom inquired, trying to use humor to move on from his frustration at Tapito forcing him to go on this trip.

"Come on, Max, give it a rest. Honestly I'm not too worried about that. I think my life is changing enough right now that I shouldn't worry about my feelings. . . if it works out, it'll work out."

"Wow, that's really mature sounding. Or are you just saying that because you're too scared to actually tell her how you feel?"

Dusty quickly looked away and gave no reply. After a moment of silence, Dusty tried to change the subject.

"I'm really sore."

Maxstrom decided to give Dusty a break from the teasing and went in the new conversational direction. "Yeah that happens to me when I control fire after taking a break for a short time; I can only imagine how sore you must feel after controlling fire for the first time."

The duo reached their home and walked into the treehouse.

"Ah, home sweet home," Dusty declared as they both walked in.

"Not for much longer though. Time to move. . . again."

"I can understand you not wanting to uproot your life, especially since it already happened to you once." Dusty said, trying to be empathetic.

"Excuse me?" A Shadican inquired as he stuck his head through the door.

"Yes?" Maxstrom inquired.

"We're about to hoist your hot rock up, assuming you need one tonight?"

Since the Shadicans in Shavi lived in treehouses built in massive trees, they did not use fire places in their homes because of safety reasons. Any fire besides candles were to be kept on the ground; this rule included fires for cooking meals, which was done on the ground either over an open fire, or at a cooking shack on the ground built sporadically throughout the town with a designated cooking spot for each family. So instead of fires to keep warm in the treehouses, volcanic stones were heated up on the ground by a fire and then hoisted up every night into each house to provide warmth. The stones were placed on a metal tray installed in each Shadican treehouse. This technique proved incredibly effective at keeping forest fires at bay, and worked well at generating heat within the thick moss insulation packed between the outer and inner wood frames of the Shadican treehouses.

"Yes please." Maxstrom responded.

"Alright, just wanted to be sure since I overheard you guys talking about leaving. Don't want to hall one of these heavy stones up if I don't need to." The Shadican said as he walked in and grabbed the metal tray that housed the volcanic stone.

"Totally understand." Maxstrom answered. "We leave tomorrow."

The Shadican nodded, and then went over to the edge of the tree-house's balcony and yelled something down to a Shadican below.

"What should I even pack?" Dusty inquired as he sat on his bed.

"Well think of it as one of the warrior survival trips. You don't want to pack too much, but you also don't want to pack too little. You want enough to fit into a survival pack."

"Do you even know how long of a journey Duba is from here?"

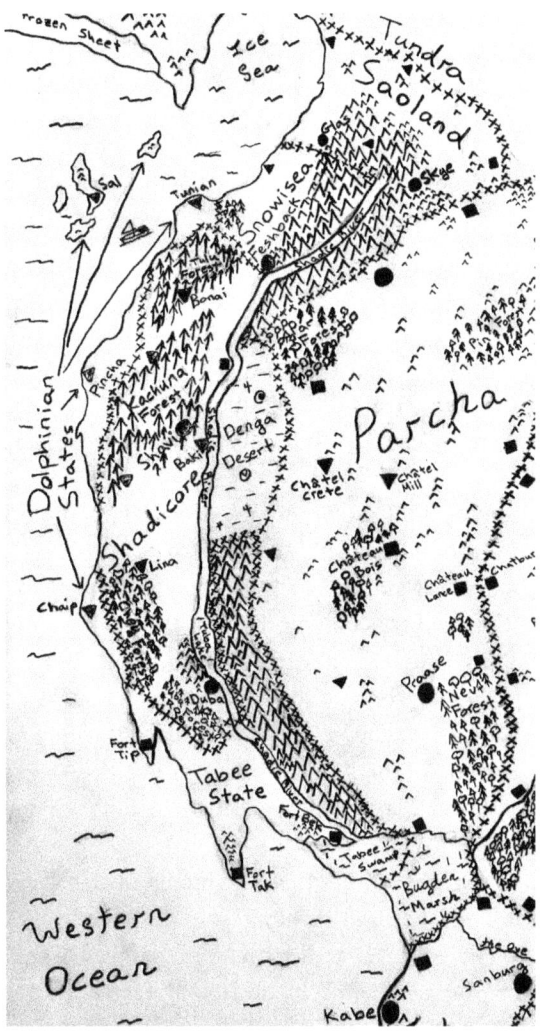

"Well on foot it'd be a long way. But we don't have to worry about that until we come back. Duba is downstream from us, so we can walk to the Shadic River, and then buy a canoe and take it down."

"Hey that's awesome!"

"Yeah, and I'm glad you're not scared of water, unlike some Shadicans. Because then I'd have to talk you into even getting into a boat."

"Nope! Less walking is good for me. I enjoy the exercise, but it does get old after doing it a few days in a row."

"Here you go." The Shadican with the volcanic stone declared as he slid the metal tray across the floor and back into place. He had thick gloves on so he wouldn't burn his paws.

"You guys are really fast. Thank you!" Dusty chimed in.

"No problem. You both have a good night now." The Shadican declared as he took off his gloves and walked out.

"You too!" Both Maxstrom and Dusty called after him.

Maxstrom then walked over to his side of the room and began looking at all of his stuff. "So I'm going to bring my hammock, and my cloak, along with some blankets. . ."

"Why blankets?"

"Dusty. You're the only one of us in this room with a cozy fur coat. I get cold really easily."

"Right. I keep forgetting that. Should I bring my water pack?"

"Sure, a water pack won't hurt. Just remember we can purify water from the river."

"Good thinking. Oh, and I'm totally bringing my root beer stash."

"You have a root beer stash?"

"Oh yeah, check it out." Dusty moved aside a screen cover at the base of his bed and pulled out a small jug. "This is the really strong brew. Strong as they come. I've been saving it for a special occasion."

"Awesome! Just don't make yourself sick. . ."

"Shouldn't be a problem, since I'll be sharing it with you."

"I like the sound of that."

Both Dusty and Maxstrom proceeded to fill their bags with their belongings.

"Hey Max, check it out. It's that old flute I got a year ago. Still haven't finished learning how to play this thing."

Maxstrom chuckled. "Yeah, I remember you were all excited and you saved up a ton of money for it. Why don't you practice with it anymore?"

"Ah, I just never had the patience. Do you think I should bring it?"

"I mean, it might be nice to have something to do when you're exhausted and sitting in front of the fire after a long canoe ride or hike."

"So yes." Dusty responded as he tossed the flute into his bag.

"Oh Max!" Dusty cried.

"What, what's up?"

"I just realized that I don't have my own actual sword yet. Which means I can't take a sword on the trip. I'll be weaponless and doomed!"

"Okay, Dusty. First off, you have claws. Those are weapons. Second, you can control fire now. You can use that as a weapon."

"Oh. Good point." Dusty responded in a somewhat dejected tone. He really wanted his own sword.

Suddenly, Dusty let out a horrid screech, and started scrambling away from his bed.

"What? What's wrong?" Maxstrom yelled as he jumped to his feet.

"It's. It's a. Spider!" Dusty exclaimed in terror.

Maxstrom's face instantly changed from concern to frustration.

"Dusty. Come on."

"Max! Kill it!"

"Fine." Maxstrom declared in a bland tone as he calmly walked over to Dusty's bed and squashed the arachnid with his boot.

"Thank you." Dusty declared as he cleared his throat and began to compose himself.

"You know, I don't get how you want to learn how to fight, yet you're so terrified of spiders."

"Bad guys and weird creatures don't scare me, Max. I don't think I'd even be terrified of a giant monster. But those, those tiny creeping monsters? They terrify me."

"I still don't get it." Maxstrom responded as he shook his head and walked back over to his side of the room. He then looked out his window through the trees and sighed. It was time for another big life change; but at least this time he would have a friend with him.

Maxstrom and Dusty woke up early the next day; well before first light. Maxstrom wanted to be sure to get an early start.

The two climbed down the net from their treehouse in the dark, and started walking towards the main road to the Shadic River with their packs on their backs. Maxstrom made a small fireball to light the way. As they reached the edge of the Shavi city limits and were about to get on the road towards the Shadic River, Maxstrom saw three pairs of eyes glimmering in the night ahead of them. He could tell they were Shadican eyes, so he wasn't alarmed. As they approached, the Shadican's figures seemed to almost materialize out of the dark; the figures of Tapito, Shacbu, and Akbu.

"Even though we said goodbye last night, I wanted to wish you farewell again." Tapito said.

"And make sure that you didn't go the wrong way or anything." Akbu added.

"I'm glad you think so highly of my navigational skills Akbu; especially since you were the one that trained me."

Akbu smirked. "I'm going to miss our sarcastic exchanges, Max. And getting you lost on purpose on those survival expeditions."

Maxstrom suddenly narrowed his eyebrows. "Wait you're telling me that. . ."

"Alright, I have a gift for both of you," Tapito interjected, cutting off the verbal banter that was about to ensue.

"For you, Dusty, a sword."

"No way!" Dusty yelled in joy as Tapito handed him the Shadican blade.

"How did you make that so quickly?" Maxstrom inquired.

"It was actually going to be a present for Dusty at the Festival of Salvation later this year since he was so enthusiastic about the mandatory warrior survival classes, but I figured it would make more sense to give it to him early. Akbu gave some input into the design and specifications." Tapito responded.

"Thank you!" Dusty exclaimed as he drew the sword and admired it with a giant grin on his face.

"And for you, Maxstrom, I had our smith make you something special. A leather suit with metal plates woven in."

"What? That's awesome! How did the smith even know how to make the suit?"

"It took him a lot of trial and error. But I figured since you're not as agile as us, you should have some kind of armor."

"Thank you, chief!"

"I wish you both the best, and I'll see you in a few months." Tapito said.

"Have a safe trip! And don't get lost this time, Max." Akbu declared, smirking.

"Thanks! See you soon." Dusty replied, and started walking off.

"I can't believe you, Akbu." Maxstrom responded, glaring at him.

Akbu maintained his smirk. "See you, Max."

After glaring at Akbu for a moment, Maxstrom turned and started walking down the road after Dusty.

"I thought you were going to give him the other thing, Tapito." Akbu whispered.

"What other thing?" Shacbu inquired in a curious tone.

"Oh, Akbu just meant a more motherly farewell." Tapito replied. Akbu shrugged his shoulders at Shacbu, and both Shacbu and Akbu started walking back towards Shavi. But Tapito stayed, and watched Maxstrom and Dusty vanish into the darkness. As soon as she knew no one was around, she pulled out a small scroll from her pack and looked down at it with a sad look. The Aceic Order's wax seal was broken, as it had been for the last two months. And even after all this time, she still didn't have the heart to let Maxstrom read what was inside.

Maxstrom and Dusty reached the Shadic River early in the evening. They arrived in Baki, a small port town, and made camp for the night just outside the town limits on the beach. Maxstrom strung up his hammock between two trees only about a foot off the ground, and Dusty formed a pile of sand into a makeshift bed. They then both dug a fire pit between them, and got a small fire going. Maxstrom then used his fishing gear to catch two fish for their dinner. Maxstrom and Dusty then gutted and cooked the fish, and Maxstrom used a packet of seasoning he had brought with him to add some flavor to their dinner. Dusty then pulled out his jug of beer, and looked at Maxstrom.

"I don't want to keep lugging this thing around with me. Let's see if we can't finish it tonight."

"I'm down for that." Maxstrom responded.

Dusty poured both himself and Maxstrom a cup, and the two drank several hours into the night. After enjoying this small feast and sharing some stories and jokes, and after a brief but failed attempt by Dusty to play his flute, the two friends decided to turn in for the night.

They both awoke with the sunrise, and were able to enjoy the pleasant surprise of sore legs from their journey the day before.

"Guess I'm more out of shape than I thought." Dusty said.

"Ah, yesterday was the only day we needed to walk. Tomorrow the rest of our bodies will be sore from rowing."

"Great, now I have that to look forward to." Dusty groaned as he massaged his leg muscles.

The duo then went into Baki and purchase a canoe along with a day's worth of food. Since there were plenty of small villages to stop at on the way to resupply, and since they could also catch fish, carrying a large amount of food was pointless. Once they had loaded up the canoe, they launched for Duba.

They made excellent time the first two days. However, right before dawn on the third day, Maxstrom awoke in his hammock to a sprinkling of rain hitting his face.

Dusty moaned. "I was in the middle of a dream about the most amazing fish I had ever tasted. Why did it have to rain right in the middle of that?"

Maxstrom looked up at the clouds. "We should probably flip the canoe and stay under there for a while."

"Why?" Dusty asked as he rubbed his eyes.

"I think it'll start pouring in a few minutes."

Seconds after those words had left Maxstrom's mouth, a deluge started to fall. Maxstrom and Dusty quickly grabbed the canoe, which was next to their campsite, flipped it over, and quickly crawled under. It was a large canoe and left plenty of room for both of them. "Well, I wouldn't advise us continuing our journey until this passes." Maxstrom said.

"That's fine with me. I want to go back to sleep and see if I can't pick up that dream with the tasty fish." Dusty replied as he curled up into a ball and closed his eyes.

Maxstrom opened his eyes slowly. It had stopped raining.

"Hey, Dusty." Maxstrom whispered as he turned to his travel companion.

"Mm, yeah?"

"It stopped raining, so we can probably resume our journey."

"Okay, works for me." Dusty responded as he let out a yawn and did a quick stretch.

"Did you ever get back to dreaming about that tasty fish?" Maxstrom inquired as he rolled out from under the canoe.

"No, sadly. I lost it." Dusty responded in a sad tone.

"Sorry bud." Maxstrom responded.

They both flipped the canoe back over, and loaded up their supplies. Even though they had lost a couple of hours of daylight, they still managed to make good time.

As the sun started to set, Maxstrom suggested to Dusty that to make up for lost time they travel through the night instead of setting up camp. He also suggested that they could take shifts sleeping.

"I'm alright with that if you are." Dusty replied.

They did this pattern through the night, and continued through all of the next day as they neared the entrance to Tuba Lake. Both Dusty and Maxstrom felt that this approach used their time more effectively, and decided to do it the following night. But as they exited Lake Tuba on their sixth day of their travel, a small setback occurred.

It was still somewhat early in the morning, and it was Dusty's shift to keep watch. However, Dusty was quite sore and tired, and accidentally fell asleep while on his shift. Suddenly, both awoke to the boat being hit violently from beneath.

"What's going on?" Maxstrom yelled, grabbing the sides of the boat. He was still laying down.

Dusty, who had just woken up, needed a moment to gather his senses.

"It seems that I may have navigated us into the rapids part of this river."

"Dusty! Why would you do that?" The canoe jolted again after impacting another rock, throwing Maxstrom into a sitting position. "All you had to do was steer us to the left side of the river and we would have missed this!"

"Well, it's hard to do anything while you're asleep."

"You were asleep?! Dusty!"

"I'm sorry okay! You can hate me later. Right now we need to focus on getting out of this mess!"

Suddenly they both heard a large ripping sound. Maxstrom looked down, and saw a fist sized gaping hole in the bottom of the canoe. Water started gushing in.

"Okay Dusty, you need to navigate us out of this. I'm going to try and stop the canoe from filling with water."

"Good plan."

Maxstrom used his ability to control water to grab the water beginning to build up around him in his right hand and throw it out of the canoe. At the same time, he used his left hand to push down towards the hole and stop any water from entering the canoe.

Although Dusty wasn't the best at staying awake, his navigational skills with a canoe were commendable. He was able to maneuver the canoe out of the rapids with ease and back into the deeper part of the river.

"Alright, head for the next bank on the right side so we can take a good look at this hole."

"Sure thing."

They had to travel about another quarter of a mile downstream before finally reaching a sandy stretch of shore with a tiny cove that they could get to without having to cross the rapids again. The cove was surrounded by brush and several normal sized trees, and shortly beyond that were the roots of several large mountains. Once they arrived on the beach, Maxstrom quickly pulled the canoe onto the shore and fell to the ground; his arms were exhausted from keeping the water out of the small boat.

"I'm sorry Max. . ." Dusty said, dejected.

"It's alright Dusty. I just wished you had told me you were tired. We could have pulled over and taken a break."

"Yeah. . ."

Maxstrom turned his head and looked at the hole in the canoe while still laying on the ground.

"Well I think the canoe is done. I don't have a kit to fix it with, and I don't see any villages nearby."

"I haven't seen any other boats on the river in a couple hours either." Dusty added.

"Yeah. So looks like we'll be continuing the rest of our journey on foot. I think there's a small cut through this brush leading toward Duba." Maxstrom declared as he looked in that direction.

Dusty moaned as Maxstrom started pulling their gear out of the canoe.

"I don't like the idea either," Maxstrom responded, "but we don't have any other choice. I think we should set up camp here and get some rest first, though. We can start at first light."

"Sounds good," Dusty replied as he let out a long yawn. "I could use a good nap."

Dusty and Maxstrom made camp in a small enclave that was almost entirely surrounded by trees and brush, but was sandy in the middle. Dusty decided to immediately lie down and go to sleep, while Maxstrom went into the small grouping of trees to collect some firewood. Maxstrom thought it was weird seeing normal trees again after all of the time he had spent in Shavi, where the trees were enormous. After about an hour of work, Maxstrom successfully brought back enough firewood to last the rest of the day and through the night.

Maxstrom awoke with a start. Something didn't feel right. He looked up, and saw that it was nighttime and overcast; there was no moon or stars visible. The fire, which should have lasted until morning, was stone cold.

"Dusty. Hey." Maxstrom whispered loudly.

"Mm. Let me sleep." Dusty replied groggily.

Maxstrom looked around. He felt an oppressive atmosphere, but couldn't figure out why. It almost felt like something was watching them. Although he was no longer afraid of the dark, the thought that something might be watching him creeped him out a little too much, and he quickly made a fire ball in his hand so he could see into the dark. He scanned the surrounding brush, but couldn't see anything.

"What are you doing?" Dusty said, sitting up and slowly rubbing his eyes.

"I feel like something is watching us."

Dusty got up and started gazing into the forest with his cat-like eyes.

"I don't see anything Max, and my night vision is far better than yours. I think you must've just had a bad dream. Can we go back to sleep now?"

All of the sudden, they both heard a loud crack to their left. Then they saw a massive tree branch fall to the ground. Even though it was dark, they could see that this branch was at least twenty feet long, and had fallen from a larger tree. They also noticed that this branch was full of green leaves, and the wood sticking out of the broken end looked fresh, and almost white.

"Max that branch was broken by something. . . there's no way it could have just snapped on its own like that."

The duo then heard sinister whispering in the wind, and the whispering's direction shifted as if it was circling them. Then, out of nowhere, a high pitched, evil shriek broke the silence, and a dark creature came flying out from the opposite direction of the broken tree branch. It was something unlike anything either of them had ever seen before. The creature was dark, yet its body was transparent, similar to smoke. But unlike smoke, the creature had a defined form. It also had glowing red eyes with no pupils. Its face was similar to a pitch black bark, and was much less transparent than the rest of its body. It hard arms, but no legs; instead of legs, the creature tapered off at the end into three points, similar to how a bat's bottom would end. It had hands with large, lanky fingers. On top of having arms, it had two thin tentacles near its shoulders. The creature glided several feet above the surface of the ground; seemingly unaffected by gravity.

The monster flew at Maxstrom with its arms extended. Maxstrom pulled his arm back to use his fireball to launch a blast at the creature; but he had no time. The monster slammed into Maxstrom and threw him against a tree, which forced Maxstrom to extinguish his fireball. With lightning speed, the creature wrapped its tentacles around Maxstrom's neck, and began to suffocate him. Maxstrom tried to grab the tentacles, but the monster's arms gripped his own, and Maxstrom was overpowered. He couldn't move, and after several seconds of struggling, his vision started to become clouded with darkness; he was about to pass out.

Dusty gave a loud yell, and the creature looked up to see the Shadican flying through the air towards him, sword raised above his head. The creature gave another shriek, but did not move. Dusty swung his sword down

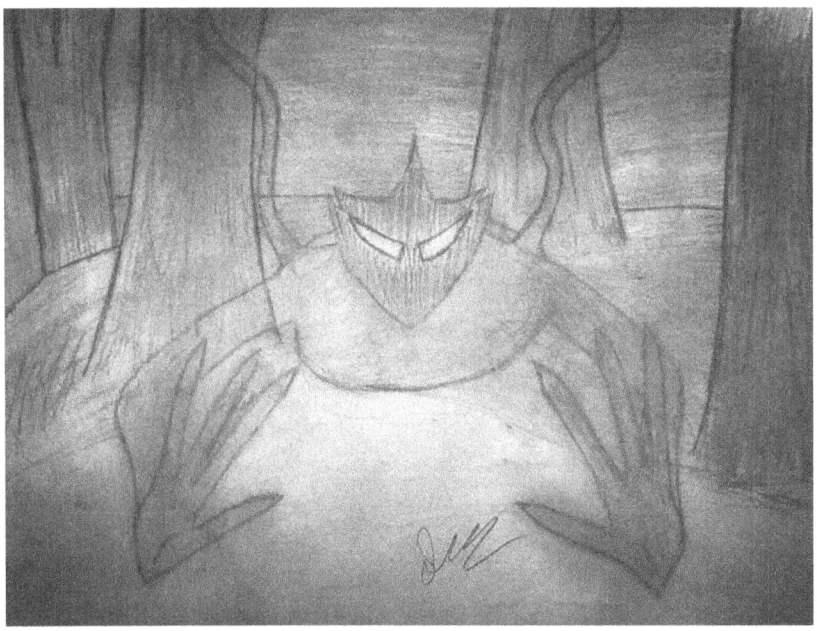

and hit the creature in the middle of the face, following his strike through and separating the creature's face into two even halves. The monster dropped Maxstrom, but stayed levitating in the air. Maxstrom struggled to crawl away and pull the tentacles off of his neck, gasping for breath.

Dusty looked up at this beast still hovering above him before moving to check on Maxstrom. But to his horror, he saw the two halves of the face begin to rejoin. Dusty was stunned; he could only stare at the monster. Within seconds, the monster's face was fully reformed and the red, glowing eyes were gazing into his own as the creature looked down on him. Dusty froze. It quickly came to his attention how big this creature was; at least triple his own size. He also noticed that the creature breathed in a heavy and forced manner. Its breath was warm, but smelled like death.

As Dusty was taking this scene in, there was one other thing that caught his eye; something bright appeared behind the see-through creature and rapidly grew in size. It was a bright stream of fire. Maxstrom, who was now standing behind this beast, had recovered his breath and was shooting a steady blast of fire at the monster from behind. The creature titled its head up to the sky and let out a loud shriek of pain as the flames began to roast it. Dusty, recovering from his stare down with the monster, grabbed his sword and stabbed the creature under the jaw and pushed his sword through the top of its head. He then pulled his sword out with all his might, and as he removed his sword, the creature fell to the ground with a thud.

Once Maxstrom saw the creature fall, he stopped his fire blast. There was a small amount of light smoke that was emanating from the creature's bottom half, but it had not caught fire. Maxstrom walked over to Dusty, and both of them looked down at the creature's face. The creature lay there, motionless. But its red eyes were still glowing.

"What do you suppose it is?" Dusty asked.

Just then, the wound to the monster's head rapidly healed itself, and the creature lifted up off the ground and lunged for Dusty. Just as its creepy fingers were about a foot away from him, a ball of light appeared all around Dusty. The creature impacted this light as if it had hit a stone wall and was instantly thrown back. There was also a loud sizzling sound that came from the creature as soon as it touched the ball of light. As it was flung back, the ball of light around Dusty disappeared. Confused, both Dusty and Maxstrom looked at the monster. The creature seemed to be burning with white light wherever it had touched the ball of light. As it burned, the monster kept crying out and tried to scratch this light off of itself, but the light started to expand and cover the whole creature, until it was completely covered with light. Once it was completely covered, the monster changed into a ball of light, which then shrunk down into nothing, and extinguished itself.

Dusty and Maxstrom were almost in a daze; neither of them knew what to do or what to make of this experience. So they both just stood there, staring at where this creature had been.

"Doesn't this thing sound kind of like those creatures we've heard stories about from the Shadican elders?" Maxstrom asked, hardly believing that these things could actually be real.

"You mean the denac? But they're spirits. They aren't able to touch things in the physical world."

"I thought so too." Maxstrom said, "But I can't think of anything else this thing could have been."

Both Maxstrom and Dusty kept staring at where the creature had been.

"I still don't get how that thing doesn't terrify you, but spiders do. Spiders, Dusty." Maxstrom declared as he looked over at his friend and pointed to where the monster had been.

"Hey come on now. We almost just died and you have to bring that up?" Dusty retorted as he furrowed his eyebrows at Maxstrom.

"Sorry bud. It just confuses me." Maxstrom responded as he looked off into the distance.

"Me too. I can't really explain it." Dusty informed as he too looked off into the distance.

Neither of them got much sleep the rest of the night, and at least one of them was keeping watch at all times. As the sun rose, the duo guessed that they had about another days' worth of walking ahead of them. They both quickly packed their gear, and began moving towards Duba. But rather than keep a casual walking pace, both Maxstrom and Dusty decided to pick up a light jog because of the fear of running into another monster, and they kept this pace the whole day. As a result, they reached Duba shortly after the sun had set. But they were both exhausted, dehydrated, and in desperate need of food.

Chapter 3

A Mountaintop Experience

B.Y. 4013

"I've faced many powerful foes; but the two greatest?
Fear, and myself."
—Shadic III

"Makbu, have you heard?" Chipo asked, smiling at his uncle, which emphasized his unique pink nose. They were both walking in the dirt street.

Chipo was always glad to see his uncle in town. Makbu often went into the mountains to be alone, but he was on one of his few trips back into Duba to spend time with his extended family and gather supplies.

"Heard what?" Makbu inquired.

"Two strangers from Shavi came into town last night. One is a human, and the other is a Shadican. Both can control fire, just like you! And they said they ran into some monster up the river a ways."

Makbu stopped walking. "What did you say?"

"Some monster! It was like see-through or something. I heard it was almost impossible to kill!"

"No, the other part."

"A human and a Shadican that can control fire?"

"Yeah, that." Makbu thought for a moment. "Do you know where they are staying?"

"I heard they're in the campsite near the fishing docs." Chipo responded excitedly.

Makbu reached inside a small pouch he was carrying and took a few coins out.

"Chipo, how about you take these coins and run to the market. Buy me three large trout, and get yourself something small with what's left over. Bring the fish to my house when you're done."

"Yes uncle!" Chipo yelled as he ran off.

"Hey. Hey, you two. Wake up."

Maxstrom jumped up and struck a fighting pose. He had been asleep, but after the night before, he wasn't about to let some monster get the better of him.

"Woah kid, calm down would ya?"

Maxstrom looked and saw that it was just a male Shadican, and an older one at that. The Shadican's yellow eyes were slightly sunken in, but they twinkled with knowledge and experience. Maxstrom noticed that this Shadican was shorter than most; he was slightly under three feet in height. The fur on either side of his face was longer than most Shadican's facial fur would normally grow. Maxstrom then noticed that the Shadican's fur in general also had a rougher look to it, but it wasn't exactly unkept. The Shadican stood tall and confidently, and had only slightly flinched at Maxstrom's reaction.

"Forgive me, elder." Maxstrom replied as he folded his right hand over his left fist and bowed slightly in respect. 'Elder' was what Shadican culture expected their wiser and older Shadicans to be called.

"That's alright, I suppose it's my fault for startling you."

"What's going on?" Dusty asked as he sat up groggily.

"I figured I'd stop by now instead of later and save you both the trouble of trying to find me." Makbu replied, for that was who this older Shadican was.

"What do you mean?" Maxstrom asked, quizzically looking at the Shadican who had startled him.

"It's not every day someone who can control fire walks into Duba, let alone a Shadican and a human. I assumed you came all this way to be trained?"

"Oh. Yes! Are you the Shadican that can control fire that Tapito told us about?"

"Yes, that's me. Ah, I haven't seen Tapito in ages. I had heard she took in a young human ace, and I was beginning to wonder if she'd ever send you to me."

"You wouldn't believe what we've been through to find you." Dusty declared as he got up from his makeshift bed on the sand and began dusting himself off.

"Would it involve you running into a denac?"

Maxstrom and Dusty looked at each other.

"We're not quite sure what it was. How did you know we ran into something on our way here?" Maxstrom inquired.

"This isn't like Shavi, boys. Word travels fast here in Duba. I wouldn't be surprised if the whole town knew about your encounter by noon."

"Ah." Maxstrom responded.

"So wait, you seem convinced it was a denac. But I thought they couldn't touch things in the physical world." Dusty declared.

"That's what most katlicans believe, and usually that's true. But once a year, a denac has the ability to muster up enough strength to manifest with physical power for up to a full day, if it so chooses. Most of the denac decide to direct their attention to influencing men from behind the scenes; but that doesn't mean all of them refuse to manifest physically."

"But how do you know that's what we ran into?" Maxstrom questioned.

"Did it have red, glowing eyes? A transparent body? Could it fly without any logical explanation?"

"Yes. . . it did." Maxstrom replied.

"The forms may vary, and the faces are often different, but the general traits stay the same. I've had several of those things try to attack me in the mountains."

"Why were you in the mountains then?" Maxstrom asked.

"Because I dislike Duba. I love the people, but society drains me. I prefer to go to the mountains to pray, train, and think. It also helps me draw closer to Abada. But enough of this small talk; I want you both come to my hut for lunch. I would love to hear about your encounter in detail over a meal of freshly caught trout."

"Sounds delicious! I'm starving." Dusty chimed in.

Maxstrom and Dusty packed up their gear, and Makbu took them both through the streets of Duba to his house. Duba, which was built on a small hill next to the Shadic River, consisted of wooden huts on the ground, unlike Shavi. Since Duba was a fishing village, the Shadicans of Duba preferred to be as close to the river as was safely possible.

As Makbu walked into his hut, he saw the three large fish he had asked for sitting on the hearth of his fireplace. Maxstrom was the last one in, and had to bend down to fit through the small doorway. To both Dusty and Maxstrom's disappointment, there was no fire going.

"I'll need a little time to prepare the meal. There's a washing room in the back of the house with two private stalls, feel free to get cleaned up back there."

Maxstrom and Dusty were both quite dirty and stinky at this point, so they were excited at the idea of washing up. They thanked their host, and then walked to the back room.

"Hey Max!" Dusty called from his stall.

"Yeah Dusty?" Maxstrom responded. The stall was just barely tall enough for him.

"Um, where's the bath water? And where is it supposed to go? There's no tub!"

"I think it's a shower."

"A what?"

"A shower. I heard some of the Shadicans talking about how they had installed a plumbing system in Duba a few years back. Supposedly it channels filtered water from the river and pours a constant deluge on you. Instead of sitting in a tub of water that quickly gets gunky, you can just stand and be cleaned by a steady stream of water. Kind of like a waterfall."

"That sounds awesome! But how do you turn this thing on?"

Dusty suddenly heard a surge of rushing water from over in Maxstrom's stall, and then heard Maxstrom let out a surprised yell.

"Max, are you alright?" Dusty inquired frantically.

"Yeah, it's just that it's colder than I was expecting."

"How do you turn it on?"

"Pull the knob in the center of the wall."

Dusty looked around, and saw the knob. He grabbed it and gave a light tug. Nothing happened. He pulled again, this time with a little more force. Still nothing. He then grabbed it and yanked with all his might, and he flew backwards against the stall wall. He heard the sound of rushing water above him, and felt as if someone dumbed a bucket of ice cold water on his head. He gave a slight yell of surprise and stood up. He then realized his paw was holding onto something, and he looked down. To his horror, he saw that he was still holding the shower knob; it had detached from the wall. He quickly tried to put it back in its place, but it took him a minute because everything in the stall was now wet. After dropping the knob several times, he finally got it to fit back onto where it had been.

"You good Dusty?" Maxstrom called.

"Yeah. Why?" Dusty asked, slightly nervous.

"There's a lot of noise coming from your stall that doesn't sound like water."

"No I'm good."

"You sure?"

"Yup. Nothing to see here. Just taking a, what's it called? A shower."

"Okay. . ." Maxstrom replied skeptically.

After spending a good twenty minutes in the showers, both Maxstrom and Dusty were summoned from their stalls by the delicious smell of spiced fish. Dusty dried himself with a towel and wrapped it around his waist while Maxstrom dried himself off and put on his spare undergarments. The duo walked back out into the main room, and to their surprise, they saw a roaring fire going. Just as they entered the room, Makbu reached into the fireplace to pull out the three fish he had been cooking. Maxstrom and Dusty then remembered that Makbu was able to control fire, and so it made perfect sense that he could quickly start a blazing fire in the fireplace.

"Good timing." Makbu declared as he turned to face Maxstrom and Dusty. "Diner is ready."

Makbu then set the fish down on three separate plates near the fire. Under the fish was a bed of steaming mashed potatoes, and melted butter was gently rolling down the sides.

Dusty and Maxstrom quickly walked over took their spots. Makbu gave a quick blessing for the meal, and then they began to eat.

While they were eating, Makbu asked Maxstrom and Dusty about their journey. He also questioned the duo on how Tapito and the city of Shavi were doing. Maxstrom and Dusty answered all of his questions between bites of their delicious meal. But before they knew it, there was nothing left.

"Thank you for the meal, Makbu. We haven't had good dinner since we left Shavi." Maxstrom said.

"Of course." Makbu replied.

"So, when do we start training?" Dusty asked, excited.

"Well I want to take you both into the mountains to train. We can leave first thing in the morning. You both have had a long journey, and you probably want to turn in early. I'll wake you when it's time to go. You both can help yourself to my stash of mats and blankets in the corner over there and sleep as close to the fire as you'd like. I'll keep it going all night. I'll also wash your garments so you don't have to put on stinky clothes tomorrow."

Dusty and Maxstrom both thanked their host, got up, grabbed several mats, came back to the fire, and quickly fell asleep.

"Come on you two, we're almost there!" Makbu called over his shoulder.

"I don't understand," Maxstrom said to Dusty in between panting for breaths, "how such. A small Shadican. Can walk. So fast!"

Dusty leaned against a small boulder on the trail and gasped for breath. "You and me both."

"Today, please!" Makbu called, almost taunting them from the next ridge.

Dusty and Maxstrom both gave each other a frustrated look, and then continued hiking up the steep path.

As they reached the top, they saw Makbu sitting with his back up against a small wooden hut, which was built against the back of the cliff face. His eyes were closed. The duo walked up to him, but Makbu didn't move a muscle.

"Makbu?" Dusty asked.

Makbu slowly opened one eye and looked at them.

"Oh, you finally made it!" Makbu declared with a yawn. "I almost fell asleep waiting."

"So, when do we start training?" Maxstrom asked, still catching his breath.

"Dusty can start immediately. I'm not training you." Makbu declared to Maxstrom.

"What?" Maxstrom asked, shocked.

"I said, I'm not training you. At least, not yet." Makbu repeated in a casual tone.

"What do you mean? Why did you bring me up here then?" Maxstrom questioned in both confusion and frustration.

"Because I have training in mind for you, just training from something other than me." Makbu responded.

Maxstrom gave Makbu with a confused look.

"By who, then?"

"Logas will be your teacher."

"Who's Logas?"

Both Dusty and Makbu looked at Maxstrom with surprise.

"It's not 'who', it's what. It's Abada's Law that was given to us. Obviously you have more to learn that I thought." Makbu said as he got up and walked into his hut.

Maxstrom's gaze followed Makbu as he walked into the hut.

"Look, I respect your religion and all, but I don't see why my knowledge of your beliefs are important for me, especially when it comes to controlling fire." Maxstrom called in a loud voice after Makbu.

Makbu walked back out, holding a small scroll in his paw.

"Look, I'm not a fan of reading." Maxstrom declared.

"That's interesting." Makbu said with an apathetic look on his face and a small shrug. He continued to hold the scroll out towards Maxstrom.

Maxstrom eventually took the scroll.

"Can you at least tell me why I have to read this?"

"Now we're getting somewhere!" Makbu exclaimed. "I will certainly tell you. Before I train you, I want to be sure you won't abuse your power. And for me to be sure of that, you need to be a follower of Abada. That is why I insist you read this scroll. I can tell you do not have a relationship with Abada, because if you did, His protection would be on you."

"What do you mean?"

"The denac. He almost killed you?"

"Yes. . .? But I don't. . ."

"Dusty had a shield of light protecting him. Because Dusty is protected. I don't know what you believe, but obviously you don't believe the right thing, otherwise you would have been protected. So I want you to read that scroll."

"So reading this scroll will give me a shield of light?"

"No, it won't. You'll just have to go read the Logas and see if you can't figure out how that works for yourself."

"I really don't want to read this." Maxstrom thought to himself as he climbed further up the mountain.

He finally spotted the next plateau, and climbed up from the south side. It was extremely quiet. The only thing Maxstrom could hear was the sound of a small spring trickling down the mountainside nearby. He looked around, and besides spotting the spring, saw that there was another path going north from the plateau he was on to the next mountain; they were connected. The highest peak was still a little ways above him, and the peak of the mountain to the north of him was only a couple miles away. Down the mountain to the east he could make out the Shadic River, but it looked small because of the height he was at. He couldn't see much beyond that, because a large light grey cloud was rolling in all around him and beginning to engulf the mountaintops.

After grabbing a quick drink from the mountain spring, Maxstrom scanned the plateau he was on and found a decent sized rock to sit on. He then sat down, and opened the scroll.

"The Law of Abada."

First, love Abada. He shall be kept first, above all else, because He is to be your Lord.

Do not worship idols, the denac, or Upa.

Love others. Do not hate, for this is the path of evil.

Honor those above you in authority, and show them respect.

Be trustworthy. Do not be a false witness.

Do not murder or hate either man, woman, or creature.

Do not desperately crave what another has, and do not steal from anyone. Instead, you should show love.

Do not become arrogantly prideful. Do all to the credit of Abada, who has given you the ability to do all things.

Honor your marriage commitments. Only for the sake of unfaithfulness can the covenant of marriage be broken.

Keep marital relations the way Abada has made them to be.

Keep your speech pure.

All of these commands can be summarized by loving one another as you would desire them to love you.

These are the commands of Abada, and this is His holy standard. Any who keep this law to its fullest will be given life after death. Those who fall short of even one standard will suffer eternal torment after death.

Unless the proper sacrifice is offered."

Maxstrom tried to continue pulling the scroll open, but nothing more came. He had reached the end.

"Well, that's bleak and hopeless."

Maxstrom thought for a moment in the silence.

"That can't be all, there has to be more." He muttered to himself.

He re-read it again. And again. He didn't know what to think. If there was a God, it couldn't be this God. Maxstrom was honest enough about himself to know that he fell short of this standard; him and everyone else. If this scroll was true, then it seemed that God simply wanted to send everyone to eternal punishment. But he had always assumed that God was merciful.

Maxstrom sat and pondered everything for some time, but he just couldn't figure it out.

"How can there be any hope if this is true?" He yelled into the cloudy sky.

Silence greeted him for a moment, and then he felt the wind pick up slightly around him. Suddenly, Maxstrom felt a hand on his shoulder, and he almost jumped. Shadicans were known for being sneaky, but he could still often hear them coming.

"You caught me by surprise there." Maxstrom stated.

"I guess I did."

It wasn't Dusty's or Makbu's voice. Yet he almost felt that he knew it somehow. He turned, and saw not a Shadican, but a grown man standing behind him. He was in a brown robe, with a rope belt fastening the garment at the waste. The man had a sword on his back. Maxstrom then brought his attention to the man's face. He had deep, penetrating blue eyes that smiled, dark brown curly hair, and a beard. The beard was full, yet fairly short; not much longer than a Shadican's hair. He had a friendly, yet faint smile. And for some strange reason, Maxstrom felt that he could trust this stranger completely.

"Sorry to bother you," the man said, almost smiling, "but I was passing through and wanted to make sure everything was alright."

"Oh. No, I'm really confused by this scroll I'm reading." Maxstrom said, taken aback by this strange man.

"Is there any way I can help you?"

"Well I don't know, are you familiar with the law of Abada?"

"I am!" The man replied, now bearing a large smile.

"Well that's what I'm reading. And I don't understand it."

"What do you not understand?" The man asked as he sat down on the ground next to Maxstrom and looked up at him.

"Okay, so I don't know what I believe. About God. About life. I think there has to be some higher being; to say that there isn't goes against reason. Something can't come from nothing."

"That's sound reasoning." The man replied.

"And I used to believe in God, as a kid. My parents taught me some about Him. But from what I remember them saying, God should be merciful. But this law doesn't sound like mercy, it sounds like judgement. And technically, isn't God responsible for evil, being the creator? So how can He judge us for falling short of His standard in that case?"

"Evil is terrible. But God did not create evil, He only allows evil on a temporary basis because He gives the gift of free will to His creation. It is an inevitable side effect of God not making mindless servants. So all the evil you see in the world is not because of God, but because of the choices of His creation."

"Okay, I suppose that makes sense. But from what I'm reading here, it doesn't matter if anyone chooses to love Him or not; no one can meet His standard, so we'll all suffer eternal punishment. It's impossible to attain eternal life! Can't Abada let some things slide?"

"Without help, you are right. It is impossible. But with Abada, all things are possible. Abada knew the people of Balyita couldn't live up to his standard, so He did something about it. You see that last part? The part about the sacrifice?" As the man pointed to the bottom of the scroll Maxstrom had been holding open, he noticed the man had a small hole in the center of the man's right hand; straight through. It was some kind of scar.

"Yeah?"

"Abada loves you. Abada loves everyone; and He doesn't want anyone to suffer eternal punishment. But a sacrifice had to be made. So He provided one."

"How did He do that?"

"How much do you know about the First Era of Balyita?"

"Not much." Maxstrom confessed.

"Upa, who you read about in the beginning of the law, was ultimately ruling at the time. Upa was a luminous being once; in fact he was Abada's right hand. But Upa become selfish and prideful, and wanted to try to become God rather than follow Abada. So Abada cast Upa out of the heavenly realms, forbidding him to return. Upa then deceived man to rebel against Abada, and man swayed the rest of creation to also rebel, which in turn destined man and creation alike for certain death. Upa convinced creation through deception to help him gain access to one of the power jewels of Balyita. As a luminous being, he could not wield an element as the humans could, but he was the only luminous being that could wield certain elements with the aid of any of the power jewels; and each jewel is about the size of two fists. He decided to steal the Tradjan Jewel, which gave him the ability to control fire and rock, as well as turn the rock into lava. So, under the deception of Upa, man and creation helped Upa claim this jewel. However, as soon as Upa had it, he revealed his true plan; to rule the world with an iron fist. Man had been tricked! But it was too late, because now Upa had power that no one on Balyita could stop."

"So what happened next?" Maxstrom asked, intrigued.

"Well with the jewel, Upa had more extreme power than any ace. Upa used this ability to create mindless monsters with bodies out of rock, and he had his spirit minions possess these creatures. These rock monsters were called magmen. With these possessed monsters and the denac who had fallen from heaven, Upa set out to rule Balyita. He had resolved that if he couldn't have the role of Abada, he would have the next best thing in his opinion; ruling the world. Man tried to fight. For almost two millennia, man struggled against evil with all their might. And because man had re-belled against Abada's standard, Abada could only help in small ways and from a distance. All hope for humanity seemed lost. But then, God did the unthinkable. He took on the form of man, not as Himself, but as His son."

"Wait, wait. Hold up." Maxstrom interrupted. "How can Abada be God yet also have a son and also be His son?"

"The answer to your question is above the understanding of creation at this time. The best way I can explain it is that God is one, yet has separate parts, all at the same time."

Maxstrom just gave the man a confused look.

"Wouldn't you expect a God who had enough power to create not only all of Balyita, but also the sun, the moon, the stars, and who existed before time, to be far above the understanding of anything in His creation?"

"I suppose that makes sense." Maxstrom said. "You can continue."

"This man was perfect, since He was God. He could keep God's stan-dard; the law you just read. But also, because this man was a man, he could intervene in man's affairs and face Upa on Balyita. And that is exactly what He set out to do. But Upa was powerful, and killed the man."

"So wait, God lost?"

"No. Because what Upa did not realize was that the death of a perfect man given in sacrifice to free humanity was enough to grant creation the gift of eternal life again. Abada's standard was met. So God, in the form of man, rose from death in a flash of light, and defeated Upa. Now, God is willing to impart the gift of life after death to any who ask Him for it."

"I suppose that makes sense." Maxstrom said as he gazed off into the cloud that entirely surrounded them.

The man gave a chuckle.

"It's a good deal to think about."

"So how does one receive the gift of life?"

"All you have to do is tell God you accept it. Just pray to Him and verbally tell Him that you accept the gift, and then do the best you can to live up to His standard."

"Okay. That's simple enough."

"It is simple, but it's not always easy."

The two sat in silence for a few moments and stared into the cloud around them, even though they could see nothing.

"Well, I must move on, my friend."

Maxstrom came out of the daze he had been in.

"Oh. Thank you so much for your time, sir."

"Of course." The man said, smiling again as he shook Maxstrom's hand.

"I never even asked your name." Maxstrom realized.

"Yasha."

"Well thank you for taking some of your time to help me, Yasha."

"Of course. I'll see you later, Maxstrom."

He then turned, started going down the northern path, and disappeared into the fog.

Maxstrom watched him go, and then sat back down on the rock.

"God," he prayed. "I know I can't meet your standard, and I accept your free gift."

Suddenly a strong wind picked up around him. Within a few seconds, the sun had broken through the clouds and a beam of light rested on Maxstrom. He looked up, and the ray of light warmed his face. Maxstrom felt strangely peaceful; it was as if Abada's presence was right next to him. He felt refreshed in his spirit.

The cloud began to move. After a few moments, the cloud around him had cleared and he could see in every direction again.

Suddenly it dawned on him that he had never told Yasha his name. How could he have known? Maxstrom ran over to the northern path and looked down. He couldn't see Yasha, which was odd since the long, windy path was entirely visible from the ridge he was on, and there was nowhere else Yasha could have gone.

"Yasha!"

There was no reply.

Maxstrom looked at the sun. He was shocked to realize he only had another hour of daylight left. It seemed like it had only been noon a few minutes ago. He still needed to get down to Makbu's hut, and he didn't dare do the climb in the dark. So Maxstrom took one last regretful look towards the northern path, and then headed to the path from which he had come.

"Maxstrom should be back by now, shouldn't he?" Dusty asked, sitting in front of the fire inside Makbu's hut after a long day of training.

"I hope he didn't think I meant for him to spend the night up there." Makbu said, looking toward the door.

Just then both of them heard a knock. Makbu walked quickly to the door.

"Who is it?"

"It's Max."

Makbu rapidly opened the door.

"We were worried you were planning on staying the night up there."

"Well you didn't say if I was or wasn't supposed to come back." Maxstrom said as he came in and took off his cloak.

"How did it go?" Dusty asked.

"Surprisingly well." Maxstrom said. "The scroll really confused me at first, but a man came along and explained everything to me."

"A man?" Makbu questioned, confused.

"Yeah, I mean, wasn't that your plan all along?" Maxstrom said as he walked towards the fire to warm himself.

"No. . . that wasn't exactly what I had expected." Makbu replied as he continued to stare at the doorway with an intrigued, yet confused look on his face.

"Well I understand now. I accepted the gift of God's son, and I have life after death now. I can't really explain it, I just know it."

"Um. . . okay. That's a lot more progress than I planned you would make today. . ." Makbu trailed off as he turned to look at Maxstrom.

"I see why you had me learn more about Abada now. Otherwise, I have no absolute of right and wrong to adhere to, and as a result, I could easily use my power for evil."

"That's good you understand. And as an added bonus, you now have that shield of light protecting you." Makbu replied.

"Really?" Maxstrom asked.

"Yes. Now Abada will shield you physically from the spiritual forces now that you're one of His. The denac can't touch you. Like what happened with Dusty. But that doesn't mean they still can't influence you in other ways."

"That's awesome!" Dusty yelled.

"I like the sound of that!" Maxstrom declared. "Oh and here's the Logas."

Maxstrom handed the scroll to Makbu.

"Thanks." Makbu responded as he took it.

"So what's next? Another scroll for me to read in the mountains?" Maxstrom inquired.

"No, I don't think you need that, at least for now." Makbu replied. "It's time for you to start fire training. You both should get some sleep, we start at first light."

Maxstrom and Dusty both snapped wide awake to the sound of metal vibrating loudly between them. They had both fallen asleep next to the fire.

"Oh good morning. Just wanted to test this thing out to see if it still worked." Makbu said while standing between them and holding a gong about half his size.

"It works." Maxstrom moaned as he began to rub his ears.

"You don't say. Well since you're both up, you should get your clothes on; the real training starts today!" Makbu exclaimed as he walked over to the door and set the gong next to it. He then walked out the door, slammed it, and let out a maniacal laugh.

Dusty and Maxstrom just looked at each other.

"What have we signed up for?" Maxstrom asked.

"I don't know." Dusty replied. "He was really mellow yesterday. You don't think he's like, mentally not all there, do you?"

"I. . . sure hope not."

After about three minutes, both had their clothes on and were outside. Makbu was sitting near the edge of the ledge facing down towards Duba.

"It was rumored that the aces of old had figured out how the science of how we could control elements." Makbu said, standing up and turning to face his students. "That secret has partially been lost to time. But there are some things that I've learned over the years. Have you both figured out that you use your muscles to control the elements?"

"That's why my muscles ached so much after I controlled fire for the first time!" Dusty yelled.

"Exactly. There is a science behind it, although I don't understand how everything works. All the muscle groups attached to any limb you have helps you control fire. That means you can control fire with not only your arms, but your legs as well."

"What? I didn't know that!" Maxstrom declared.

"Shooting fire from your legs is similar to a kick, except you tense your muscles up to shoot fire; like how you shoot fire with your hand or fist."

"That's awesome!" Maxstrom replied. "Can we start working on that now?"

"Oh I'm sure you'd like that." Makbu responded with a sly grin. "But no. No, because controlling an element is connected to muscle groups. That means if you have weak muscles, your ability to control fire will also be weak."

"Uh oh. . ." Dusty groaned.

Makbu smiled. "We're going to do intense strength building and cardio exercise the next two weeks. It'll be fun!"

"Great. . ." Maxstrom countered.

"We'll start off with some pushups. You both have until before noon to complete two hundred."

"Two hundred?" Dusty cried. "But my arms will hurt. . ."

"Oh I wasn't finished." Makbu declared, the smirk growing on his cat-like face. "You also have to count slowly to fifty while planking, do twenty pull-ups, and one hundred squats. I'd advise you both get started. Take as many breaks as you need in between, just make sure you reach the quota by noon."

Maxstrom and Dusty looked at each other, and reluctantly got on the ground to start doing push-ups.

It was only about five minutes from noon when Dusty finished his last squat. Makbu had been watching for most of the time; and when he had not been watching them, he had been doing push-ups, pull-ups, planks, squats, and sit-ups.

"Cutting it a bit close there." Makbu informed Dusty.

"Please." Dusty panted. "Don't tell me. That this is going to be our regular routine."

"Oh but it is." Makbu smirked as he placed his paws on his hips.

Both Maxstrom and Dusty grimaced.

"Now, time for a short five mile jog! Let's go." Makbu said as he started sprinting away from them on all fours. Since most adult katlicans only run in a fight, and because most katlicans carry a weapon while running, it is not common to see one of the kind running on all fours. But since Makbu's weapon was his ability to control fire, he had no problem running on all fours, as he didn't need to carry anything. Dusty felt more comfortable keeping his front paws free so he could grab his sword if he needed to, so he started running after Makbu on his back feet with Maxstrom.

The next seven weeks led into what Maxstrom and Dusty would later describe as the "most painful experience of their lives up until that point." Makbu put them through an intense training course, doing push-ups, pull-ups, sit-ups, squats, planking, running, and even had them lifting heavy rocks to build strength. Makbu didn't even begin teaching fire techniques until halfway through week four. But the intensive training had a purpose; by the time Maxstrom and Dusty began training with fire they had more strength and stamina then when they met Makbu, so they could train longer, and more efficiently.

"Dusty, you're up! Give it your best shot."

Dusty ran towards the target and launched a powerful kick. Fire immediately appeared in a quick blast and impacted his target, a large rock. It was a direct hit, and the rock slid back slightly.

"Good! You both have improved immensely in the last seven weeks. I'm proud of how far you've come."

"Yeah, but I'm still not as good as Max is. I still can't split a rock in half." Dusty declared, somewhat disappointed.

"It'll come with time. Remember, Max has been controlling fire a lot longer than you. It's more natural for him."

Dusty looked at Maxstrom to hear his thoughts, but Maxstrom was staring at the valley to the south, seemingly uninterested in the conversation.

"Max?" Dusty asked.

"Um, guys. The south part of Duba is on fire." Maxstrom declared in a concerned tone.

"What?!" Makbu cried, as he ran to the edge. "We have to get down there. Let's go!"

Makbu sprung over the edge and started bounding down the mountain on all fours with his students right behind him. As they were descending down the mountain, Dusty looked over to Maxstrom and yelled "you know, I never thought I'd be happy for Makbu's rigorous training, but it looks like today it finally paid off!"

As they reached the north side of Duba, they saw flocks of female Shadicans and kits fleeing the town.

"You all ready to put your training into practice?" Makbu asked, looking at his students as they jogged into town.

"I was born ready!" Dusty yelled.

"No you weren't." Maxstrom exclaimed between breaths.

After a few minutes of running through the streets, they were near the fire. But then Maxstrom had an idea.

"I'm going to split off from you guys and go towards the river; I think controlling water is better than fire for this situation." Maxstrom shouted out.

"Sounds good Max, go!"

Maxstrom took the next left, and continued running full speed down the small hill Duba was built on; the river was about of an eighth of a mile straight ahead. But as he was running, something jumped in front of his path. He quickly skidded to a stop about ten feet from the creature, and could hardly believe his eyes. Before him stood a rock monster, approximately six feet in height. It had the form of a human, except its right hand wasn't a hand; it was a large mace. The creature was a dark dull grey with veins of glowing red cracks sparsely interjecting the bland rock color. These veins were more numerous at joints and points of mobility.

The rock monster hadn't seen Maxstrom, and was looking to the north. But as Maxstrom was taking this scene in, the monster saw him out of the corner of his eye. The creature quickly turned its head to face Maxstrom. Its eyes were glowing red with no pupils, similar to the denac. It had no mouth, and only a tiny protrusion for a nose with two red slits directly beneath it, which glowed like its eyes.

"And what are you?" Maxstrom asked, slightly horrified.

Suddenly, a mouth appeared on the creature's face with a cracking sound; as the rock at this location had to split slightly to form a mouth. The mouth then formed into a jagged, evil looking smile. The creature then swung the large mace over its head and charged at Maxstrom. Maxstrom stood his ground and launched two fire blasts at the monster. The monster dodged one blast, but the other landed on the creature's left shoulder and blew its arm off. The rock monster lost its balance as result of this blow, and skidded past Maxstrom's left side, coming to a halt. The creature was still glowing red at various spots, but it lay motionless on the ground as a small amount of lava poured out of its left shoulder. Maxstrom smirked. Makbu had taught him well. He then directed his attention towards the fire; the houses on the south side of the street he was on were in flames.

But then Maxstrom heard a noise behind him, and he turned just in time to see the rock monster back on its feet, swinging the mace horizontally at Maxstrom's face, lava spurting from its other arm. He threw himself to the ground to avoid the strike, and as Maxstrom landed, his sword flew out of its sheath and landed on the ground just above his head. The monster then picked the mace above its head, preparing to crush Maxstrom beneath it. Maxstrom did a backward roll while grabbing his sword, dodging the strike just in time. After recovering his stance, he swung his blade straight for the monster's core, and the creature was cut in half with a loud cracking sound. The two halves of the monster fell to the ground; lava gushing out. After a couple seconds, all of the brightness had completely vanished. Maxstrom's foe was becoming a permanent rock on the street.

"These have to be the magmen Yasha was telling me about." Maxstrom mumbled to himself as he caught his breath.

Maxstrom then glanced at his sword to see if it needed cleaned, and then suddenly realized that the top half of his blade had completely broken off!

"That's fantastic." Maxstrom muttered to himself sarcastically.

He then felt a wave of heat from the houses burning next to him, and realized he needed to get to work on putting out this fire. So he tossed his broken sword aside and ran for the river. Once he arrived, he quickly pulled out a ball of water and threw it at the nearest burning Shadican hut. The fire responded with a large hiss and rapidly died out.

"One down, only several hundred more to go." Maxstrom whispered to himself as he grabbed another ball of water from the river.

"Dusty! Behind you!"

Dusty turned to see a magman swinging a rock sword for his face. Dusty rapidly bent back and cleared the strike by an inch. He came back up and jammed his sword into the magman's face. The magman went limp, and lava started spurting out. Dusty tried to pull his sword out, but couldn't. Realizing it was his sword or his life, Dusty jumped to the side just as a spurt of lava shot out from the monster's face and landed exactly where he had been standing.

Dusty heard a loud crack behind him. He spun around and saw that Makbu had successfully split another magman open with a fire blast.

"How do you do that?!" Dusty exclaimed, wishing he had mastered that skill.

"Time and practice." Makbu responded, as he pulled both his fists together and shot a quick fire blast at a magman running at him. The blast impacted with another loud crack and the magman flew back to the ground, splitting open.

"Makbu, look up!"

Makbu looked up to see a magman jumping towards him from the top of a hut. Makbu fell to the ground, pulled his paws and feet close together above his chest, and shot them all up at once, sending out a huge burst of flame. The strike hit the magman right in the face and blew his head into a thousand pieces. The limp body continued falling and landed at Makbu's feet.

"That was amazing!" Dusty cried.

"Focus, Dusty! We have to stop this fire." Makbu yelled back.

Just then they both heard a loud scream come from one of the burning huts.

"Dusty there's someone in there! Help me put the fire out!"

The hut was almost entirely engulfed with flame. Even the heavy curtain in the doorway had already burnt up. Makbu and Dusty ran over and pushed the flame back.

"Dusty, can you hold the flame away from the door?"

"I think!"

"It's not 'I think', its yes or no!"

"Yes! I got it!"

Makbu sprinted in, pushing the flame aside as he went. After about twenty seconds, Dusty was struggling to keep the flame away from the door. And just when he thought he couldn't hold it any longer, he heard a sound behind him. He turned his head and saw a magman with an injured leg limping toward him.

"Makbu!" Dusty cried.

The magman kept coming closer, slowly, and raised a broken mace above his head to strike Dusty.

"Makbu, I need help!"

The magman was right next to Dusty. And just as it raised its arm back a little more for extra force on the strike, Dusty saw a stream of flame shoot past him and hit the magman in the face. The magman fell back and split his head on the ground, spewing lava out. Dusty turned and saw Makbu walking out of the hut with a female Shadican leaning on him.

"Are you alright?" Makbu asked the Shadican that had almost been burnt alive.

"Yeah I'm good." Dusty said as he stopped holding the fire back from the doorway.

"I wasn't asking you, Dusty." Makbu responded curtly.

"Oh."

The female Shadican coughed for a moment, and then looked at Makbu and said "I'm alright. Thanks, Makbu."

Makbu smiled. "You better get out of here, it's not safe."

The female Shadican nodded and began running to the north, away from the fire.

Suddenly Dusty and Makbu both felt a light mist spray them. They looked over and saw the house next to them was no longer fully on fire.

"I don't. Think. This is. Working fast enough."

They both turned and saw Maxstrom, panting for breath. He'd been running back and forth with large amounts of water for several minutes now.

Makbu looked at Maxstrom and thought for a minute, and then got on his knees.

"What are you doing?" Asked Maxstrom.

"Praying. We can't do this alone." Makbu replied.

Both Dusty and Maxstrom looked at each other as Makbu sat in silence for a few seconds. The fire raged all around them.

"God, could you please send a heavy downpour of rain? We desire to save Duba, but it's more than we can handle. Thank you for hearing me."

Makbu then looked up to the sky. Dusty and Maxstrom also looked.

"It doesn't look like it's going to rain." Maxstrom declared. The sky looked almost entirely clear beyond the thick smoke that was bellowing into the sky.

"Just wait and have faith." Makbu said.

Suddenly, they noticed a shift in the wind. The wind, which had been blowing from the south, suddenly shifted and began blowing from the north. Makbu looked up towards the mountains, and smiled.

"My help," Makbu said, "comes from the maker of heaven and earth."

Maxstrom and Dusty looked as well. They saw huge black clouds rolling in rapidly from the north.

"Woah." Dusty declared.

"Well it's time for us to do what we still can. Dusty, let's see if we can hold back this fire for a little longer. Max, keep doing your runs to the river!"

Maxstrom sprinted for the Shadic River as Dusty and Makbu ran back to the houses to try and hold the fire back.

About a fourth of Duba was destroyed in the fire, but the rest of the town had been saved. The rain that came was the heaviest downpour anyone had ever seen, and it extinguished the fire completely. Only about twenty Shadicans had died in the fire. The real death toll was due to the fighting; a hundred and thirty-three Shadican warriors had fallen fighting the magmen. All the magmen had been killed, and totaled a hundred and forty-five.

"We haven't ever been attacked like this before!" Lazda, the elder of Duba, declared. All the prominent Shadicans still alive in Duba were gathered in the town hall, which was located in the north of town, and thus was untouched by the fire. Makbu was there, and had invited both of his students.

"How did these monsters even get here? And when did the magmen return? They were wiped out thousands of years ago!" Lazda questioned hysterically.

Silence fell on the room.

"My concern isn't how they got here, or if these are magmen." Puka declared. Puka was the highest ranking Duban warriors still standing. "My concern is that we only have about sixty warriors left. If we get attacked like this again, we won't be able to stop them."

"Why do they have so few of warriors here?" Dusty whispered to Makbu.

"Duba is a fishing village. And although it's one of the largest Shadican cities, because of its location in relation to mountains and the border, it's deemed a minimally threatened town. Most of the Shadican soldiers are elsewhere, at places like our borders."

"So how did the magmen get through our borders without anyone sending word?" Dusty inquired.

"I don't know. . ." Makbu whispered back.

"We need to get more troops here!" Lazda declared.

"But if we draw forces from the border then we leave ourselves open to attack!" A Shadican cried from the back of the room.

"What do you call what happened today?" Lazda retorted with his fists clenched. "We need more soldiers, and we need builders to fix our homes!"

"Excuse me." Makbu interjected in a calm voice.

Everyone fell silent. Even Lazda looked over at Makbu quietly and respectfully. The whole of Duba already respected Makbu before the fire, and since he had played a pivotal role in interceding with Abada to put out the fire, he had everybody's attention.

"I think we're wasting our time debating useless points. The fact is, we were attacked, and Duba is in need of aid. We need to send word to local towns, and to Shavi."

"Here, here!" Several Shadicans yelled.

"We also need troops. Somehow there is a gap in our defenses, but until we figure out where that gap is we need to have troops in every town ready to fight off any threat."

"I agree with you entirely." Lazda declared as he hit his fist onto a table.

"I'll send my two students back to Shavi with the news. Tapito will send whatever help she can."

Maxstrom and Dusty looked at each other, surprised. They weren't expecting to go back so soon.

"Sounds good to me." Lazda replied.

"Makbu?" Dusty inquired in a soft voice.

"Let's go outside." Makbu replied as he got up.

Maxstrom and Dusty followed him to the door and went outside.

"You're sending us away?" Maxstrom asked.

"You both have already learned so much. There's always more to learn but I'm satisfied with your progress."

"Satisfied?" Dusty asked. "But there's so much more I want to know! I couldn't even split the magmen open."

"I know. Times have changed, though. You need to go back to Shavi and get help. And Max, you need to start your water training."

"What? There's a Shadican that can teach me water?"

"No, but I think there's a human in the far north that can teach you. Tapito can tell you how to get there."

"But. . . Makbu. I. . ." Dusty stammered.

"Yes, Dusty?"

"I feel like there's so much more I need to learn."

"Just keep getting stronger and you'll be fine. I want to keep training you both. But now is not the time. Max, as good as you are with fire, I think you'll be even better with water. And I don't want to see your gift wasted. There's so much more you have to learn about controlling water."

Maxstrom and Dusty both stood in silence.

"Well I guess this is goodbye then." Maxstrom declared.

"Indeed. I'd say you should wait until morning, but time is of the essence. You need to start as soon as you can. Head up the mountain and grab your supplies while it's still light."

Dusty ran over and gave Makbu a hug. Makbu was surprised, but quickly returned the hug.

"Once this crisis has passed, we can consider resuming training." Makbu reassured. "Until then, I have something for you."

Makbu reached into his small pouch, and pulled out two tiny scrolls, and gave each of his students one.

"These contain some more fundamentals for you, Dusty. If you practice these techniques, you should be able to split rocks open in the near future. And Max, yours contains some techniques for getting hotter fire blasts. If you practice what's inside, it may be possible for you to generate blue fire since you are so much bigger and stronger than us katlicans.

"I remember my dad being able to do that! Thank you for everything, Makbu." Maxstrom responded.

"You are quite welcome. Oh, and Dusty?"

"Yes?"

"One of the Shadican soldiers found this and gave it to me. There's still some rocks you'll need to chip off; but the blade looks to be intact." Makbu informed as he grabbed a sword that was laying against the town hall.

"My sword!" Dusty exclaimed in excitement. "I was sure it was destroyed."

"Now go get your things and get started on your journey." Makbu ordered with a grin.

In response, Maxstrom and Dusty bid their teacher a final farewell, and then started walking towards the mountain.

Chapter 4

A Friendship for Generations to Come
B.Y. 4013

"A friend that helps you in the fire is a friend for life."
—Fire Phoenix Proverb

"We need to retaliate. Tapito, you are showing weakness to the humans!" Turibu exclaimed as he angrily tensed his eyebrows, which narrowed the white patch of fur that surrounded his left eye.

"Turibu, I understand you are upset about this small trapping excursion on our land." Tapito replied as she sat on her mat with her paws resting on her lap. She was in her treehouse hosting another meeting.

"Upset? No! I'm furious! We need to go across the Shadic River and slaughter these humans! Do you realize this is the fifth trapping raid this month in Shadicore alone? The Snowiseans report having sustained over double what we've had!"

"I'm aware. . ."

"I don't think you are." Talican interjected as he folded his paws behind his back. "Tapito, we can't keep taking raids like this. We've been put up with raids on and off for centuries, and now it's time to change that once and for all!"

"But we haven't lost any lives this time." Tapito replied calmly.

"Not yet. But we can't keep fighting defensively. We need to go and send a message!" Turibu countered.

"You see, that's the problem." Tapito replied. "We are at peace with Parcha, and these raids are not an act of Parcha. We are being raided by bandits, not an army."

"I don't care!" Turibu yelled as clenched his right fist with his left paw. "Parcha needs to pay because their citizens are attacking us!"

"I will not condone an act of war like that. You are seeking revenge for something that is not worth our time."

"Not worth our time? So the katlicans aren't worth your time? And regardless of whether or not you 'condone' an act of war, they are at war with us!" Turibu questioned as he frantically threw his paws up.

Akbu had had enough, and decided to step in. Turibu's tone had become quite aggressive, so Akbu's paw had been resting on his sword for some time now.

"Turibu, I'm sorry, but are you deaf? Tapito just told you that these attacks aren't from Parcha. So, logically, Parcha shouldn't have to pay."

"Yes they should! Raid a town. Burn it to the ground. That'll teach them to leave us alone."

"No, that will only incite more violence. And then Parcha would actually have a reason to attack us."

"Unbelievable." Turibu muttered as he walked out of the house with Talican and Nandu right behind him.

"Well, that went well." Wachuna, a member of the Elite Guard, remarked once the trio had gone.

"You don't say." Shenabu responded from the corner. "I was having a hard time keeping up with writing everything down!"

"I really would love to just punch him in the face." Akbu declared, getting up and starting to pace the room.

"Yes, but that would resolve nothing." Tapito replied.

"Oh I'm aware. If I actually thought it could do something, I would have already done it." Akbu informed.

Suddenly, Akbu stopped.

"Shenabu! Don't write that down! That's off the record." Akbu ordered, pointing a finger at her.

"Oh! No. I hadn't. Written that. Yet. Don't worry. Off the record now. Got it." Shenabu stammered in response as she frantically scratched something off of the page in front of her with her claws.

"Shadan, you've been the elder of Shavi for a long time. What do you think?" Tapito questioned.

Shadan, who had been sitting crossed legged in the corner the entire time with his head bowed, bobbed his head slightly.

"Shadan?"

Shadan didn't move.

"Um, so I'd say the pleasantries put our dear elder to sleep." Akbu remarked with a chuckle.

"Shadan!" Wachuna barked loudly.

Shadan snorted. "Huh? Oh is he gone yet? Thank goodness. I don't like that feisty kit."

"Me either." Tapito remarked.

"Say, what's the ruckus down below?" Shadan asked.

"What ruckus?" Wachuna asked. He couldn't hear well because his ears had gotten damaged by cold water in the Shadican River as a kit.

"Wait. I know that voice!" Akbu declared. "Max and Dusty are back!"

"Dusty!" Dusca cried as she ran in and hugged her older brother, looking up at him with her big, orange eyes.

"Good to see you too you big cry baby!" Dusty responded as he hugged his younger sister.

"Max, good to see you're back." Shacbu said, giving Maxstrom a hug.

"Good to see you too Shacbu."

Dusty simply looked sheepishly at Shacbu and said "Hi."

Shacbu let out a small, awkward laugh and said "Hi" in return.

"Well look at this." Akbu declared, climbing down the net that hung from the Tapito's treehouse.

"Akbu!" Maxstrom yelled.

"We weren't expecting you back for a while." Akbu remarked as he gave Maxstrom a hearty handshake.

"Well we wouldn't have been back this soon either, except. . . there's a problem."

"Problem?"

"Is Tapito in her treehouse?"

"Yes, and so is Shadan and Wachuna."

"That's actually perfect. I need to talk to you all."

"Hey Max, is it alright if I take my stuff back to our treehouse?" Dusty questioned.

"Yeah no problem, I'll talk to Tapito."

"Thanks, I'm exhausted."

"So how long was the trip back?" Akbu asked, as he and Maxstrom started climbing the net.

"About two weeks."

"That's pretty good time."

"Yeah, well we had an emergency down in Duba."

"So what happened?" Akbu inquired, as he reached the balcony and extended a helping paw to Maxstrom.

"Duba was attacked." Maxstrom responded as he grabbed Akbu's paw and reached the entrance of Tapito's house.

"What? How did they get through the Tabees at the border?" Tapito, who was standing by the door, inquired. The Tabees were one of the four katlicans tribes; the Tabees are known for being muscular, and have light grey fur interjected by black stripes.

"We don't know. But these rock monsters attacked and burned down a quarter of Duba. And they looked like magmen." Maxstrom declared as he walked into the treehouse. All the Shadican's faces immediately displayed looks of shock.

"Wait. So you're telling me Duba was attacked by magmen? They've been extinct for a couple thousand years! And the Tradjan Jewel was destroyed!" Tapito exclaimed.

"Well from what I saw, the magmen somehow still exist. Thing ruined my sword too; basically split it in half."

"And . . . Tapito made you a custom Shadican blade." Shadan remarked quietly as he stroked the fur on his katlican face.

"I thought we had border patrols for this sort of thing." Wachuna interjected.

"We do." Tapito and Akbu responded simultaneously.

"So how did they get through, Max?" Wachuna asked.

"I don't know. All I know is that Duba is calling for aid. Builders and warriors. And Makbu wants me to go train with water."

"In this time of crisis?" Tapito inquired, raising an eyebrow.

"Those were more or less his parting words to me."

"Well, if Makbu thinks that's what you should do, then I agree." Tapito responded.

"So, where do I go to find my teacher?"

"Saoland." Tapito replied.

"Saoland? The vicious tribesmen of the north?" Maxstrom inquired in a concerned voice.

"That's the place." Tapito responded in a serious tone.

"Is that my adopted brother?" Ipachoo asked as he ran over with uncontainable excitement and hugged Dusty. He then proceeded to give Dusty a friendly bite on his ear.

"Hi Ipachoo. Yes, I'm back." Dusty responded as he pushed Ipachoo's head to the side. His adopted brother's habit of ear biting was quite annoying, even though Ipachoo did it out of affection.

Ipachoo was not a Shadican; he was a Dolphinian. Dolphinians are predominantly grey furred with no stripes, and are known for their love of water and remarkable sailing abilities. Usually, each katlican sub-species lives with their own kind, but Dusty's family found Ipachoo abandoned as a kit, so they took him in. Ipachoo was still technically a kit, since he was only eleven years of age, and katlicans mature at the age of thirteen. Ipachoo always had a bright and happy personality around everyone in his family; he was overjoyed to have been adopted by Dusty's parents. It was his biggest dream after he was abandoned to be a part of a loving family, and Dusty's family was the perfect fit for his dream.

"How was the trip? Are you a fire master yet?" Ipachoo questioned energetically.

Dusty chuckled. "Not yet."

"So any fun adventures?" Ipachoo asked with interest.

"Hey you big dope." Dusca said, sticking her head through Dusty's door.

"I've been back two minutes, can't you at least knock?"

"Tapito wants to see you. Immediately."

"I'll be right there." Dusty said, letting out a huge groan. "I just want to sleep!"

"We can catch up later, brother." Ipachoo stated.

"Yeah, definitely. Oh and to your previous question; yes. There were lots of adventures. I almost died like, three times."

"What? Dusty you can't leave me with that!"

"See you later Ipachoo!" Dusty shouted, running off.

"Dusty!" Ipachoo hollered after his brother in a frustrated tone.

"I'd like to leave tomorrow at dawn." Maxstrom said to Tapito as Dusty walked into the treehouse.

"So soon, Max?" Dusty asked.

"Yeah, I want to keep moving. And I'm also kind of excited to see what this new teacher has to show me."

"I'm going to miss you." Dusty declared. "So why did you want to see me, chief?"

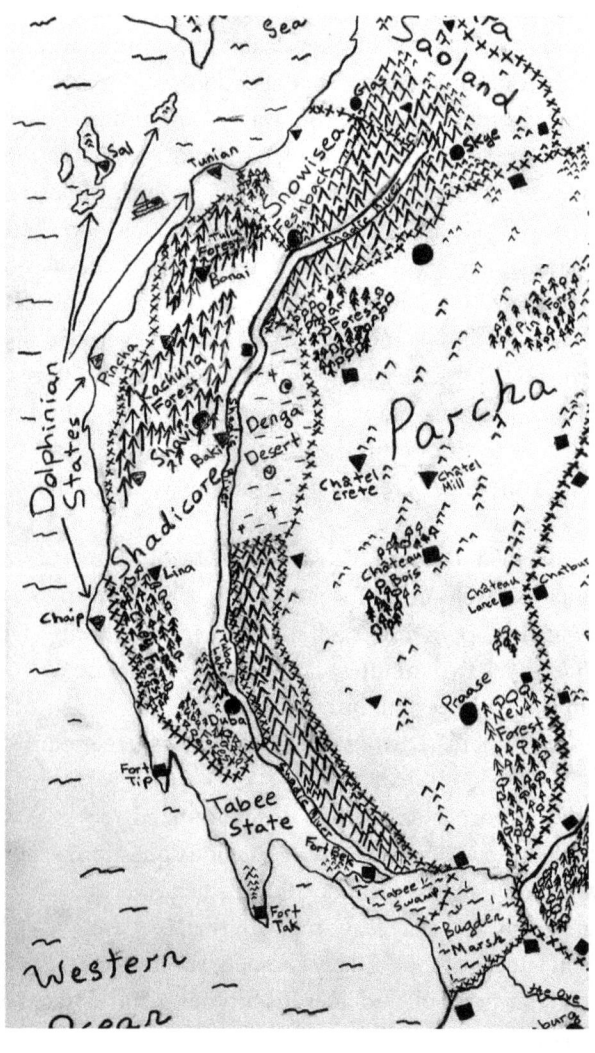

"I'm trying to figure out how to divide the forces in Shavi so we can send help down to Duba." Tapito responded. "I'm sending two hundred Shadican troops, and I want you to go down as well."

"But I just got back." Dusty answered in a tired groan.

"I know, but Max told me how you wanted to stay and continue your fire training with Makbu, and even though he'll be busy, I'm sure he can still give you some pointers. Tell him it's a humble request of mine that he continue training you anyway he can."

Dusty couldn't help but smile.

"That is amazing! Thank you so much."

"You're welcome. Now Max; your water teacher."

"Yes?" Maxstrom perked up.

"His name is Rayduan. You'll have to cross the border to find him. As I'm sure you know, the Saoland tribespeople can be quite aggressive. And for good reason; they had to fight long and hard for their freedom from Parcha several hundred years ago."

"I've heard the stories. . ." Maxstrom remarked as his voice trailed off.

"Remember, they won't hesitate to kill you if they deem you a threat." Akbu cautioned.

"Fantastic." Maxstrom responded.

"Just be careful, Max." Tapito warned with a stern look. "And always try to find the peaceful way out. We are at peace with Saoland, so if you don't appear to be a threat to them, you shouldn't have any trouble."

"Well, make sure you come back in one piece, Max!" Dusty interjected.

"I'm sure I'll be fine." Maxstrom replied, masking his concern.

Maxstrom awoke early the next morning and started his journey north towards Saoland. Tapito couldn't give him a specific location to travel to; all he knew was that Rayduan was somewhere near the border of Saoland and Shadicore, and that he lived on the shore. Maxstrom's plan was to follow the dirt road near the Shadic River all the way up to Feshback, and then head North West and skirt the foot of the mountains until he reached the town of Glas in Saoland. Feshback was in Snowisean territory, and although Maxstrom had only seen a couple Snowiseans before, he had heard they were usually as hospitable as the Shadicans were.

Although he missed Dusty's company, Maxstrom found he was able to make much better time on his own since he didn't have walk slower for his short Shadican friend. By dusk of the tenth day, he had managed to reach the outlying farm fields of Feshback. But for some reason, the Snowisean farmers seemed less friendly towards him than the Shadicans did in the South. In fact, many would not even speak to him; they often ran into their homes as Maxstrom passed by.

Suddenly, as he was continuing his journey, three Snowiseans jumped out from the surrounding bushes and blocked his path. Two were male, and one was a female.

"Stop!" One of the Snowiseans yelled.

Maxstrom stopped. "Is there a problem?"

"Yes. You cannot pass. How did you even get into our country, you mud pile?"

"Woah, calm down now. I'm a friend of Tapito. . ."

"Liar!" The Snowisean yelled as he charged at Maxstrom with his sword drawn.

Maxstrom had no weapon with him except a walking stick he had made from a small tree during his journey, so he quickly pulled it up and aimed it at the three Snowiseans in front of him as if it were a spear. The Snowisean charging him stopped.

"I am not a liar." Maxstrom declared. "And to be honest I'm surprised you don't know who I am. I. . ."

All of the sudden, Maxstrom felt a dart go into his neck. He pulled it out of his neck, looked at it, and felt his legs go numb. As he collapsed to the ground, he realized it was a sleeping dart; but by the time his face hit the dirt, he was unconscious.

Maxstrom awoke to loud cheering. He struggled to open his eyes, but quickly winced them shut again, because there was a bright light below him. After a moment, he was able to open his eyes. As he opened them, he realized that he was being suspended upside down over the Shadic River, which glistened with the light of the late-morning sun.

"How things have changed, eh?" One of the Snowiseans on the shore yelled.

As the rope suspending Maxstrom tensed and spun him toward the Snowiseans, he saw the Snowisean who had confronted him the night before holding a rope tied which was tied to a tree.

"Hey, get me out of here!" Maxstrom yelled.

"I don't think so. I think it's time you and your bandit friends learn a lesson."

"Drop him in! Drop him in! Drop him in!" The Snowiseans on the shore started chanting.

"Wait!" Maxstrom yelled. "Can I at least. . ."

And Maxstrom could not finish his sentence, because the Snowisean released the rope and he dropped into the river. Immediately, he began to sink, and quickly realized this was because the Snowiseans had weighted him down with a large stone. Maxstrom struggled to get himself turned upright. Although Maxstrom was able to control water, his arms were bound. He was sinking fast, and his mind raced for possibilities. Suddenly, he had an idea. Makbu had shown him you could use legs to control fire, what if the same was true with water? Maxstrom had never tried this technique before, but he figured now was as good a time as any to test this theory. He pulled his knees to his chest, and shot them down towards the bottom of the river. To Maxstrom's surprise, his plan worked, and his body rocketed up, but he was still underwater. He repeated the action again, and his head broke through the surface. He then angled his head towards shore, and shot his feet downward a third time. He shot through the water and ran aground on the shore, gasping for breath. Maxstrom tilted his head up to see what was in front of him, and his glance was returned by almost fifty flustered Snowisean faces.

"What. Just. Happened?" One of the Snowiseans questioned loudly.

"If you had only. Let me finish." Maxstrom said, still gasping for breath. "My name. Is Maxstrom. I'm the human Tapito took in eight years ago."

All of the Snowiseans stared at him in silence, with looks of horror on their faces.

"In that case, you have my formal apology, Maxstrom." A voice declared from in the crowd.

The group of Snowiseans in the front moved aside to reveal an older Snowisean that was hunched over and hobbling on a cane.

"Aren't you Gumabu? The elder of Feshback, and recognized governor of the Snowiseans?" Maxstrom asked.

"I am."

"I remember you, although it's been several years. You came down to visit Tapito for some urgent business."

"Oh dear, you really are Maxstrom then. Please, I offer you the humblest of apologies on behalf of all of Feshback." Gumabu declared as his blue eyes reflected his regret.

"All is forgiven." Maxstrom responded. "You don't suppose you could untie me now?"

"Of course." Gumabu motioned to several Snowiseans near Maxstrom, and they ran over to cut him loose. "Your forgiveness is undeserved and greatly appreciated. Would you please allow me to make restitution by inviting you to my house for a meal?"

Maxstrom, who had just been cut loose, stood up. "Of course. But could I have a minute to dry myself off?"

"Please. Take all the time you need." Gumabu replied.

At this point Gumabu gave a brief gesture to dismiss the Snowiseans, and the white furred katlicans turned to go back to Feshback. As they left, Maxstrom, who was still in several inches of water, walked onto dry land and used his fire ability to send a blast of flame around him into the sand in an attempt to dry himself off. He performed this action several times, and his effort was mostly a success. He looked up to see the Snowisean that had stopped him on the road waiting for him to finish.

"I also feel that I also must offer my formal apology." The Snowisean declared.

"It's alright." Maxstrom said, still slightly frustrated at the whole incident, but choosing not to hold a grudge.

"I am Habu, captain of the Snowisean forces in Feshback."

"So why did you deem me as such a threat, Habu?"

"Well, we've been experiencing numerous raids from across the river. Humans have been coming over and trying to take any katlicans they can hostage. We can only assume it's for slavery; to force us to entertain them and serve them."

"That's awful."

"Indeed."

"I can understand why you attacked me if that's the case. But what about the execution without any form of trial?"

Habu stopped and looked at Maxstrom with a horrified look.

"You don't really think we were executing you, did you?"

"Yes. . ."

"Oh no." Habu declared as he put his face in his paws. "The rope that was around your hands and supporting the rock was also connected to the rope we were suspending you by. We were going to pull you up after about half a minute."

Maxstrom started laughing.

"What's so funny?" Habu asked.

"This whole thing." Maxstrom replied.

"You're telling me you've never seen them do that down at Shavi?"

"No, I've never seen any intruders apprehended. I know there's been some trouble recently, and some magmen attacks, but that's about it."

"Magmen attacks?" Gumabu inquired as his jaw dropped. Habu and Maxstrom had reached his house.

"Yes, Duba was attacked by magmen. They burned down a fourth of the town."

"Is there an invasion? Do I need to rally the soldiers we have here to aid the Shadicans? How did they get past the Tabees?"

"No, Tapito didn't give me any instructions for you. We think that they somehow snuck past the outposts, because we received no warning."

"That would make sense, since there's no way magmen could have destroyed the Tabees with how vicious of a reputation the Tabees have."

"The whole situation is quite confusing." Maxstrom explained.

"Please, have a seat." Gumabu instructed. He had poured tea out for him, Maxstrom, and Habu, and it was sitting on a dining matt on the floor. There was also a small meal of beans.

"Thank you." Maxstrom responded as he walked over to his place and took a seat.

"So what brings you up to Feshback in this time of crisis?" Gumabu asked.

"Well, I was instructed by my fire teacher, Makbu, to start training water with a water ace. I was told that there was someone in Saoland who could teach me."

"Ah! Makbu. How's he been? I haven't seen him in at least fifteen years!" Gumabu declared.

"He's well. He spends most of his time in the mountains training. He's quite extreme."

"Still crazy as always?" Gumabu questioned.

"Yes. Very." Maxstrom answered in between bites of his meal.

"Well. That's something. So you're looking for a water teacher then?"

"Yes, I am."

"And you say there's someone in Saoland?"

"That's what Tapito told me."

"I can't think of anyone off the top of my head. But then again, my memory isn't what it used to be. Do you know of anyone, Habu?"

"I heard of someone a few years ago, but I have no idea if he's still there."

"His name is Rayduan." Maxstrom interjected as he finished his meal.

"Ah! Yes. Now I remember." Gumabu declared with a full mouth of tea. As a result, he spilled some on his chin. He quickly wiped away the mess.

Maxstrom took a final sip of his tea and set the cup down next to his mat, as was the katlican custom.

Gumabu smiled. "Well, I can see you are a fast eater, and probably eager to get back to your journey. Thank you for joining me for a meal. And again, please forgive the actions performed by me and my captain. I guess I haven't journeyed down to Shadicore enough in recent years."

"You are welcome, Gumabu. And you have nothing to worry about, all is forgiven."

"Splendid. Now, I insist upon making arrangements to have two of my soldiers escort you to the border as travel companions. I would not want you to run into any more trouble along the way."

"Oh, that won't be necessary. . ."

"But it is! It's the least I can do to pay you back for the trouble I've caused you. Nacha! Arkana!"

Two Snowisean came to the door. Maxstrom looked up and realized they were the other two Snowisean soldiers that were with Habu the night before.

"You both are to travel with Maxstrom north and be sure that he arrives to Saoland safely." Gumabu declared.

"Yes sir, as you wish." Nacha responded with a slight head bow.

"We'll also give you some supplies for your journey." Gumabu said, turning to Maxstrom.

"That would be greatly appreciated."

"Good! Then it's settled. We'll send you off no later than noon."

Then next thirty minutes involved Gumabu yelling loudly for several of his assistants and sending them running all over Feshback collecting beans, bread, berries, and smoked fish for Maxstrom's journey. After this frenzy had taken place, Gumabu gave another formal apology to Maxstrom, and then sent the group on their way.

"Dudanca, you have no clue how to set a katlican trap."

"Shut up Klanab. I was doing this years before you entered the business."

"So, how much do you suppose one of these creatures will go for?" Ofpila asked.

The group of three trappers were deep in Snowisean territory, in a tiny forest near the base of the mountains.

"A lot. I know some circuses and high end officials that would pay a fortune to have any kind of katlican, especially a Snowisean."

"The problem is catching them." Dudanca remarked. "They're very feisty."

"Should we use bait?" Klanab asked.

"No, they'll see that a mile away and know to avoid it." Dudanca remarked.

"Well, hang on." Ofpila interjected. "I got a diamond we could use. That's not super obvious."

"Ofpila, katlicans are simple creatures. They won't care."

"Oh come on Dudanca. You're telling me a sparkly little rock won't catch a sweet little katlican's attention?" She asked as she blinked her eyebrows in an attempt to appear sweet.

"Fine. Whatever. Let's keep setting traps."

"So how long have you both been in the army now?" Maxstrom asked his escort as they were walking. The early evening sun was lighting the dirt path.

"I've been in three years." Nacha, the female Snowisean, replied.

"I've only been in ten months." Arkana declared.

"Neat." Maxstrom remarked. Neither of the Snowiseans were talkative, and he'd been trying to start a decent conversation for the past four days with little success.

"The mountains look astonishing." Maxstrom remarked.

"They look just as good as when you said so yesterday." Nacha responded.

"Okay, so do you guys usually not talk much?" Maxstrom questioned in frustration.

"Not when we're on assignment. That and we don't like humans." Nacha replied curtly.

"Oh? Why is that?" Maxstrom inquired politely.

"Because a human kidnapped my sister, Sancha, two years ago." Nacha replied as she glared at Maxstrom. "And even though Gumabu has allowed several stealthy excursions into Parcha, we haven't been able to find her."

"I'm sorry." Maxstrom replied. "I can understand how you feel, but I'm not like that."

"Which is irrelevant to me." Nacha responded coldly.

An awkward silence fell on the group as they kept walking.

"What's that?" Maxstrom asked. He heard some type of bird screeching from the woods in distress.

"Probably some finch becoming lunch." Nacha remarked snottily.

Maxstrom stopped and listened, and then heard a voice faintly call out for help.

"Still think it's a finch?" Maxstrom asked, looking at Nacha.

Nacha and Arkana both drew their swords.

"Let's go!" Maxstrom declared.

The trio took off running into the forest. It took them a few minutes to reach the source of the call, but they finally found it near the top of a small, sloping hill.

"It's a fire phoenix!" Arkana exclaimed in surprise.

"Snowiseans! I should have known." The fire phoenix yelled, suspended in the air by a net. "And colluding with a trapper. For shame! When my kind get word of this treachery, there will be war! My father leads the mightiest Phoenix clan!"

"What? No, we're here to help you." Maxstrom explained with a confused look.

Nacha ran over to the net and tried to cut it with her sword.

"It's made of metal! I can't cut it."

"Wait, you're here to rescue me?" The fire phoenix inquired as he raised his eyebrows.

"The trap has to be tied off somewhere." Maxstrom informed. He looked around and saw a rope fastened around a tree to the left. He ran over, set his walking stick down, and untied the knot. After this was complete, he slowly lowered the fire phoenix to the ground. Nacha and Arkana ran over and quickly removed him from the net.

"Oh. Well, thank you. Ow! My wing. It hurts."

The three looked at the fire phoenix's left wing, and could instantly tell that it was broken.

"We need to get that fixed." Maxstrom declared.

"I have some medical training." Arkana replied, and went over to take a look.

"I'm Feftan, by the way." The fire phoenix remarked.

"I'm Maxstrom, and this is Nacha and Arkana."

"Nice to meet you all. Thank you for getting me out of the. . . Ow!"

"Sorry." Arkana replied. "I'm going to have to slide your bone back into place before I can splint it."

"Will that hurt?"

"A lot."

"Could we maybe not do that?" Feftan inquired politely.

"Well if I don't, your wing won't heal right, and you'll never be able to fly again."

Feftan's face reflected the deep thought he was in as he weighed his options.

"Okay katlican, but let's make it quick, alright?" He finally responded.

"Nacha I'm going to need your help."

Nacha came over. "What do you need me to do?"

"I need you to hold him in place. He's going to change his mind once I start."

"I won't change my mind!" Feftan declared, mildly offended.

Nacha grabbed Feftan's left shoulder and braced herself. "Got him."

Arkana started to pull the bone back into place.

"Ah! No! I changed my mind!" Feftan screamed.

"Hold him!" Arkana yelled.

"I'm trying! He's almost twice my size you know!" Nacha retorted.

Maxstrom ran over and grabbed Feftan, who was about to slip out of Nacha's grip.

"Got it!" Arkana declared.

Nacha and Maxstrom both let Feftan go.

"Wow. That. . . hurt."

"Yeah. Now sit still, I have to make you a splint."

"Wait, is there more pain?" Feftan asked as he retracted from the group in horror.

"No. This will be quite painless actually. I just need to put a splint on your wing so it has a guide to heal correctly."

"Oh, good. Well that sounds, simple enough, I suppose."

Arkana grabbed two sticks laying nearby and tied them around Feftan's wing to make a loose splint.

"There's a town not too far from here. We can take you there and get you a safe place to stay until you're healed."

"But my sweetheart is going to be worried sick about me! I was just trying to get her that diamond in the trap! Without that I don't know if I can win her wing in marriage!" Feftan declared.

"Well we certainly can't take you on foot up the mountain, if that's what you want. Sorry about your love problems, but that's not my concern." Nacha responded.

"There is a lot more at stake than my feelings, as fragile as those may be. . ."

"What's that?" Arkana asked suddenly, cutting Feftan off.

The other three fell silent and listened for the noise Arkana had picked up on, but they heard nothing.

"It sounded like a twig snapped." Arkana remarked, skeptically gazing into the thin forest.

All of the sudden they saw a tiny red object fly through the air and imbed itself into one of the sticks in Feftan's splint. Everyone looked at the projectile; it was a large dart; too large to be a Snowisean sleeping dart.

"Trappers! Run!" Nacha yelled.

Both the Shadicans took off running, but Maxstrom stopped for a second to grab Feftan, and then started running back toward the road. Maxstrom looked as he ran, but he couldn't see either Nacha or Arkana. Although running with a nearly five foot fire phoenix in his arms was awkward, he made it back to the road fairly quickly. He looked over and saw Arkana running towards him.

"Where's Nacha?" Arkana yelled.

"I thought she was with you!" Maxstrom replied.

"Oh no. . ."

"What happened?"

"We got split up. She should be here by now. And trappers rarely set just one trap. . ."

"Let's not jump to conclusions just yet." Maxstrom stated as he looked back into the forest. He couldn't see Nacha.

"Okay, here's what I want you to do Arkana. I want you to hide Feftan and keep him safe. I'm going back for Nacha."

"But Max, you shouldn't. . ."

"Listen, we don't have time for this right now. Feftan is hurt, we need to hide him; otherwise they'll see his bright red feathers from a mile away."

"Hey now." Feftan interjected. "I've been told that my red feathers are very handsome. And my best feature."

"You don't say." Arkana remarked dryly to the fire phoenix.

"Arkana. Keep him safe. Okay?"

"Yes sir."

Maxstrom quickly turned and started running back into the woods.

"Well, well, well, what have we here?" Klanab asked as he leaned towards Nacha. She was hanging from another trap.

"Looks like we got ourselves a Snowisean." Ofpila remarked in a taunting voice.

"Indeed!" Dudanca exclaimed with delight.

"Let me go, you monsters!" Nacha yelled.

"Oh we will." Ofpila informed. "After we sell you to the highest bidder."

"You got her paws, Klanab?"

"Aye, I do. . . Ow!"

"Ooh, looks like we got a feisty one here." Ofpila declared.

"You don't say. You good Klanab?"

"No! That thing cut my arm open!"

"Let me see. Oh stop your whining, that's barely a scratch. Now get her paws. And be more careful this time."

Klanab slowly returned to the suspended trap and fearfully looked at the Snowisean.

"Want to try your luck again, or just let me go?" Nacha questioned with a smirk.

Klanab froze, and looked into Nacha's eyes with terror.

"Guys, there has to be an easier way to do this." Klanab remarked as he backed away from the net.

"There is; we just like messing with you." Ofpila replied.

"What? Come on!"

Ofpila walked up to the net, took one of the sleep darts out of her ammo pouch, and jabbed Nacha in the side with it.

"Nap time, katlican."

Maxstrom finally arrived at the net that Feftan had been caught in, and saw his walking stick sitting where he had left it. He went over to pick it up, and then turned to look in the direction he thought Nacha had run, and something caught his eye. He walked over to one of the pine trees, and saw that several branches had been freshly broken, almost as if someone had been dragging a net with something in it. He looked to the ground and saw both drag marks and human footsteps heading in the same direction, so Maxstrom started to track the trappers.

He was able to gather a few more clues along the way until he managed to locate the trappers by their voices. The tones were hushed, but still rather careless because of their apparent triumph. Maxstrom quietly worked his way toward where the voices were coming from until he came to a small meadow on the slope of a gradual hill. In the middle of the clearing was a sloppily put together shack surrounded by dirt; the hunters had used the immediately surrounding grass, mud, and branches to make the shack. Maxstrom dropped to the ground and slowly began crawling towards the sloppy shelter. As he was moving, he found he was close enough to the trappers to hear what they were saying.

"Man did you see those katlicans run?"

"I know right? So much for Snowisean comradery."

"I wonder what that human was doing with them. You don't suppose it was another trapper, do you? Trying to steal our catch?"

"No, if anything it was a Saoland tribesman."

"This far south?"

"I'll tell you what, I'm glad he ran away. Saoland people scare me."

Maxstrom reached the side of the house. He thought for a minute about the next course of action. He figured the best way to rescue Nacha was to get the trappers out of the house, and the only way he could think to do that was to start a fire. He created a small fireball in his right hand and moved it next to a section of dry wood on the shack. It quickly caught on fire.

"So, when are we going to go back to Parcha to sell this katlican?" Ofpila asked.

"Tomorrow, first light. It's already well past noon; the sun will be going down soon." Dudanca responded.

"Hey guys, do you smell something?" Klanab questioned.

The three fell silent for a moment. Then Dudanca yelled "Fire! Get out!"

All three of the trappers quickly ran for the door. Klanab was the first one out, and he was greeted with a blow to the face from Maxstrom's walking stick. Klanab slid to the ground, unconscious. The next one out of the shack was Ofpila, who almost tripped over Klanab's body. She quickly whipped her dagger out and ran at Maxstrom, which caught him by surprise. She swung her dagger at Maxstrom's chest as he staggered back; but since Maxstrom was still wearing the Shadican armor Tapito had given him, this attack did nothing other than tear the fabric covering the metal plate. Maxstrom and Ofpila stared at each other for a moment, and then Ofpila ran at Maxstrom again. This time, Maxstrom was ready. He blocked her strike, and then grabbed Ofpila's wrist to get control over the hand she was holding the knife in. He then quickly swung his right elbow in and hit her in the face. She staggered back and dropped the knife. Maxstrom then took a step forward and kicked her in the face with his left foot, and Ofpila flew to the ground. She was unconscious.

Finally, Dudanca, the third opponent, came through the door carrying Nacha, who had just started to wake up. He saw Maxstrom standing above his two comrades, and dropped Nacha to the ground. Dudanca then pulled up his fists; ready to fight. Maxstrom realized that Dudanca was in shape, yet quite heavier than him, so rather than get into a fist fight,

Maxstrom decided to try and catch his opponent off guard by launching a fire blast combo.

The double blast surprised Dudanca, but he reacted quickly by throwing himself backward to avoid the attack. In doing so, he crashing into the shack, and it collapsed. Dudanca then reached into the burning wreckage, picked up a large branch which had broken off of the structure, jumped up, and swung it at Maxstrom. Maxstrom had no time to react, and clenched up to absorb the blow. The strike hit Maxstrom's right shoulder and threw him on the ground. Dudanca walked over to Maxstrom with the beam poised over his head, ready to strike. Maxstrom quickly recovered his senses and threw a forceful fire kick with both legs right into Dudanca's belly. Dudanca went flying back and landed on the ground. Maxstrom stood to his feet, and slowly walked toward his foe.

"Stay down." Maxstrom commanded in an authoritative tone.

Dudanca didn't listen. Instead, he reached for his knife and jumped up. But Maxstrom was ready, and kicked him in the face. Dudanca flew back to the ground.

"I said stay down."

"I don't listen to punk kids." Dudanca mumbled, wiping his mouth with the back of his hand.

"Well this punk kid just beat you and your two thugs."

"Did you, though?" Dudanca chuckled, looking behind Maxstrom.

Maxstrom turned to see Ofpila with a large branch, ready to swing for his head and split it open. But suddenly, her muscles relaxed, and she dropped to the ground; which revealed that a knife had been thrown into her back by Nacha.

"No!" Dudanca yelled.

"This is your fault. You're the one that came here to kidnap katlicans!" Maxstrom declared, pointing his finger at Dudanca.

Dudanca simply glared at Maxstrom.

"Nacha, can you bring me some rope?"

"It'd be my pleasure."

"Okay this is lame."

"Feftan. I generally don't like to be blunt. But could you please shut up? You've been complaining about every possible thing for the past fifteen minutes."

"Arkadoodad. Whatever your name is. I'm complaining because this sucks."

"It's Arkana. And just because a situation may not be ideal, doesn't mean your attitude shouldn't be."

"You took deer feces and smeared it all around our hiding spot!"

"To help conceal our scent."

"From humans? Wow; for a Snowisean that's traveling with a human you sure seem to know nothing about them."

"What do you mean?"

"Humans can't smell."

"Um, yes they can. They have bigger noses than us katlicans!"

"No, they can't. Come on, I live in the mountains away from humans and even I know this. Their nose is just to accent their face."

"Are you sure they can't smell?"

"Yes. Why do you think humans use dogs to chase things down most of the time?"

"I always just thought they did that because humans are slow runners."

"Well, you know what they say about thinking." Feftan remarked with a snort.

"That. . . everybody does it?"

"What? No. I mean, yes."

"Shh!"

"Really? Now you're going to shh me? Just because I'm smarter than you? Well shh to you too!" Feftan exclaimed as he looked down at Arkana.

"No! Shh I hear something." Arkana whispered and gave Feftan a frustrated look.

"Oh!" Feftan responded sheepishly, and quickly fell silent as he ducked his head down.

"Hey! Arkana! Where are you?" Maxstrom called.

"That's Max, we're good." Arkana declared as he got up.

"Oh cool." Feftan said, getting up and following Arkana. He then let out a terrified screech at the sight of two trappers standing in front of him, and quickly jumped back into his hiding spot.

"Feftan. They're tied up." Arkana stated blandly.

"Ah. Right. Gotcha. Carry on!" Feftan responded and hopped back out into the open.

"You okay, Nacha?" Arkana asked.

"Yeah, just a little groggy. That trapper jabbed me with a sleeping dart."

"Oh, that sounds miserable. Where is she anyway?"

"I killed her." Nacha replied.

"Nacha saved my life." Maxstrom explained.

"And you saved mine. So thank you." Nacha declared, looking at Maxstrom.

"You're welcome." Maxstrom responded with a smile. He then scrunched his nose as he sniffed the air.

"Say, what's that smell?" Maxstrom inquired as he covered his mouth and nose.

Arkana glared at Feftan. "I told you they could smell."

"Wait, you can smell?" Feftan asked Maxstrom in surprise.

"Yes. . . why wouldn't I be able to smell?"

"I mean, humans use dogs to track stuff when they hunt, right?"

"I grew up with Shadicans, Feftan. I have no clue what normal humans do."

"Oh."

"We sometimes use dogs to hunt." Klanab interjected.

"You do?" Maxstrom asked.

"Aye. But we left them on this trek because stealth is key when trying to successfully trap katlicans."

"Please, let me slit his throat." Nacha inquired calmly.

"What? No! Don't let her!" Klanab yelled, horrified.

"No, Nacha. Let's take these two to the nearest town; the Snowisean elder can decide what to do from there."

"As you wish. Oh hey, Feftan. I have something for you." Nacha remarked.

"You got me a present?"

"Sort of. I found that diamond you wanted to take to your sweetheart."

Feftan let out a shriek of joy. "Thank you so much! My mission is well on its way to being completed!"

Nacha simply smiled as she handed him the diamond, and Feftan took it with his beak.

"Finally, now that he has something in his mouth, this negative bird will stop complaining." Arkana declared.

"Hey." Feftan tried to say as he rolled the diamond around in his beak.

"Alright, let's get going. I want to get to the next village before sunset." Maxstrom interjected.

"Sounds good. Lead the way, Max." Nacha responded as she looked up at him with respect.

"I still can't thank you enough, Maxy." Feftan declared, enjoying the ride on Maxstrom's back. Maxstrom had made a comfortable sling for Feftan to rest in on the outside of his pack.

"It's Max. And you're quite welcome."

"Max. Got it."

Maxstrom had agreed to take Feftan part of the way home; to the foot of his mountain chain. The Snowisean elder had decided to hand the two trappers over to the Parchan government, since they were residents of Parcha. Even though trapping was becoming a fad amongst Parchans, the government itself frowned upon this activity and severely punished anyone caught in the trade. Maxstrom had also decided to part ways with his guard.

"Which peak did you say was yours again?" Maxstrom asked. Maxstrom was standing in a meadow, looking up at the mountains before him. He had paused both to catch his breath and to get directions.

"We call it Nuna Peak." Feftan responded, not even looking.

"Yeah, but which one of the peaks is it from what's in front of us?"

"Oh. It's the really big one behind this tiny one we're looking at." Feftan informed as he gestured with his one good wing.

"This is going to be so much fun. . ." Maxstrom remarked.

"I know right! I've never ridden a human before."

Maxstrom turned his head to glare at Feftan.

"What? Was it something I said?"

Maxstrom simply rolled his eyes and resumed walking.

"So. We should have a conversation."

Maxstrom stopped walking and looked back towards Feftan again.

"How about you do most of the talking since you're not the one carrying a twenty pound bird on your back?" Maxstrom questioned in exasperation.

"That's fair. Can I tell you about my sweetheart?"

"Sure. Go for it." Maxstrom remarked as he started walking again.

"So, I first saw her in my clan's migration from the Southern Peak. It was love at first sight. But the problem was that she's from another clan. There are three fire phoenix clans. And, while we don't fight, there's a lot of tension between the groups."

"Why is that?" Maxstrom asked.

"Because, a long time ago, the three clans were one clan. A family. But then, three brothers got into an argument, and each went their separate ways. So the problem is that the clans haven't mixed in marriage for about a hundred years."

"So your family doesn't approve?"

"Exactly the opposite. My dad, the clan leader, thinks it's a fantastic idea. A chance to reconcile and merge our clans together. And the other clan leader thinks it's a great idea too."

"So I don't see the problem then."

"Well, the problem is that the other clan leader is playing hard to get. He wants me to present my sweetheart with some trophy as payment to be allowed to marry her."

"Ah. I see."

"Exactly. So that's why I went for the diamond when I saw it in the trap."

"Makes sense."

"So enough about me. I think you've got a much more interesting story. Raised by Shadicans?"

Maxstrom was just reaching the top of a small hill and starting to walk down, so he decided to engage in the conversation more.

"Yeah, for the last eight years."

"And how old are you now?"

"Sixteen."

"Wow. Do you remember your parents?"

"Vaguely."

"Don't you want to find them?"

"Well, they sent me away. So I figure when the time is right, they'll come get me."

"Why did they send you away?"

"There was a change of power in my country, and an evil ruler took over."

"Oh. Hate when that happens."

"You've had that happen in one of the fire phoenix clans?"

"Huh? Oh no, not at all. I just meant that in a hypothetical sense."

Maxstrom turned his head towards Feftan to reveal the befuddled look on his face as he continued walking down the hill.

"So anyway Max, how did you come to live with the Shadicans?"

"I was sent to them."

"Wait, your parents are friends with the Shadicans?"

"My dad. He's part of the Aceic Council. And since the Aceic Council helped the mass migration of the katlicans to their current home, all of the katlican tribes think highly of the Aceic Council. That relationship has been around for quite a long time, just at a distance."

"Mass migration of katlicans? What are you talking about?"

"Well the katlicans didn't always live here."

"I'm going to be totally honest with you Max. I didn't know that."

"Really? You've never heard the story?"

"Never."

"I'll have to tell you all about Shadic the Third some other time, it looks like we've got company." Maxstrom declared as he looked to the sky.

Feftan looked up as well, and saw several large birds circling about a hundred feet in the air.

"Hey that's my family!"

Feftan then gave a loud call, which was returned by several faint calls. The birds above began to slowly descend down toward them.

"Feftan!" An older fire phoenix exclaimed in a deep voice.

"Hey dad!" Feftan responded. "So I had a little accident on my journey."

"I've gathered as much. Who's this human?" Feftan's dad inquired with great suspicion.

"I'm Maxstrom."

"He was raised by Shadicans." Feftan threw in.

"Oh? That's a first. So what happened to your wing, Feftan?"

"I broke it."

"I knew something like this would happen." Feftan's dad declared as he rubbed his wing over his face.

"But I got something of great value!"

"Did you?" Feftan's dad perked up.

"I got a diamond! Max, show him!"

Maxstrom pulled the diamond out of a pouch on his belt, and showed it to the fire phoenix clan leader.

"Beautiful!" He remarked. "Well, thank you Maxstrom for bringing my Feftan home safely."

"You're welcome."

"Um, dad. How am I going to get to the top of the mountain with a broken wing?"

"Feftan. We can pick you up and fly you there."

"Oh. Why didn't I think of that?"

"Maxstrom, is there any way we can return the favor you have done for us?"

"Well, I could use some directions. Although I'm not sure if you'll know exactly where I'm going."

"I'll do my best." Feftan's dad responded as he leaned in.

"I'm a water ace, and I'm heading to Saoland to try to find a teacher by the name of Rayduan."

"Ah! It would seem Abada brought us together. I know exactly where you can find him."

"Really?"

"Indeed. He's been a friend to the fire phoenixes. So you'll follow the foot of the mountains up into Saoland, and shortly after you cross the border you'll hit a town. I believe the town is known by the name of Glas. But after you hit that town you'll need to head due west until you reach the ocean. Rayduan's home should be right around there."

"Thank you, I appreciate your help." Maxstrom declared as he set Feftan on the ground.

"It is my pleasure, and thank you for everything you've done for my family, water ace. Know that you've made a friendship for generations to come with the fire phoenixes."

"Thank you. Well, farewell Feftan!"

"Farewell to you as well, Max! I'll miss you."

The group of fire phoenixes gently grabbed Feftan. Then they all simultaneously burst into flame while lifting off from the ground, heading towards Nuna Peak with Feftan waving goodbye to Maxstrom beneath the fiery group.

It had been raining for almost three days straight, and Maxstrom was soaked. Even a water ace couldn't keep dry in a constant deluge. He was freezing, and starting to get sick. There was no shelter anywhere, and no place for him to get warm. His joints felt achy. Maxstrom could only guess that he had a fever, and he felt exhausted. And to make matters worse, he had several blisters that had formed on his feet. But as far as he could tell, he had crossed the border into Saoland.

Suddenly, he tripped and collapsed on the muddy trail. He tried to get up, but he didn't have the strength. He'd been shuffling along all day at only a fraction of his usual pace. And now, he was exhausted. He didn't have the ability to go any further.

"Help!" He yelled faintly, with a raspy voice. He cleared his throat, and yelled again.

He gave several more desperate calls for help before he let his face rest on the mud. He knew it wasn't likely there was anyone around; but it was worth the try. He closed his eyes from exhaustion, and lost consciousness almost instantly.

Chapter 5

Refining a Student

B.Y. 4013

"Everyone needs a good teacher."
—Akbu

Maxstrom slowly opened his eyes, and realized he was on his back instead of on his face. There was something above him, and it took a moment to figure out what it was; wood support beams to some kind of house or hut. He heard a light crackling, and looked over to his left. A safe distance away was a fireplace with a cozy fire going, and his clothes were hanging nearby, drying out.

As he was taking in this scene, the door, which was opposite the fireplace, swung open. Two figures entered the hut. It took Maxstrom a moment for his eyes to adjust enough to be able to clearly see their faces. One was a young man about his age, and the other was a middle aged woman. The woman had a bowl in her hands.

"He's awake." The woman remarked to the young man.

"Good. Now I want to know what. . ."

"Nathar, calm down. He's obviously not well." The woman scolded as she walked over to Maxstrom. "Here, I brought you some soup. Can you sit up?"

Maxstrom tried to speak, but nothing came out, so he nodded, and slowly sat up.

"Good. Its beef and lentil, with a little bit of lemon in it. It'll help you warm up and restore your strength."

Maxstrom quickly devoured the large bowl. Once he had eaten, his voice came back.

"Thank you." He managed to say.

"You're welcome." The woman said, taking the bowl. She walked back to the door and went outside.

"Okay so who are you?" The young man, whose name apparently was Nathar, asked in an agitated tone.

"My name is Maxstrom."

"Maxstrom. Sounds like an interesting name. Where are you from?"

"Do you want the short version or the long version?"

"Does it look like I'm here to play games?" Nathar yelled as his eyes narrowed.

"No. I'm sorry, it's just complicated."

"Well, uncomplicated it for me."

"I'm from Dauchenland, but I've spent the past eight years of my life living with the Shadicans."

Nathar scoffed. "That's impossible, the Shadicans don't accept outsiders."

"They accepted me. I'm an ace."

Nathar suddenly became more friendly and intrigued. "You are? What kind?"

"Fire and water."

Nathar raised his eyebrows. "That's impressive."

"Thanks." Maxstrom replied, unsure of what else to say.

"So what brings you to my country?"

"I'm looking for Rayduan."

"Oh, well that makes perfect sense then."

"Yeah. I'm looking for a water ace to help me hone my skills."

"He's all the way at the shoreline. About two day's walk from here."

"Where is here?" Maxstrom inquired.

"You're in the town of Glas. Well, on the edge of it anyway."

The door opened again, and the woman returned.

"I brought you some water."

"Thanks." Maxstrom responded.

She handed him a large cup, and he quickly drank the whole thing.

"Don't drown yourself now." The woman said, jokingly.

"I'll try not to."

"Rina, he says he's a fire and water ace." Nathar said excitedly.

Rina, who was the woman, raised her eyebrows in surprise as this information.

"And he says he's looking for Rayduan."

"See Nathar? I told you that he intended us no harm."

"Well," Nathar said, glaring at Maxstrom, "he seems friendly enough now. But I'd like to see his abilities before I'm going to trusting him."

"I'm not sure how much I can do for you at the moment, I feel pretty weak."

"Nathar!" Rina yelled. She then looked at Maxstrom. "Don't trouble yourself. You just need to rest for now."

"That actually sounds like a good idea." Maxstrom replied, yawning.

"Before you go back to sleep, I have an herb that will help restore your strength. I'll be right back." Rina said, going to the door again.

Once she had left, Nathar looked at Maxstrom skeptically and said "Show me what you can do."

Maxstrom, realizing that the only way he would be believed by Nathar was if he proved he was an ace, took out his hand and made a weak fireball in it. It sputtered out after a few seconds time.

"Sorry, I don't have much strength at the moment." Maxstrom informed apologetically.

"No, no! That's fine. I've seen enough." Nathar responded.

Maxstrom started coughing.

"You alright?"

"Yeah, I'm good." Maxstrom declared as he recovered his breath.

"So how did you find out you were an ace? Like, what's the process?"

"Well my dad controls fire, and since abilities can often be passed down genetically, he tested me."

"Tested how?"

"He brought me a candle and had me try different methods of pushing and pulling the flame. After about twenty minutes of trying different things, I found that I could move the flame."

"Wow! And how about for water?"

"I figured that one out on my own actually, while I was in Shadicore. I wanted to test and see if I was a water ace."

"And how'd you do that?"

"Same idea as with the fire, I just spent a couples hours trying to move a small stream, and eventually I had some success."

"So if I wanted to test and see if I'm an ace, all I need to do is go try and move stuff?"

"Yeah that's it. Why, do you think you're an ace?"

"No. . . it'd just be cool to check, ya know?

Nathar and Maxstrom both heard the hut door open. It was Rina; she had returned with a small bowl, and she brought it over to Maxstrom.

"It's spicy, but it will help your body fight off the sickness."

In the bowl there were several small leaves from an herb. Maxstrom took the small leaves and ate them. After he swallowed his mouth started to burn.

"Oh. That is spicy!"

"The burning is a sign that it's helping your body fight off the sickness. Now, you need to get some rest. Come on Nathar, let's leave our guest be."

"See you ace, have a good nap!"

Both the Saolanders went to the door, and walked out. Maxstrom's eyelids bobbed down several times, and he quickly fell back asleep.

"Hey there, sleepy."

Maxstrom struggled to open his eyes.

"You've been sleeping for two days."

"Two days?"

"Aye." Nathar replied. "How do you feel?"

"I feel a lot better. But I'm hungry."

"I thought you might be. Here's some stew." Nathar declared as he offered Maxstrom a bowl.

"Thanks." Maxstrom said as he took the meal and started to eat.

"So I hope you're feeling good enough to travel."

"I think I should be soon, why?"

"There's a few wagons heading west towards where Rayduan lives. They leave at noon, which is in about two hours."

"That would be great. I'm tired of walking."

"I can imagine. How far did you walk from?"

"Well technically I came from Duba."

"Isn't that like, in the south of Shadicore?"

"Yeah."

"Woah. That's a ways."

"Yeah, it was. Thanks for the stew."

"Oh sure! You want more?"

"Do you mind? I still feel a bit weak."

"Not at all!"

Seven bowls of stew later, Maxstrom finally had enough strength to get up and walk around a little.

"Want to see the town?" Nathar asked.

"Sure." Maxstrom replied.

Nathar took Maxstrom through the door and out into the bright daylight. Maxstrom winced as he waited for his eyes to adjust to the light.

"Oh, sorry, forgot you'd been in there so long."

"It's fine, just give me a minute." Maxstrom replied.

As Maxstrom's eyes adjusted, he could see several dozen of lean-to cabins made of wood and stone staggered across the rolling hills and rocky terrain. Towards what he assumed was the center of the town, he saw a large wooden fort. In the far distance Maxstrom could see several gigantic mountains.

"I'm guessing that's east?" Maxstrom asked as he pointed to the mountains.

"Indeed!" Nathar replied. "Your navigational skills are impressive."

"Well I was following the mountains up through Snowisea, so I should be fairly familiar with them."

"That's a good point."

"Nathar! You should be letting our guest get his rest." Rina declared, coming up behind the two.

"Mom, he's fine."

"I'll be the judge of that. How are you feeling, Maxstrom?"

"Much better, thank you."

"You're very welcome." Rina responded as she scanned Maxstrom from head to toe. "Well I suppose you look alright. Should be good enough to travel with the wagon train if you're up for it."

"I think I am. How can I repay you for your hospitality? I don't really have any money. . ."

"Oh nonsense!" Rina responded. "You were a person in need, and we helped you. We did what any civil person would do. Now I want you to head back inside; I have some more herbs for you to take to help boost your strength. Then we can help you set up travel arrangements with the wagon train."

The wagon train wasn't going directly to Rayduan's residence, so they dropped Maxstrom off after about a day of travel. Maxstrom continued to head west until he hit the shore; and it was quite a beautiful shore. Maxstrom had never seen the ocean before. There were spurts of various rock formations lining the coast interrupted by occasional stretches of sandy beaches.

After spending a few minutes admiring its beauty, he decided to start searching for Rayduan. Maxstrom couldn't see any man-made structure on the part of the beach he was on, so he decided to start walking around. He walked about a mile south and found nothing other than more beautiful scenery. So he decided to retrace his steps and head north. By the time he passed the point he had arrived on the beach, it was getting close to sunset.

"I need to find Rayduan soon." Maxstrom whispered to himself.

All of the sudden, Maxstrom heard a yell come from the ocean. He quickly turned and looked, but it was hard to see anything since the sun was starting to set in that direction.

He heard another yell, but it wasn't a cry for help, it was a yell of enjoyment. Maxstrom squinted his eyes and scanned the waves. Finally, his eyes adjusted to the bright light, and something caught his eye; it was a person. The person was standing on some board and riding a large wave coming in.

Maxstrom watched in amazement. The person moved along the wave easily, and did several snaps up to the top of the wave. Then, all of the sudden, the wave started to collapse and it formed a tube over the person. Maxstrom lost sight of the wave-rider for a moment, and then saw him shoot out of the tube the wave had formed, and jump off of the object he had been standing on into the water. It seemed that the person had finished the odd activity, so Maxstrom decided to try and talk to the stranger.

"Hello!" Maxstrom called loudly.

He saw the person look toward him, and then grab the object he had been standing on and start swimming to the shore at an unusually rapid pace. The person stopped about fifteen feet from land, hopped off of his wooden board, and stood waist deep in the water.

"Can I help you?" The stranger yelled to Maxstrom.

"Yeah, I'm looking for Rayduan. Would you happen to know where he is?"

The person hesitated for a moment.

"No, no one by that name lives here."

"Are you sure?" Maxstrom questioned.

"Indeed."

"Great." Maxstrom muttered to himself.

Maxstrom decided to ask this person for some advice before moving on. "I'm not from around here, could you tell me where I should go if I'm looking for Rayduan?"

"You should try the town of Glas." The stranger replied, still in the water.

"I just came from there!" Maxstrom yelled back. "And they sent me here!"

"They sent you here?"

"Yeah!"

The stranger started to wade in towards Maxstrom.

"What's your name, kid?"

"Maxstrom."

The stranger stopped about five feet from the shore. Maxstrom could make out a blonde goatee on the stranger that matched his light blonde hair. The stranger's hands hovered above the water.

"That's not a Saolander name. What do you want?"

"I want to find Rayduan."

"I got that part, but why do you want Rayduan?"

Maxstrom hesitated. This stranger was acting weird, and he wasn't sure if he should tell him about his abilities or not. After thinking for a moment, Maxstrom decided to go for it.

"Because I need a teacher, and he's the only water ace in this corner of the world."

"Who told you he was a water ace?"

"Tapito, head of the Shadican tribe."

The stranger's eyes got big.

"You met Tapito and didn't die?"

"Well, my father was on the Aceic Council in Dauchenland, and he worked hard to maintain a relationship with the Shadicans. . ."

"What's your father's name?"

"Ottokar."

The man came out of the water and onto the shore with a smile on his face.

"Ah, Ottokar. I remember him. He was a good guy."

"You know my dad?" Maxstrom asked excitedly.

"Aye. He was a good Aceic soldier."

"So were you an Aceic soldier too then?" Maxstrom inquired.

"Oh no, I never wanted to get involved with all those politics. I just helped your father with a peacekeeping mission here."

"What do you mean?"

"Your father was stationed here, in Saoland. You didn't know?"

"I think I vaguely remember hearing something about that. . ."

"Well your dad was stationed at the capital of Saoland, Skye, for about six months. He also met his wife there, Retta. Who I assume is your mother?"

"Yeah! She is!"

"Well anyway, it's getting dark. We should probably head to my cabin."

"I was looking for a cabin around here and I couldn't find anything." Maxstrom declared.

The man smiled.

"That's good! I purposefully tried to hide it."

"Why is that?"

The man suddenly became more serious. "We can talk about that later. I have a fish stew cooking, and you're probably starving."

"I am." Maxstrom replied, realizing that his stomach was growling.

The man then led Maxstrom a little ways into a grouping of trees and bushes.

"So, just to be clear, you are Rayduan, right?" Maxstrom inquired as he followed the stranger.

The man laughed.

"I suppose I didn't make that very obvious, did I? Aye, I am."

"Okay. Just making sure."

"It's right here." Rayduan declared, and walked through two bushes.

Maxstrom stopped for a moment, looking after Rayduan with a confused look.

"You coming, kid?" Rayduan called.

"Yeah." Maxstrom replied as he walked through the bushes that concealed the doorway to Rayduan's cabin.

Maxstrom awoke with a start. He looked around and didn't know where he was. Then he remembered, and relaxed. He was in Rayduan's cabin. He had been so exhausted from walking yesterday that after they had eaten, he immediately fell asleep.

Maxstrom was lying in a cozy bed surrounded by animal furs for warmth. He looked over and the fire was still going. But Rayduan was not in the cabin.

Maxstrom got up and walked to the door, which he realized was a thick bear skin curtain. He pushed this curtain aside and walked out. A bright late morning sun greeted him, which forced him to squint his eyes. The cabin didn't have any windows, so the difference in brightness outside was stark.

Once his eyes adjusted, he looked around. At first he could see little other than the beautiful and sporadically rocky beach that was around him. But then Maxstrom directed his gaze towards the waves and saw Rayduan walking on the beach towards him.

"Good morning!" Rayduan called.

"Good morning!" Maxstrom yelled back.

"Glad to see you're up. I got breakfast!" Rayduan said, and held up a large bunch of seaweed.

"Great, I'm starving."

"Just give me a few minutes to roast this stuff and we can eat." Rayduan declared as he walked passed Maxstrom.

"Is there anywhere I can get some water to drink? Is the ocean safe to drink from?" Maxstrom inquired, realizing he was quite parched.

"Oh, no! No, the ocean has too much salt. Look over there, you see that large rock formation? There's a natural spring in there; it has fresh, cool water. Use that to drink and wash up."

"Thanks!" Maxstrom responded as he walked towards the rocks.

After a few minutes of washing up and quenching his thirst; Maxstrom returned to the cabin.

"The seaweed is almost ready." Rayduan said as Maxstrom walked in.

"Good!"

"But in the meantime, we should talk about our journey."

"What journey?" Maxstrom inquired, confused.

"I'm going to take you to my training ground." Rayduan declared. "It's just over a day's walk up the beach."

Maxstrom tried to mask his disappointment. He was feeling tired of all the traveling he had to do, and the blisters on his feet still hadn't fully recovered.

"I know you probably don't want to do anymore walking," Rayduan said, noticing the look on Maxstrom's face, "but I want to go to a more ideal and secluded spot for all that I'm going to teach you. How much do you know about your abilities?"

"That I can pick up water, and that I can use my ability to swim faster?"

"Good start! But there's so much more than that. You've just scratched the surface."

"What, really?" Maxstrom asked. "My fire training had a few surprises. . ."

"You can control fire too?" Rayduan questioned with an intrigued tone. "Who trained you?"

"Makbu."

"Ah! I've heard of him. One of the few Shadicans that can wield two elements. So what did you learn from him?"

"A bunch of powerful moves, that controlling elements is linked to the muscles, and that I can use my legs to shoot blasts of fire."

"Good! You've made some progress then. I assume he probably put you through some physical training as well?"

Maxstrom groaned. "Yeah, a lot of it."

"That's very good! I won't have to put you through all that then; I can get right to teaching you. Oh and you might want to change out of your armor after we eat; we'll be in the water a good deal, and that might weigh you down and tire you out needlessly. I have a spare set of clothes I can give you."

"Alright, thanks."

Rayduan looked at the seaweed he was roasting.

"I think it's about ready. Let's eat so we can get on our way."

Maxstrom and Rayduan traveled north up the beach for about a day and a half before reaching their destination. When they decided to take a break and sleep, Maxstrom noticed that Rayduan set up camp in a secluded spot. He also dug a fire pit so it would be less visible to anyone in the vicinity. Maxstrom tried to inquire if there was a reason behind this behavior, but Rayduan simply looked around with a worried look on his face and told him he would explain everything later.

After some hours of walking the next day, the duo arrived at an unusual section of the beach. There was still sand, but there were dozens of massive rocks strewn about the shore. There was also a small freshwater stream running towards the ocean, but it disappeared under a pile of massive rocks.

"We're here." Rayduan declared.

"Here? This is it?"

"It is indeed!"

"This is just a bunch of rocks."

Rayduan simply smiled. "That's what it's meant to look like."

Maxstrom stared back in confusion as Rayduan walked over to one of the nearest boulders, and climbed up and around to a small ledge a third of the way up. He was now out above the water, and he looked down at the sloshing waves that were beneath him, as if he was deep in thought.

"What are you looking at?" Maxstrom asked, confused.

Rayduan simply looked at Maxstrom, smiled, and then jumped into the water head first.

Maxstrom quickly ran up to see where Rayduan had gone, but he couldn't see him anywhere. After some climbing, Maxstrom looked at what was under the surface where Rayduan had jumped, and saw that there was a huge hole going straight down. The water below was deep.

Maxstrom was hesitant to follow Rayduan under water, because Maxstrom wasn't the best at holding his breath, and didn't like the idea of being underwater again after his incident in Snowisea. So instead, he waited for a few minutes to see if Rayduan would come back. But he didn't. Eventually Maxstrom realized he would have to face his fear and jump in. So he took a deep breath and plunged in head first, pack and all.

He swam straight down for about twenty feet, and then hit the bottom. He looked around and saw that the tunnel continued horizontally, so he continued in that direction. After using his ability to control water to rapidly swim for about another fifteen feet, the walls of the tunnel opened up, and he could tell he was in some kind of cavern. Maxstrom quickly swam for the surface, and his head broke through. He immediately took a deep gulp of air.

"You made it!" He heard a voice call, even though both of his ears had water in them.

"Yeah." Maxstrom replied, wiping his eyes so he could see. He looked around, and saw that he was in an enclosed cavern, with no way out except the way he came in. In the center and going up to the back of the cavern was a rock peninsula which led into a small enclave; and this is where Rayduan was standing. At the top of the cavern there were several tiny holes letting in a small amount of light.

"Woah." Maxstrom declared. "This is pretty cool."

Rayduan smiled. "Glad you like it. Now come on over and let's get started!"

Maxstrom swam over to the peninsula and stood on the rocky shore.

"How are you dry?!" Maxstrom exclaimed as he looked at Rayduan. There was no evidence he had even been in the water.

"Stand still." Rayduan replied, and walked towards Maxstrom.

Rayduan parted all of his fingers, and began pulling all of the water off of Maxstrom while walking around him in a circle. After about a moment, he was finished.

"That's really cool. You need to show me how to do that."

"At some point. But first, I have to make sure you have all the basics. When you build a house, you can't start with the roof. You have to start with the foundation."

"Makes sense." Maxstrom replied.

Rayduan walked over to the edge of the water, and pulled a large stream out, and kept it close to the ground. He then stopped and began turning it into ice; quickly molding it into a pillar about six feet high.

"What?!" Maxstrom exclaimed. "You're going teach me that too, right?"

Rayduan simply chuckled. "At some point. But for now, I want to see how you throw water."

"You don't want me to hit your ice pillar, do you?" Maxstrom inquired, not wanting to destroy it.

Rayduan chuckled. "Yes. As hard as you can. I can always make more if you manage to break this one."

Maxstrom reached his right hand toward the pool and pulled out a ball of water. He then aimed, and threw it at the pillar. The water splashed aside, but the pillar remained intact.

"Not bad. Good accuracy. But keep in mind, we are using water now, not fire. You have to hit hard with water."

"That was as hard as I know how to hit." Maxstrom responded, slightly dejected.

"Okay, and that's fine. That's what I'm here to teach you. Now watch me."

Rayduan pulled a ball of water out of the pool.

"Now you're using a closed-handed technique, which isn't my favorite, but that's fine. We'll work with that."

Rayduan took the ball of water and pulled it close to his face as if he were about to punch something in front of him. He then launched his fist forward, but at the last second opened his palm out and gave the ball of water an extra thrust. The ball of water hit the ice pillar and shattered the top foot of it off.

"Woah!" Maxstrom exclaimed.

"So two things you need to do differently. First, you're letting the water go too soon. You need to hold onto it and give it momentum all the way up until the last second. Then, you not only release you're grip, but give it a push with an open palm. And second, rotate your foot and hips with each strike, it helps build extra momentum."

"Okay, got it."

"I assume you learned as well that controlling the elements means that you not only can pull them towards you, but also repel them?"

"Yeah, I saw that I could do that with fire."

"Good. So remember, you have that same ability with water. Use that to help you."

Maxstrom grabbed another ball of water and tried again, following all of Rayduan's instructions. The pillar cracked upon impact.

"Better!" Rayduan declared. "Keep practicing; work on that release and your footwork."

Rayduan quickly repaired the ice pillar.

"Go for it!"

Maxstrom launched another attack, and knocked the top of the pillar clean off.

"That's what I'm talking about Maxstrom! Just don't forget your footwork. Now, I want you to do that with your left hand."

Maxstrom grabbed water with his left hand and attempted to launch it as he had just done, but the ball of water merely splashed into the pillar.

"That's okay, one hand usually comes easier than the other. Just try again."

Maxstrom grabbed another ball of water and threw another attack. It also merely splashed against the pillar; doing nothing.

"Alright, here's what we're going to do. We're going to keep drilling the left side until you get it, and then we'll do one hundred strikes with each side. I'll stand here and fix the pillar; you just focus on getting your form right. Take your time."

Maxstrom tightened up his stance, pulled another water ball out of the pool, and launched another attack.

"Good job, Max."

"That is quite a workout!"

Rayduan smiled. "Well, we're not finished yet. I want you to look behind you."

Maxstrom turned around and looked. "It's basically just a rock wall."

"You see that bar about seven feet off of the ground in that dead-end doorway?"

"Yeah?"

"That's for you to do pull-ups. I want to see you do thirty."

Maxstrom groaned.

"Take your time. Take as many breaks as you need."

After about seven minutes, Maxstrom finished his thirty pull-ups.

"Alright, now let me show you the open palmed form." Rayduan stated.

Rayduan then reached down towards the pool and grabbed a stream of water by only slightly bending his fingers and spreading them apart. Instead of a ball, it was in a long, ovular shape. He then began passing it around his body from one hand to the other.

"That's impressive." Maxstrom remarked as he watched.

"Thanks. Now you give it a go. Take your time."

"I don't think I can do anymore. I feel exhausted." Maxstrom moaned as he rubbed his arms. They felt incredibly sore.

"You should be." Rayduan declared. "We'll call it a day."

Rayduan walked over to the right side of the rock peninsula, and then jumped into the water.

"Wait!" Maxstrom called. "Isn't the exit on the other side?"

Since Rayduan was already in the water, Maxstrom was greeted with silence. Maxstrom ran over and watched the exit to see if Rayduan swam over there, but after a moment of watching, he saw nothing. He then walked over to the edge Rayduan had jumped off of, and looked down. He thought he could make out another tunnel, but this time it went under the peninsula he was on.

"Well, here goes nothing." Maxstrom said as he grabbed his pack and jumped into the water, blindly following Rayduan again.

There was indeed a second tunnel, and it went under the island for about twenty-five feet, and then made a sharp left. The next section was another twenty-five feet, and then the tunnel opened into another cavern. Maxstrom was almost out of breath, and quickly went to the surface.

As soon as his face broke through the surface, he was greeted by Rayduan laughing at him.

"You know, I like you as a teacher, but I'm not a fan of you disappearing like that." Maxstrom remarked.

Rayduan just chuckled. "Come on out, Max."

Maxstrom came out of the pool, and this time he was in a room about the same size as Rayduan's cabin. There was a pile of furs and other odd supplies over in one corner.

"You want me to dry you off?" Rayduan asked.

"I think I'll actually give it a shot, if you think I can do it."

"Go for it." Rayduan replied.

After a few failed attempts, Maxstrom had mostly dried himself.

"Not bad for your first day."

"Thanks. We wouldn't happen to have any food in here, would we?"

"Indeed we do!" Rayduan informed as he went over to tiny pool on the other side of the room, froze some of the water, and pulled out two large frozen rocks of ice.

"What's in there?"

"Fish." Rayduan replied as he walked over to an empty hole that didn't have any water in it.

"What?!" Maxstrom exclaimed. "That's amazing!"

Rayduan then dropped the balls of ice onto the ground and quickly killed and gutted both the fish. Instead of using a regular knife, he created one out of ice. He then dropped the fish into the empty pit, pulled some water over from one of the pools, dropped it in, and after he aimed his arms at the water for a moment, it started to boil.

"Just give it a few minutes." Rayduan declared.

"This is really a lot to take in. . ."

"I can imagine. A lot of stuff you might not have even thought of before. But really, controlling water has a plethora of uses."

"You don't say."

Both sat in silence for a few moments.

"So why were you so keen on getting here secretly, Rayduan?"

Rayduan hesitated for a moment.

"I suppose I do need to tell you sooner or later."

Maxstrom leaned in, waiting to hear what Rayduan had to say.

"Assassins." Rayduan whispered.

"Assassins?"

"That's the main reason, anyway. That and not all the tribes like me; but that's a different story."

"So, assassins are after you?"

"Aye. One almost killed me eight years ago. Then shortly after, I noticed I was being followed. So I left society."

"That's creepy. What did the assassin look like?"

"He was in a black cloak with a white mask. Others have described them as ghosts; but it wasn't. It was a human."

"How do you know?" Maxstrom asked.

"Because I've seen spiritual forces, and this figure was vastly different." Rayduan replied.

"What exactly happened?" Maxstrom inquired.

"Alright, I'll give you the whole story. Nine years ago, I sent your father a letter that I had discovered a new ace in Skye. The family was willing to send him down to become an Aceic soldier. But Ottokar sent me a letter back informing me that it wasn't the best time, and that things were becoming tense in Haiedenburg and Dauchenland. He asked me to keep an eye on the future ace for the time being because there had been rumors of ghostlike figures going after future aces and either killing or kidnapping them Since I trusted your father, I did as he asked; I stayed with the family, and decided I would start working for a hunting crew. But after about eight months, the assassin appeared.

One night, I came home earlier than usual, and noticed the house was abnormally quiet. As I approached the door, I saw that it was open. I walked in, and that's when I saw him. He was standing over the child I was supposed to protect. The kid was dead. The figure turned and aimed some weapon and me, and shot me in the shoulder. There happened to be a bowl of water off to the side, so I grabbed it, made a sword, and charged the soldier. He drew a dagger, and we fought for a moment. But he got the upper hand, and stabbed me in the side. I collapsed. He pulled his dagger up, ready to strike me, but I grabbed my ice sword and lunged it into his abdomen. The assassin staggered back, clutched his gut, and ran out. I tried to go after him, but I blacked out by the door."

"That's horrible." Maxstrom replied.

"And I feel like it's my fault. If I had taken your fathers request more seriously and not taken up a job for some money, maybe that kid would still be alive."

"It sounds like you did everything you could, though."

Rayduan stared into the distance for a moment, and then changed the subject.

"Looks like the fish is almost ready."

Rayduan walked over, got the fish out, and seasoned them. "Here ya go, get your strength back, Max. You're going to need it for tomorrow."

"Thanks." Maxstrom responded as he began to eat.

"Today we're going to build on what we did yesterday. I want you to spin the water around you and then strike the ice pole."

Maxstrom, who had just repeated a condensed version of everything he did yesterday, was still catching his breath.

"You alright, Max?"

"Yeah, just recovering."

"Alright. So the purpose of this attack is to gain extra momentum. The more momentum you have, the harder the impact of your attack will be. We'll do fifty, and then switch to the other hand. And don't forget to rotate your hips and foot for each strike."

Over the next week, Rayduan went over how to make attacks more powerful by condensing water attacks into a smaller surface area, and taught Maxstrom several other water techniques, including how to use his legs to control water. However, Rayduan informed Maxstrom that legs were generally not the most effective for controlling water, and that when it came to legs, he should use them primarily for keeping a strong stance.

"So, Rayduan, I have a question." Maxstrom grunted as he was working on pull-ups.

"Aye?"

"Why do you think my dad sent me to Shadicore rather than to Saoland?"

Rayduan stood silent for a minute as he thought about the question.

"Probably because of the assassins. After I wrote him about what happened, he wrote me back and informed me that what had attacked the kid matched the description of the assassins who had been going after other ace children; and he even informed me that one of those assassins had attacked Maskima."

"That's when I left Dauchenland; I remember my mom telling me Maskima had been attacked." Maxstrom declared as he kept working on his pull-ups.

"Really? That's interesting." Rayduan replied. "Bottom line, I think your dad realized that Shadicore was safer than Saoland. That and Saoland is more spiritually dark than Shadicore."

"Oh? Because I got attacked by a denac in Shadicore."

"You what?" Rayduan raised an eyebrow.

"Me and my Shadican friend, Dusty, were both attacked by a denac."

"How did that go?"

"Not very well for me, because I hadn't accepted God's free gift of salvation at that time, so I didn't have any protection."

"How did you manage to fight it off then?" Rayduan inquired with surprise.

"Ultimately, I didn't. Dusty had accepted the gift, and the denac tried to attack him. That didn't work out for the denac."

"Wow. So now you're a believer in Yasha?"

"Yeah. Wait. Hang on." Maxstrom inquired.

"Aye?"

"I know what happened and I understand what I believe and all, but that name. Yasha. I recognize it. What does it mean again?"

Rayduan gave Maxstrom a surprised look.

"I'm surprised you don't know who He is. He's the man that was God and that slayed Upa."

"Wait. What?!"

"Aye. Why is this a surprise to you?" Rayduan inquired, confused by this conversation and Maxstrom's lack of knowledge on the topic.

"Because I met someone named Yasha in the mountains."

"Wait, back up. What happened?"

"My fire teacher, Makbu, wanted to make sure I understood what I believed about God before he trained me. So he gave me a scroll of God's commands and sent me into the mountains to read it. While I was there, a man named Yasha came along and explained everything to me, and that's when I accepted God's free gift."

"I've heard rumors that Yasha still walks around and interacts with people from time to time; but until now, I'd never met anyone that had actually experienced it." Rayduan declared with a look of surprise on his face.

"So you're saying that was Him?" Maxstrom exclaimed in shock.

"I think it was. Max, that's a unique experience. He doesn't do that often. Hold onto that."

"I will."

Rayduan stared off into the distance for a moment, and then realized Maxstrom was done with his pull-ups.

"Well, we should keep training. Today I'm going to show you how to take water and turn it into both ice and steam. This is a difficult skill, so don't be disappointed if you don't pick it up right away."

"Alright. So how does it work?"

"So many years ago I actually talked with an Aceic Order soldier that had studied into how controlling the elements actually works. He explained the prevailing theory of the science was something like this: a drop of water is made up of thousands of building blocks. Each building block is water in the smallest form it comes. And each building block has an amount of power, so to speak. It basically vibrates in place. The more energy the building blocks have, the more they move around. If it gains or loses enough energy, the drop will either become steam or freeze, respectively. Make sense so far?"

"I think so." Maxstrom said, furrowing his eyebrows as he tried to process everything Rayduan had just said. "But why do I need to know all of this?"

"Well, if you have an understanding of what's going on when you're trying to do make steam or freeze water, you may find it easier. It helps me. So, the excitement level can be defined as how much heat each building block does or does not have. In other words, if you were to take one drop of water, isolate each building block and stop each's vibration, you will freeze the whole drop. And conversely, if you excite each building block, it will get hotter until it turns into steam."

"Okay, I think I get that."

"So in essence, you're control the temperature of the object. Give it a shot."

Maxstrom reached down and grabbed a ball of water.

"Just take a large drop of it and work with that. Start small."

Maxstrom dropped most of the water ball, only holding a few drops. "Now you're not really worried about keeping these drops as a whole still. You're worried about each component that builds up the water being still."

"Got it." Maxstrom replied, and started focusing on turning the large drop of water into ice.

An hour later, Maxstrom still hadn't gotten it.

"You're sure I can do this, right?"

"I'm sure, Max. Maybe we should take a break for today and try again tomorrow."

"If you say so." Maxstrom responded in a dejected tone.

"I did tell you this would take a while to figure out. Give it time.

Three days later, Maxstrom's patience was wearing thin.

"I still can't get this!" He yelled, and threw his drop of water down.

Rayduan walked over to the drop that Maxstrom had thrown on the peninsula, and felt it.

"Max."

"What?"

"It's cold."

"What?"

"It's cold. Colder than the pool water. Whatever you were doing was on the right track. Try again."

Maxstrom grabbed another drop, and focused as hard as he could on it. Suddenly, it turned into a drop of ice.

"No way!" Maxstrom declared. He then took it and started moving it around.

"You can use that to make swords, spears, arrows, or any weapon you like. You can use it to create ladders or other useful objects, just keep in mind the ice can be quite slick. You can even use it to stop bleeding as well."

"How do you stop bleeding with it?"

"Throw some water into a gaping wound, freeze it, and you got yourself a temporary bandage right there."

"Wow. That's cool."

"Now that you got that down, let's teach how to make objects. You have to take it piece by piece. Start by freezing several drops, and then position the liquid water where you want from there, and just keep doing that."

"Sounds simple enough."

"We'll see if you still think that by the end of today." Rayduan replied.

"Alright Max, now that you're comfortable with making objects out of ice, and turning water into steam, there is one last thing about water I have to teach you."

"Really? It's only been four and a half weeks!"

"Well, I'm not a water master, and you are somewhat of a natural at this."

"Thanks Ray. So what's the last thing?"

"Well, similar in form to steam, water is already in most of the air around you as vapor."

"Really?"

"Indeed. See how much water you can pull out of the immediate air."

Maxstrom moved his right hand around slowly and began attracting drops of water and consolidating them into a ball above his left hand. It was fairly small, about half of the size of his fist.

"It's not ideal, but still better than nothing." Rayduan declared.

"I think it's awesome."

"Well Max, it's been great getting to know you and training you, but I think it's time I sent you back to Shadicore."

"I thought I'd be excited about going back, but honestly I'm beginning to like it here with you."

"I'm glad to hear that my personality isn't entirely repulsive!" Rayduan responded with a smile.

"Not at all."

"Max, there's actually something else I want to tell you about."

"Sure, what is it?"

"It's about the denac, especially since you've seen them."

"Yes?"

"I've been on this world for over forty years, and the biggest lesson I've learned is that people, no matter how corrupt, aren't the ultimate enemy. The denac are."

"What do you mean?" Maxstrom inquired, confused.

"Max, God has a big plan for your life. But to help you reach your highest potential, I want to tell you about spiritual warfare. You see, although man is corrupt and has evil in him, man is not the ultimate enemy.

Some men can become corrupt; so corrupt they choose to be beyond redemption. But only God knows when they reach that point. The real evil is the denac, who work behind the scenes tirelessly, corrupting man subtly, giving him evil ideas and thoughts, and tricking him or tempting him to doing evil things."

"So you're saying people aren't responsible for what they do?"

"Oh no! Not at all. We each have free will, and are fully responsible for what we decide to do. But at the same time, there are evil forces working in the background in deeper ways than you or I could understand. And they are working to convince and trick each individual into becoming evil. My point in all of this is that if you ever need to take a life; that course of action should be your last resort. People are not the real enemy; the denac are, and they can move so subtly and patiently that most men fail to recognize their work."

"I suppose that makes sense." Maxstrom replied. "So how do I fight them?"

"There are several ways, but one of the greatest is through praying to God and asking Him for His help. He has an army of angles at His disposal, and He wants to help mankind. But He wants man to want Him to help; He doesn't like to step in without anyone asking."

"That makes sense. When Duba was on fire, Makbu prayed to God, and then rain came and put the fire out."

"Exactly. But don't just pray to God to get things. Pray to have a conversation. Yasha, who is God, is your friend."

"That's good to know. Thanks Ray."

Rayduan smiled. "You're welcome, Maxstrom. But now, we should start our journey back to my house. And then it's off to Shadicore with you."

Chapter 6

The Betrayal

B.Y. 4013

"Those closest to you have the ability to hurt you the most.
—Tapito

"I don't like the atmosphere here in Shavi, Tapito." Akbu declared with frustration as he paced around the room and slicked back his Mohawk.

"Well if you wanted more sunshine, you shouldn't have made your home in a forest." Tapito replied with a smirk. She was looking out the window of her house.

"Very funny chief. You know what I mean. I don't like the unrest that has been building. Shadicans have been talking. Gossiping. Reports from the border and news about the attack on Duba are becoming exaggerated."

"What do you propose?" Shacbu interjected from near the door.

"Shacbu, know your place!" Wachuna yelled in anger.

"Wachuna!" Tapito barked. "Silence! Shacbu will almost certainly be my heir; and I will not have you disrespect her. She needs to learn to think, lead, and ask questions."

Wachuna simply bowed his head toward the high chief in respect.

"Go on, Shacbu." Tapito encouraged.

"I was just asking what Akbu had in mind to do about all of this."

"I don't know." Akbu grunted. "I'm just telling you about the problem. Popularity hasn't really been much of a problem for a Shadican leader before."

"Popularity?" Tapito inquired in a confused tone.

"The Shadicans are not your biggest fans as of late, chief."

"But I have the elder's approval and I passed all of their combat tests!"

"Chief, with all due respect, that was fifteen years ago."

"So?"

"So," Akbu stopped pacing to look at his chief, "and these are their words, not mine, but they are saying that you are no longer fit to lead us. That you are a senile old katlican."

"Do you think there is war on the horizon?" Tapito asked, as she thought about all of this.

"War?" Shadan interjected.

"Oh Shadan, glad you're still with us. I thought you had nodded off again." Wachuna declared with a smirk.

"War. The Shadicans have lived in peace with each other since Shadic the Third. At least for the most part. I do not think it will come to a war, my chief." Shadan declared in his old, crackly voice.

"With all due respect, I think you are wrong. Things change with time. Just because a war hasn't happened in the past, does not mean it is out of the realm of possibilities." Akbu responded in a serious tone. His face displayed the concern he felt.

"That is a worryingly accurate statement." Wachuna added.

"Okay, okay. You both need to calm down. I don't think it will come to that." Tapito assured.

"How can you be so sure?" Akbu asked quizzically.

"The people are believing lies? Then so be it. I'm unpopular? Then so be it. These things are easy to fix. Akbu, what are you always saying about lies?"

"Not. . . to tell them?" Akbu inquired, slightly confused.

"No, the other thing."

"Oh! The best way to deal with a lie is to tell the truth?"

"Exactly!" Tapito declared in triumph as she slapped her right fist into her left paw.

"So you're going to tell the truth. How do you plan on doing that?" Wachuna inquired.

"At the festival of Salvation, I shall address the Shadicans." Tapito declared.

"The festival of Salvation is a week away. . ." Wachuna interjected.

"And the Shadicans might not be planning to wait that long to take action." Akbu added.

"There is no better time. It's the largest meeting of Shadicans all year, and it's the perfect time to address any falsehoods. I do not see how I can do it any sooner."

"Good point, chief." Akbu replied.

"By the way, how are our efforts going to find the breach that the mag-men used?" Shadan inquired.

"There are no updates. The Tabees are double checking every fortification on their end, and there haven't been any breakthroughs on our end of the border."

"Odd. They couldn't have just materialized behind our borders. Akbu, I need you to see if there's anything else you can do to speed up this process. I want to have more information to offer the people next week." Tapito ordered.

"As you wish, chief."

Akbu awoke with a start. A floorboard was creaking; almost as if someone was walking on it. From what he could hear, it sounded like it was on the balcony. He reached for his sword, which was always within arm's reach of his bedside, and slowly got out of bed. His Mohawk was mostly flat; what remained of it leaned towards his left ear.

"What are you doing?" Niba asked her husband in a soft tone.

"Quiet. I thought I heard something."

"Akbu, it's probably just one of those squirrels again."

Akbu didn't bother to reply, but instead started quietly walking towards the door as he slicked his Mohawk back up impulsively. Maybe all of the unrest in Shavi had him on edge, but he figured it was better to be safe than sorry; especially since his house was at a dead end amongst the rope bridges, and he had pulled his house's rope to the ground up for the night. He quietly drew his sword, and used his ability as a Shadican to redirect the light around him, making himself entirely invisible. The only thing he did not hide was his eyes, since he needed to see. After he had become invisible, he quickly stepped outside. His treehouse, like most Shadican homes

in Shavi, was circular in shape, so he could only see a little around either corner. He turned to his right and looked at the rope bridge tethering his home to the rest of the village. It was swaying slightly, as if someone had recently been on it.

Akbu suddenly heard something around the corner, just out of his sight. He moved quickly and stealthily past the rope bridge and pulled his sword close to his chest, ready to fight off whatever foe lie ahead. Controlling light was incredibly difficult, and took a massive amount of strength and concentration to use, so Akbu knew he would have to become visible to attack whatever was before him. And as he swung around the corner, his eyes found the culprit; it was a squirrel.

"Really?" Akbu muttered as he revealed himself to the visible world.

The squirrel, who had patches of skin under either arm for flight, was terrified by this sudden appearance of a Shadican, and ran for the edge of the balcony in horror. The poor creature then quickly jumped off the balcony, and glided away into the night.

"Unbelievable." Akbu grumbled as he walked back around the balcony.

"You were right, it was just one of those pesky squirrels." Akbu declared as he walked through the doorway.

All of the sudden, Akbu heard something behind him. He quickly spun around and received a kick to the gut. The blow threw him on his back into the middle of the room. Winded, Akbu gasped for breath, and then looked up. He saw a Shadican wearing a cloth grey mask over the bottom half of his face. This Shadican was standing in the doorway, and a half moon glistened ominously behind him.

"Who are you? What do you want?" Akbu questioned as he recovered his breath.

The Shadican responded by drawing his sword.

"You don't want to do that." Akbu cautioned.

The Shadican took no heed of this warning, and charged at Akbu. Akbu quickly looked around; his sword had gone flying out of his paw from the kick and was across the room. So Akbu jumped to his feet and decided to try and disarm his attacker. The masked Shadican swung his sword to try and slit Akbu's throat, but Akbu ducked under the attack, tackled his opponent, and slammed him into the wooden floor. The sword went flying out of the masked Shadican's paw, and Akbu began swinging claw strikes at his opponent's face. The masked Shadican moved his paws up to cover his face, but not before Akbu ripped the mask off of the Shadican's mouth. Suddenly, Akbu stopped. He recognized this Shadican.

"I know you. It's Fesha, isn't it? What are you doing here, kid? Don't you work at the trading post?"

Fesha responded by throwing Akbu towards the doorway. Akbu quickly jumped to his feet to see Fesha charging him, sword in hand. But then Akbu heard a loud battle cry, and saw Niba flying through the air and land a solid cut right across Fesha's abdomen and side. Fesha collapsed to the ground, dead.

"Thanks." Akbu said, taking a deep breath. "I told you it wasn't a squirrel."

"Actually, you said it was a squirrel. And then you got kicked into the middle of the room while managing to lose your sword." Niba replied with a smirk.

"I had it under control." Akbu claimed as he stood up and moved towards Niba.

"Well as a member of the Elite Guard, I'm sure you would've figured it out." Niba responded as she set her sword down.

Akbu gave her a hug and gazed into her eyes, "You know, for a regular Shadican soldier, you're pretty handy with a sword."

"I am married to the best sword fighter in the nation, and he taught me a few things." Niba replied, touching noses with Akbu.

All of the sudden, Akbu heard the patter of several Shadican feet coming from the open door behind him. He quickly picked up Niba's sword and aimed it right at the throat of the Shadican about to enter his home.

"Woah." The Shadican said, shocked at how quickly Akbu had reacted. It was the night watch. "What's going on, Akbu?"

"I was attacked." Akbu responded. "I need to see the chief, immediately!"

Akbu walked into Tapito's treehouse and was greeted by a scream of terror.

"Oh, it's you, Akbu." Shenabu exclaimed. Shenabu was known for being easily frightened in stressful situations.

"Where's Tapito?" Akbu inquired.

"Hiding. There were a couple of masked Shadicans here that were looking for her, but she used her ability to control light to hide, and I told them she wasn't here. After searching around for a while, they left. I'm not sure where exactly is in the room she is, though."

Akbu scanned the room for any odd shapes; even a master at controlling light couldn't entirely vanish without a trace. But it took an experienced eye to pick up on any clues, which usually consisted of faintly distorted shapes in the environment. After a few seconds, he noticed that the shape of the window seemed off; indicating that Tapito was hiding between him and there.

"You can come out now, chief." Akbu declared, looking at where he thought Tapito's eyes were.

Suddenly, Tapito appeared about two feet from Akbu, and instantly opened her eyes to meet his stare. Shenabu let out another scream.

"Shenabu. Calm down." Akbu grumbled, rubbing his ears.

"Sorry."

"Glad you're still alive, Akbu." Tapito smirked.

Suddenly Wachuna and Nakbu came into the room. Nakbu was another member of the Elite Guard. Shenabu let out yet another scream and then quickly covered her mouth.

"Where's Mabo and Shacbu?" Akbu asked the night guard that followed Wachuna and Nakbu in.

"Mabo is dead. One of my guards went in to wake him up, but he had a knife in his chest. Shacbu was nowhere to be found."

"Great." Akbu remarked in frustration. "Alright, what's your name?"

"Me?" The night guard inquired.

"Yes, you."

"I'm Sheni."

"Alright Sheni, how many Shadicans do you have under your command for the night watch?"

"There's three others besides me. They're all outside awaiting your orders."

"Perfect. Okay, we need to move."

Out of nowhere, a loud drum began to sound in the distance. The group halted to try and determine the origin of the noise.

"It's the attack drum!" Shenabu cried with a look of terror on her face. "Shavi is under attack!"

"No kidding, Shenabu. What do you think has been going on?" Akbu questioned.

"Oh. Now I feel dumb." Shenabu responded sheepishly.

"Alright, let's move! We need to get Tapito out of here." Akbu ordered

"I'm not leaving Shavi." Tapito declared resolutely.

"Chief," Akbu responded as he walked over to Tapito, "you are our leader. Our job as the Elite Guard is to keep you safe. Let us our do our job."

"And my job, as the leader of the Shadican people, is to be here when they need me, especially in times of crisis and battle. I'm staying."

Akbu put his paws over his face and rubbed his eyes for a moment, and then looked at Tapito.

"Chief, you can't lead if you're dead." Akbu whispered.

Tapito smiled. "You're skilled enough that you can keep me alive whether I stay or go. The attack bell means that all Shadican civilians are to gather at the great hall. So let's go and figure out what's going on."

"Alright, but we're stopping at a barracks for more troops on the way." Akbu ordered. "That's not up for discussion."

138

As Tapito and her guard crossed over to a barracks treehouse, they saw several Shadicans standing outside. One of them turned to look in their direction, and Akbu saw that he had a grey mask on.

"Stand down!" Akbu commanded from the front of his group as he drew his sword.

In response the masked Shadicans drew their swords.

Akbu quickly counted. There were nine opponents. So although Shenabu couldn't fight, their numbers were closely matched.

The leader of the masked Shadicans charged Akbu, and Akbu quickly threw his opponents sword to the side and stabbed him in the chest. As this happened, the rest of the masked Shadicans attacked. Akbu looked over to his left, and saw one of the masked Shadicans running for Shenabu. He quickly reacted and threw himself into a side flip that sent him spinning through the air, and he cut the back of the masked Shadican's neck. The Shadican fell to the ground.

Shenabu, who had been screaming with her eyes closed, suddenly fell quiet and looked up.

"Thanks, Akbu!"

Akbu turned around and saw that the rest of the masked Shadicans were dead; but that the three night watch soldiers had also been killed. Only Sheni remained from the night watch. Akbu quickly ran inside the barracks, and saw that the soldiers stationed there had all been killed in their sleep.

"They're all dead." Akbu said, coming back out of the barracks.

"We need to get to the great hall, Akbu." Tapito declared. "I have a responsibility to the Shadicans."

"Alright, fine. Let's go!" Akbu commanded.

It took the group a few minutes to arrive at the great hall. Unlike most Shadican treehouses, the great hall was built entirely around the tree, and the massive tree was partially hollowed out inside. Once the group had arrived, they began stealthy walking around the balcony to the front, but Akbu put his paw up to halt the group as soon as he saw the door. There were two masked Shadicans standing guard, and the door was bolted shut.

"Wait here." Akbu told the group as he went invisible. He quietly walked over to the door and got behind one of the Shadicans. Akbu then revealed himself, and stabbed the first Shadican. The other masked Shadican looked over in shock and tried to grab his sword. But Akbu was too quick, and threw his sword into the Shadican's chest. The Shadican collapsed to the ground, and Akbu retrieved his sword.

"All clear!" Akbu yelled. He could hear voices inside the great hall, and he pounded on the door as Tapito and the rest of the group came around the corner.

"Open up!" Akbu called to the gatekeeper inside.

The doors swung open and revealed thousands Shadicans inside the massive treehouse. But on top of a platform, Akbu saw Turibu. It looked like he had been in the middle of a speech.

"Tapito!" Turibu called from the podium. "You have not fulfilled your duties as chief. And as such, I challenge you to a duel for your position!"

"You! You are behind all of this!" Akbu declared, pointing his bloody sword at Turibu.

"The only thing I am behind is the Shadicans, who are fed up with Tapito's failure. The chief cannot refuse a duel from one of her kind, according to Shadican law."

Akbu's face turned grim; Turibu was right. The high chief had an obligation to not only care for the people; but also to be most adept to defend them. As Akbu thought about everything, he started to worry. Turibu was a great warrior, and Tapito was not as young as she once was.

"Well then, Turibu," Tapito responded from behind Akbu, "let's head to the ground and get this duel started."

"Tapito, are you sure you're up for this?" Wachuna asked his chief in a concerned tone.

"I don't really have a choice, Wachuna."

The duel zone was being drawn by Akbu and Talican. Talican was one of Turibu's soldiers, and apparently his right hand in the rebellion.

"Now, remember the rules." Tapito ordered Turibu. "When I win, your sympathizers need to surrender to me."

"And when I win, you will be executed for your crimes!" Turibu snapped back.

Akbu glared at Turibu. "The ring is set, chief."

"Soon you'll be calling me that." Turibu claimed as he smirked and pointed a finger at Akbu.

"You better start your fight with Tapito before I step in and beat that smirk off of your face." Akbu growled through his teeth.

Turibu simply let out a laugh.

"Are you ready?" Tapito inquired.

"Are you?" Turibu fired back.

"Then let's get started."

Tapito and Turibu both walked to the center of the large fighting circle. Akbu and Talican had marked off a circle thirty feet in radius for the fight. For the most part, the terrain was flat ground covered with pine needles.

"Talican, you can call it." Akbu declared with his arms crossed.

"Get in your stance! Go!" Talican barked.

Turibu wasted no time and charged straight for Tapito, sword drawn. Tapito, who was crouched low to the ground in her fighting stance, swung her sword in front of her face to block the attack. She then threw her sword forward to try to stab Turibu in the face; but Turibu ducked to the side and dodged the strike. Turibu then swung another attack for Tapito's neck. Tapito threw up another block and clashed swords while taking a step back. The two opponents stared at each other for a moment.

"You give up yet?" Tapito questioned with a smirk.

Turibu gave no reply. Instead, he took a step back, and then drew his sword over his head to swing at Tapito. She threw up a block just in time, and caught Turibu's sword. Then she threw herself backward onto the ground and kicked Turibu in the gut. He staggered back, winded.

"Get him, Tapito!" Akbu cried.

Tapito jumped to her feet, and rushed towards Turibu. But apparently Turibu was less winded then she had guessed; he quickly stepped to the side to avoid her attack, and sliced her arm. Tapito dropped her sword and let out a cry of pain. She couldn't close her right paw; Turibu must have severed something.

"Chief!" Wachuna let out a worried yell.

Tapito spun around and faced Turibu. She couldn't get to her sword; Turibu was too close to it. She realized that she would have to disarm him if she was going to survive.

Turibu was motivated because of his newfound advantage. He lost no time and swung his blade at Tapito, and she jumped back. He swung again, and she repeated her dodge.

"Coward!" Talican yelled, taunting the chief.

Tapito was near the edge of the fighting arena, so she knew she had to act. If she stepped out of the marked zone, she was automatically disqualified. Turibu pushed his advantage, and swung again. This time Tapito ducked under his blade and lunged forward. She quickly cut his wrist with her claws. Turibu dropped his sword and screamed in pain; the cut was deep. Tapito didn't hesitate to push the advantage, and struck with her left paw again, this time clawing him across his chest. She then swung her right forearm into the side of his neck. This blow threw him to the ground.

"Yeah!" Shenabu cried, along with a large crowd of Shadicans.

But Turibu was up in an instant. Once he had recovered his stance, Turibu kicked towards Tapito. She was prepared, and grabbed his foot with her good arm. Tapito then swung her right elbow into his knee, which made a loud cracking noise. Turibu let out a cry of pain, and Tapito let go of the leg. He collapsed to the ground.

"It's over!" Tapito declared.

"Not yet. Turibu responded. Tapito hadn't noticed that Turibu was next to her sword, and he grabbed it and thrust it towards Tapito. However, Tapito's reflexes were quick enough to respond to this attack, and she moved to the side easily. She then kicked his paw with her foot, and the sword went flying. Tapito then walked after the sword, picked it up, and came back to Turibu, resting her sword on his neck.

"Do you concede?" Tapito questioned.

Turibu realized that this was his only chance to avoid death. Tapito was showing him mercy.

"I do." He grunted.

Tapito lowered her sword, and then cleared her throat.

"I hereby banish you from Shadicore and the katlican tribes. You are to wander in the wilderness for the rest of your days for this betrayal!"

"No!" Talican cried, and ran into the ring at Tapito, sword drawn. Akbu ran in and body slammed Talican to the side. Talican scurried back to his feet, and then sprung at Akbu with his sword. Akbu instantly drew his sword and blocked the attack; locking himself into a sword match with Talican.

The civilian Shadicans let out cries of terror and began to run as they realized standing outside of the fighting ring was no longer safe. As they ran, masked Shadicans emerged and charged towards Tapito. However, there were also soldiers loyal to Tapito who had been watching. These soldiers ran after the masked Shadicans to save their chief.

"I'm going to kill you, Akbu!" Talican yelled as he charged at his foe.

As Akbu was about to swing his sword, his paw got hit by a fast, yet small rock, and he lost his grip. His sword went flying to the side. He looked over and saw a masked Shadican with a slingshot glaring at him.

"Twice in one day? Come on." Akbu grumbled.

"Ha! What are you going to do now, sword master?" Talican taunted as he moved closer.

Akbu's mind raced. He knew he couldn't last long against Talican without a weapon; Talican was a good fighter. And Akbu couldn't go invisible; doing so would put a lot of strain on his already tired muscles, and he couldn't move fast or attack while doing that. He figured his only strategy was to dodge Talican's strikes for as long as he could and look for an opening.

Talican swung for his neck, and Akbu jumped back.

"Come on, Akbu, die like the coward you are!" Talican taunted.

Akbu saw out of the corner of his eye the masked Shadican with the slingshot launch another rock, and Akbu ducked. But this time, the masked Shadican had aimed for Akbu's knee. The rock hit with a loud crack, and Akbu dropped to the ground with a cry of pain.

"Time to die!" Talican screamed with an evil grin.

Talican raised his sword, ready to cleave Akbu's head in two. Akbu glanced around to see if there was something he could use as a weapon, or if there was any way he could try and block the strike. The only thing near him was water from a spring; but that was useless to him.

All of the sudden, as Talican swung his sword for Akbu's neck, Akbu saw a stream of water go flying past and slam into Talican's face, throwing him backwards to the ground. He then saw another stream go flying by and hit the masked Shadican with the sling, throwing him to the ground as well.

"Looks like I got here just in time." A voice declared from behind Akbu.

"Max." Akbu chuckled, and looked behind him to see his friend next to the spring.

"What happened? Are you alright?" Maxstrom asked as he ran over to Akbu.

"Turibu started a rebellion. And yes, I'm good." Akbu responded as Maxstrom helped him stand to his feet.

"What?!" Maxstrom exclaimed.

"Yeah, tell me about it."

Akbu took a moment to test to see if his knee was broken or if anything was torn; it was not.

"And this'll be a nasty bruise tomorrow. But I'm glad you're here, Max. Let's get back to the fight; we need to keep Tapito safe!" Akbu informed as he started running towards where Tapito had been.

❖❖❖

Tapito was cornered; she was surrounded by five masked Shadicans. On top of that, she was stuck with only using her left paw due to her injury from the duel, and she had no weapon. As the masked Shadicans closed in, one stepped forward.

"I want to do it." He declared.

"Who are you?" Tapito questioned. "If you're going to kill me, at least show your face!"

The Shadican pulled of his mask to reveal himself. It was Nandu.

"Nandu! I should have known you were in on this!" Tapito yelled.

"You should have listened to Turibu's suggestions to secure our borders, and then none of this would have happened!" Nandu retorted angrily.

"You and I both know that Turibu would have tried to overthrow me anyway. He just needed a good excuse!"

"Lies!" Nandu yelled, and pulled his sword back to thrust at Tapito.

Suddenly, a blade appeared through Nandu's chest, and then the blade retracted. Nandu collapsed to the ground, dead. Everyone looked and saw that Shacbu was the one who had slain Nandu.

"What?" One of the masked Shadicans exclaimed. "Kill her!"

Shacbu was standing in the middle of the group, with two masked Shadicans on either side. As they swung their blades for her, she disappeared using the ability to control light. But as she did this cloak, she also threw herself backwards out of the way of the Shadican blades. Instead of the strikes hitting her, the two closest Shadicans missed, and killed each other as a result.

"I thought only Tapito and Akbu where the only ones in Shavi who could do a full body cloak!" One of the living masked Shadicans yelled as he looked around in horror, not knowing where Shacbu was.

Shacbu then revealed herself again, but this time she was standing between Tapito and the masked Shadicans. She then quickly swung her sword and killed the two dumbfounded enemies in front of her.

"You alright, chief?" Shacbu inquired, walking over to Tapito.

"We thought you were dead!" Tapito declared with raised eyebrows.

"Nah. I'm not that easy to kill! You and Akbu trained me well."

"But I thought you hadn't mastered the ability to control light. I've been trying to teach you that for a year now!"

"I woke up to a large group of Shadicans whispering outside my window, and after listening in I realized they were arguing about how to kill me. I didn't think I could take that many, had nowhere to run, and I was desperate. But then everything you taught me just sort of clicked when I needed it to, and here I am." Shacbu responded and then gave a shrug.

Tapito smiled. She then looked and saw Akbu and Maxstrom running towards them.

"Max! You're back! Thank Abada for that perfect timing." Tapito called.

"Thanks. So, what's with this rebellion?"

"It seems that we have it pretty well in hand." Tapito declared, looking around. Her Shadican troops were routing the enemy.

"I think it's over." Akbu replied.

"No, Akbu." Tapito responded. "The real fight is just beginning. We're going to have to rebuild and grieve the loss of life. And I'll have to address the people to stop Turibu's lies."

"Where is that rat, anyway?" Akbu asked.

The group looked around.

"I don't see him anywhere." Shacbu said after a moment.

Suddenly they heard grunting from behind one of the large trees. They all looked and saw Wachuna dragging Turibu by his scruff.

"Chief! We are routing the enemy as we speak. And I caught this one trying to sneak off."

"You!" Akbu yelled, approaching the helpless Turibu with his sword aimed at his heart.

"Akbu, stand down." Tapito commanded.

"Chief, banishment is too good for him! We need to execute him."

Turibu suddenly had a look of horror come across his face.

"No! Don't do that!" He cried.

"Quiet!" Tapito yelled at Turibu, pointing a finger at him.

He fell silent.

"We could sentence him to life in prison." Shacbu suggested.

"I actually like that idea." Tapito added.

Maxstrom walked over to Turibu, and squatted down so he could look the Shadican in the eye. "Help me understand something. Why? Why would you do this? You used to be such a friendly Shadican and lead games for all the kits."

"Because I was tired of taking orders from this lowlife!" He yelled, gesturing his head at Tapito.

Maxstrom suddenly remembered what Rayduan had taught him about the denac; that they sought to corrupt from behind the scenes. He also recalled what Rayduan had told him later that evening; that if he ever ran into someone he thought was under the influence of a denac, to rebuke it in the name of Yasha.

"In the name of Yasha," Maxstrom declared "I command you to leave!"

All of the sudden the group saw a denac come out of Turibu and float behind him for a moment. Its tentacles were wrapped around Turibu's neck and head, but it quickly loosened its grip. The denac then looked at Maxstrom for a second, let out an evil shriek, and then took off into the night.

Shacbu shivered. "What was that? That was creepy!"

"Max, what did you just do?" Wachuna questioned, stunned.

"That was something I learned on my trip. Rayduan told me that the denac could corrupt good people. I figured if they could corrupt people, they could also corrupt katlicans. He told me that if I ever ran into one that I should rebuke it in the name of Yasha, and it would leave."

"He taught you well." Tapito encouraged. "I don't think we've ever had a Shadican get corrupted by a denac, at least as far as I remember."

"What, what have I done?" Turibu mumbled to himself.

"You caused a rebellion! Don't think you can get out of your punishment because of this denac!" Wachuna yelled.

"Wachuna, calm down." Tapito warned.

"No, I know what I've done. I let pride and greed consume me. Punish me any way you see fit." Turibu said, dejected.

The group stood in silence, staring at Turibu.

Three hundred and fifty-seven Shadicans had died in total. The next few days were extremely somber as many grieved, and burial ceremonies were commenced. Since Akbu was the spiritual leader of the Shadican tribe, it was his job to lead the burial ceremonies; so he was quite busy. To make matters worse, the Festival of Salvation was right around the corner, and it was supposed to be a joyous occasion. Tapito decided to put a hold on preparations for the festival until the day before the Festival would start, so that all the Shadicans who needed to could have time to grieve.

Tapito also called all the Shadicans in Shavi together the day after the rebellion and addressed the people on the issues Turibu had lied about. She told the people that the reports from the border were largely exaggerated, and reassured them that she was still able to lead the Shadicans competently. Turibu also limped up, due to his broken knee, and admitted to the Shadicans that he had mislead them all. Because of this action, and because Turibu was under the influence of a denac when everything had happened, Tapito decided to show him mercy, and only give him several years in prison.

"His guilt, and broken knee will be punishment enough. I want you all to forgive him, and to treat him with kindness." Tapito ordered the Shadicans.

"Max!"

Maxstrom slowly opened his eyes and rolled over in bed. He could make out the figure of a Shadican in the doorway.

"Max!" The voice repeated.

Maxstrom was still waking up, so it took him a moment to gather his senses and figure out who was calling his name.

"Dusty!" He exclaimed after a moment.

Dusty came running over and gave Maxstrom a big hug.

"I missed you, man!" Dusty cried.

"I missed you too!" Maxstrom responded.

"Where are the festival decorations?" Dusty inquired.

"You didn't hear?"

"Hear what?"

"There was a rebellion lead by Turibu."

"Wait, what?"

"I got here just in time to save Akbu."

"Oh wow! That's not good. I mean, the rebellion part. Akbu not dying is good."

"Over three hundred Shadicans died in the battle."

Dusty fell silent.

"That's terrible." He said after a moment.

"We'll begin decorations tomorrow. Tapito just wanted to give everyone time to grieve."

"That makes sense." Dusty responded.

"So tell me about fire training with Makbu." Maxstrom said.

"It was fun. I really like Makbu. We did most of the stuff we had been practicing when you were there, along with some agility training. I needed that extra time to learn the fire techniques."

"Well, that's good then!"

"Makbu also helped me improve my technique so I can split a mag-man open!"

"Great! Glad you finally got that down." Maxstrom replied.

"Of course! Oh and Makbu started showing me some light controlling techniques. I can make my paw invisible, but that's about it."

"Really? Awesome! Show me."

Dusty straitened his paw, and after a few seconds it went completely invisible.

"Woah. That's impressive."

"Thanks! Honestly it wasn't that hard to pick up since it was vaguely similar to controlling fire and we'd already trained up most of the muscle groups I needed. I do have to spend some time at the light school to finish my training though. Oh and I finally started getting half decent with that flute. But enough about me; how was water training?"

"It was great! I learned so much. I can even turn water into ice now!"

"What? No way! Do it for me!"

Maxstrom looked over and saw a bucket in the corner was full of drinking water, so he walked over and pulled out a stream. After a moment, he had turned it into a sword.

"Woah! No way!" Dusty yelled as he got off the bed and ran over.

"Now just don't grab it without a. . . glove." Maxstrom trailed off, because Dusty had already grabbed it.

"Why not?" Dusty inquired.

"Try to let go of the sword."

Dusty opened his paw, and the sword stuck to his katlican paw pads.

"Ah! Help!" Dusty yelled to Maxstrom in horror, trying to shake the sword loose.

Maxstrom reached out and quickly turned the sword back to water, and then put the water back in the bucket.

"Thanks."

"No problem bud." Maxstrom responded.

"Hey I'm kind of tired though, so if it's alright with you I'm going to crash." Dusty informed.

"Yeah of course! Any time in particular you want me to wake you up by?"

"Sure. Tomorrow. I'm exhausted." Dusty responded as he threw himself onto his bed.

The next day was filled with busy excitement. The Festival of Salvation, which took place about a month before the New Year, was the biggest celebration the katlicans did all year. katlicans from all the tribes came for the celebration; from as far north as the Snowiseans, as far west as some of the Dolphinian islands off of the coast, and as far south as some of the Tabees stationed in the swamplands.

Much had to be prepared. Fish had to be caught and cooked, pine branches had to be trimmed and dyed various colors, old cloth decorations had to be unpacked and displayed. Pine nuts had to be roasted, musical talent had to be rehearsed, and gifts had to be wrapped in packaging.

Years ago, the Shadicans had decided on a rule for the giving of gifts, and that rule was that only one gift be given from one to another. The Festival of Salvation celebrated two major events in history, and the Shadicans wanted to be sure to never let these events become overshadowed with material possessions. The first and primary reason for the celebration was the birth of Yasha as a man thousands of years before. When he entered the world, man and creature alike had a chance at redemption, and to defeat Upa and the denac. The second reason for this celebration was that it was on the same day, several hundred years before, that the katlicans had arrived to their present home. The arrival at this safe haven was because Shadic the Third had rallied all of the katlican tribes together and lead them to safety with the help of Abada.

"Did you get me something cool, Max?" Dusty questioned, sitting on Maxstrom's bed.

"You'll find out tomorrow." Maxstrom responded as he wound some colored fabric around their balcony railing.

"I can't wait. It's going to be so much fun!"

"I sure hope it is." Maxstrom replied. "The Shadicans need some joy and excitement to get their minds off of the horrible events from this week. Hopefully no one is spending this time alone."

"I'm sure Tapito is taking care of that. Are you going to the chief's dinner tomorrow night?"

"Of course! Are you?"

"Wouldn't miss it! I love the way they serve the fish there. They have that delicious mustard sauce."

"Oh, I almost forgot to tell you Dusty. Ipachoo is coming over to exchange presents with us around noon tomorrow along with Shacbu and Shenabu."

"Shacbu is coming?" Dusty inquired, raising his eyebrow.

"Yup." Maxstrom replied with a smirk.

"Hey could you pass me some candles?" Dusty asked, trying to change the subject. Candles for the Festival of Salvation were the one exception to the rule of no fire in the treehouses.

"Sure bud. Here." Maxstrom replied as he slid the box towards his friend.

"You know it's so cool not needing these matches to light a fire anymore." Dusty declared as he set a candle up near their window and lit the wick with a quick gesture of his finger.

Thousands of katlicans arrived in Shavi throughout the day. Once the sun had set, the katlicans headed south outside of the Kachuna Forest to a small hillside, and then the ceremony celebrating the eve of the coming festival began. Tapito, Akbu, Shadan, and about seventy other Shadicans, who were all part of the ceremony, stood on top of the hill so they could be seen and so the acoustics of their voices would travel. Behind them stood a single normal sized pine tree and a small glass pyramid.

Akbu led the crowd in a prayer.

"Abada, we thank you for all the gifts you have given us. You are amazing, and I'm sorry that I sometimes take you for granted. However, while we are here to celebrate, there are many here who are also grieving. Be with them in this time, and make yourself real to them. I thank you that you are always good!"

The crowd responded with a "Thank you Abada!"

Tapito then stood. "Thank you all for coming. I want to take this time to remind you that Yasha, our savior, came down on this night, thousands of years ago, to save us physically from Upa and the denac, and that he also saved us eternally. He is good! We don't have much prepared for tonight, but we wouldn't want to deprive you of our usual light show; so here it is."

Akbu, Tapito, and the seventy other Shadicans stood. Five of the Shadicans began shooting light through the glass pyramid near the pine tree. A beautiful rainbow shot out, and the rest of the light controlling Shadicans curved the rainbow around the pine tree in a circular pattern. Each Shadican on the hill was assigned to a group, and each group controlled a different color of light. They then shot the light out from the top of the tree, covering the audience in a mix of color. The crowd let out a wild yell. Then, after a moment, everything fell dark.

All of the katlicans knew this was their cue. Each had a candle with them, and they each pulled their candle out and lit it. After a moment, the hillside and field below were covered with thousands upon thousands of candle lights.

Shadan stood up, and hobbled over to a spot where everyone could see him. He then led the katlicans in a song.

As they were singing, several of the Shadican light experts walked towards the crowd, grabbed the light coming from the candles, and then sent it through the glass triangle. Others from the group stood next to the pyramid, and shot the colored light back to the audience. The group was again covered in a mix of colored brilliance; but this time, the light was much brighter.

When the song finished, the light show also ended. Everyone sat perfectly still, waiting for what was about to come next.

All of the sudden, the heavens burst into a beautiful light show, filled with colors of every type. Behind them, the stars were twinkling, and the colors of the galaxies were amplified behind them.

"It's so cool when this happens." Dusty whispered to Maxstrom.

"I know! Its Abada's way of saying you're welcome. It's so beautiful."

Chapter 7

War on the Horizon

B.Y. 4013

"Evil needs to die."
—Bezka

Bezka stood confidently, his large muscles and Tabee stature were contrasted against the night sky. His short tail bobbed in the breeze. He then both wet and wrinkled his nose, and his blue eyes narrowed as he thought about the scent he had just caught. It was the smell of burning rock in the distance.

"We're close." Bezka remarked, and looked back through the cold, windy night at the squad of eight Tabee soldiers that were with him. All of the Tabee soldiers were muscular, like their leader, as was typical of their kind.

"Are you sure?" Fika whispered to his commander as snow began to fall.

Fika couldn't smell anything; but it wasn't that Fika didn't trust Bezka. After all, Bezka was the most experienced in the group, as well as nephew to General Tak, the Tabee tribe commander. Beyond that, Bezka was good friends with Fika.

"I'm sure."

"There's no way the magmen could have gotten across the Tabee State and onto the peninsula of without us hearing of it. We're near Fort Tak." Zepak, another one of Bezka's soldiers, interjected.

"That was General Tak's response to the attack on Duba. But that doesn't change the fact that magmen somehow got past the Tabee's defenses and attacked our Shadican brothers." Bezka responded as he continued staring straight ahead.

"What are your orders, sir?" Fika asked.

"Let's get moving. There's a battle ahead!" Bezka yelled as he turned to his troops.

The Tabees let out a war yell, and then started running into the snowy night.

"Max, I love it!" Dusty exclaimed with excitement. He had just opened Maxstrom's gift; it was a pair of Snowisean combat gloves. The gloves allowed for extra protection and warmth of the paw while also allowing the katlican to use their claws.

"I got a pair on my way back from Saoland. Now you can hold my ice swords without having to worry about it sticking to your pads."

"Thanks so much, Max!"

"No problem bud!"

Dusty reached over and gave Maxstrom a package. "Now here, open this."

Maxstrom opened it, and saw that it was a pack of throwing stars.

"These are amazing!"

"Yeah, I just didn't think about you being able to make those out of ice until like, right now." Dusty responded, dejected.

"No I love them! I'd rather have a metal sword or metal throwing stars than make ice ones. Ice is a last resort."

"Oh! Good!"

"I brought you both some roasted seaweed I got off of one of the Dolphinian traders." Ipachoo declared as he poked his head through the door.

"Yes! I love that stuff! Thanks Ipachoo." Maxstrom responded.

Ipachoo smiled. "You're welcome! Will anyone else be joining us?"

"Yeah, Shacbu and Shenabu will both be coming shortly."

"Sweet, the more the merrier! Besides, Shenabu is kind of cute." Ipachoo remarked as he walked in.

"Am I now?" Shenabu questioned as she crossed her arms. She had just appeared in the doorway behind Ipachoo.

Ipachoo spun around with his eyes open wide in horror. "Uh, no. I meant cut! She's pretty cut. As in she can cut. With her claws. While assisting Tapito. In a non-combat role. Uh. Yeah!"

Maxstrom and Dusty were both struggling to stifle laughter. Ipachoo looked back at them and let out a soft growl.

"Anyway, I brought you all a present." Shenabu declared, entering the treehouse. "Where's Shacbu?"

"Here I am." Shacbu announced, running in slightly out of breath. "Sorry I'm late; Tapito had a quick meeting and it went longer than I expected."

"No worries." Maxstrom responded. "We were just about to enjoy some of Ipachoo's Dolphinian style roasted seaweed and exchange the rest of our presents."

"Guess I have perfect timing then." Shacbu responded with a smile.

"Hey guys! It's starting to snow!" Dusty exclaimed in excitement.

Shenabu shuddered. "I don't get how you like water."

"It's not water! It's frozen water!" Dusty responded.

"Same difference, Dusty." Shacbu interjected.

Maxstrom walked over to the window and looked up at the clouds. "It looks like there's a big snow storm coming in from the southeast."

"Let's open gifts and get over to the celebration hall as soon as possible then!" Shenabu exclaimed.

"Tracks!" Bezka declared triumphantly as he examined a broken pine branch and then looked down at the snow below. They had entered a small grouping of trees about a day's march north of Fort Tak. But unlike the trees in the Kachuna Forest, these trees were normal sized.

Zepak knelt down to examine Bezka's discovery with his orange eyes.

"There's not much left of these tracks; the snow storm has mostly covered them. But it certainly is like a human footprint." Zepak informed.

"So magmen got through our defenses, but they're just far away?" Fika asked.

"No, they're close. It's been snowing hard for some time now, so it makes sense the tracks would be almost invisible." Bezka responded.

"What kind of tracks are these ones?" Fika inquired, looking at a different set of tracks that were almost the size of a katlican.

Bezka raised an eyebrow in confusion as he examined the track. Then suddenly, he smirked.

"What, did you figure it out?" Fika inquired.

"No, but I can tell you that we're about to."

Bezka then let out another Tabee war yell, and ran off into the snow storm.

"Happy Salvation Day!" Tapito yelled, raising her glass filled with root beer in her left paw.

"Happy Salvation Day!" Everyone responded, each raising their glasses and then taking a swig. The evening festivities had begun.

"Mustard sauce, mustard sauce, mustard sauce!" Dusty started chanting to himself.

"You really like this stuff, huh?" Maxstrom remarked.

"It's the best stuff I've ever eaten!" Dusty responded.

Ipachoo leaned over and said "As long as I get to chew food, I don't really care how it tastes."

"He could chew on anything and be happy." Dusty whispered to Maxstrom.

Dusty and Maxstrom nearly burst out laughing at this, and had to work hard to keep their composure and maintain the professional atmosphere that this dinner required.

"Max, you guys should really get ahold of yourselves." Akbu commented, leaning over. He was sitting next to Maxstrom.

"Sorry Akbu." Maxstrom replied.

"Quiet! I see them." Bezka whispered to the Tabees as he approached the edge of a clearing.

"How many?" Fika asked.

"Hard to tell with all of this snow. There's at least fifteen, maybe more." Bezka responded.

"You do realize there are only nine of us, right?" Zepak remarked.

"Since when have numbers ever been a concern of the Tabees?" Bezka responded. "We are warriors. There could be two hundred in front of us and we could still defeat them all."

"I don't question our tribe's reputation, just the lack of experience some of our troops have in the squad." Zepak whispered to his leader.

"I know." Bezka answered. "Which is why I'm going to face them alone."

"Wait what?!" Fika asked in a loud, high pitched voice.

Bezka and Zepak both turned and shushed Fika.

"I'm not actually going to fight the whole time alone. I'm just going to get warmed up while you guys split up and attack from either side." Bezka informed.

"I guess it's out of the question to try and debate this plan?" Fika inquired.

Bezka responded by drawing his heavy, Tabee sword and walking into the clearing. The snow storm around him suddenly got heavier; but he could still see the glowing red eyes and mouths of some of the magmen in front of him. As Bezka approached the enemy, he spotted a large rock between him and his foe, and stepped on it in one quick, fluid motion.

"Hey rock heads! Come and get a taste of my blade!" Bezka yelled with a grin.

He saw the numerous red, glowing eyes turn and meet his glare, and heard an evil shriek come from in front of him. The group of magmen started charging towards him, weapons raised. As Bezka waited for the fight to arrive, he started seeing more red eyes and mouths in the distance through the storm.

The closest magman finally got within striking distance and tried to swing a giant spike mace at Bezka's head. But Bezka was ready, and quickly jumped to the ground while swinging his sword into the magman's face. The magman's whole face crumpled, and magma splashed to the side as Bezka swung his blade into the face of a second magman, splitting his head open as well. A third magman swung a sharp rock blade for Bezka's head, but Bezka quickly ducked to avoid the strike, and then drove his sword into the magman's chest.

Zepak ran out of the woods and decapitated a magman from behind. The other three Tabees behind him took this attack as their cue to join the fight and sprung from the forest, slamming into the magmen force charging Bezka.

Fika, who was on the opposite flank with the rest of the Tabees, saw that he was missing out on the action and let out a Tabee war yell as he ran out of the woods, sword first. He swung and cut a magman's leg clean off at the knee, and then took his sword and drove it into the monster's head.

"Come on!" Bezka yelled in his deep voice. He wanted to keep the magmen focused on him, and not the Tabees that were on either flank.

Two more magmen were running towards Bezka, and he grinned at the coming challenge. He started running at one of the magmen, but just as Bezka was in range of the magman's mace, Bezka dropped down and slid into the snow past the magman while slicing his feet off. The former magman sputtered and crashed to a halt. The second magman also stopped, turned towards Bezka, and started charging at the Tabee again. Bezka, who was already back on his feet, simply stood his ground. As the magmen closed the distance, he took his blade and stabbed the magman in the chest. The magman desperately thrashed at Bezka for a moment, and then his rock head was crushed by a Tabee blade from behind. The magman fell to the ground, revealing Fika.

"Bezka! Watch out!" Fika yelled.

Bezka turned quickly and saw a magman running for him. He quickly threw his sword in a spinning motion for the magman's head and dove to the side. The flying sword made contacted with the magman's neck, decapitating the monster. Bezka's sword landed a few feet from him.

"I think that's all of them. Good throw, by the way." Zepak declared, emerging from the snow storm.

"Thanks." Bezka declared, and looked over to see a magman missing both feet crawling towards Fika.

"Hey Fika, you might want to put that abomination out of its misery." Bezka ordered as he gestured with his head.

"What? Oh." Fika inquired as he looked down to a magman trying to grab his feet. He took his sword and stabbed the monster in the head, killing it.

"Sir! You should get over here!" One of the Tabees yelled through the snow storm.

The trio took off running in the direction the voice had come. As they approached, they saw the remaining six Tabees had cornered some massive and hairy creature.

"What. . . what is that?" Fika asked Bezka.

"I'm a tunnel mole!" The creature screamed as it used its massive, shovel-like feet to cover its face.

"Please, don't kill me! I don't want to fight."

"Stand aside!" Bezka barked at his troops.

The Tabees backed up, but kept their swords leveled at the creature.

"What is your name?" Bezka asked the tunnel mole as he approached.

"Dubger." The creature responded, relaxing a little.

"What are you doing in the Tabee State? I've never seen your kind here before."

"What's the Tabee State?" The creature asked, confused.

"This is not the time for games! I am Bezka, leader of these Tabee warriors that slayed your magmen monsters, and we. . ."

"My monsters? No, no! I was a captive."

"What? Explain!" Bezka yelled.

"I was ambushed and captured along with one of my friends in the mountains east of the Dactalyon Wasteland, and we were forced to dig tunnels for hundreds and hundreds of miles for the magmen."

"That's how the magmen got into Shadicore and attacked Duba." Fika mumbled to himself.

"I'm not a fighter. None of my kind is. I don't even want to be here! I want to be home; underground." Dubger responded.

"Well, Dubger, I'm going to have to take you back to. . ."

"What? No! We can't leave my friend behind!" Dubger cried.

"Where is your friend?" Bezka inquired.

"He was also captured. He's with the larger group of magmen!"

"Where are the other magmen now?"

"I'm not sure. These creatures don't really talk, they only make screeches and shrieks along with hand gestures."

"So there's nothing you can tell me about where they went?"

"I think they started going north-ish."

"Duba is north-east from here. Do you think. . .?" Fika trailed off.

"Dubger, how many magmen were there?"

"If I had to guess, at least three thousand."

Fika's jaw dropped in shock.

"That's too many for us to handle." Zepak muttered.

Bezka looked up at the snow storm around them.

"We need to head to Fort Tip to get more troops. Three thousand is indeed a bit too many, even for us. But the storm doesn't look like it'll let up any time so, so let's make camp and then head out once it's clear." Bezka declared.

Dusty smacked his lips. "I love this sauce!"

Shacbu overheard Dusty and looked in his direction from across the table with a raised eyebrow. Dusty returned the glance. Shacbu smiled, and then quickly looked down.

Suddenly, their peacefully dinner was interrupted by the sound of a loud drum being sounded.

"What's going on?" Tapito asked.

Suddenly Sheni burst into the room. She was on night watch again.

"We've got trouble!" Sheni declared, gasping for breath. "There's a group of rock monsters coming from the south with red eyes and mouths. They're just a couple of miles out from Shavi. I think they're on their way to attack us!"

"Magmen." Maxstrom mumbled to himself.

"Not again. . ." Dusty responded, recognizing the description all too well.

"Everyone, please remain calm and move to the great hall in the center of Shavi. That is our stronghold; you will be safe there." Tapito instructed the horrified katlicans.

A hurried frenzy followed as the katlicans got up and moved toward the exit of the celebration hall. Maxstrom and Dusty walked over to the window and looked out. The snow storm was too thick to see much.

"It seems so tranquil. It's hard to believe that more of those magmen are out there right now." Dusty remarked.

Tapito and Akbu walked up behind them.

"I don't understand." Tapito declared. "How does this keep happening?"

"Do you think they got through the Tabee defenses?" Akbu asked Tapito.

"I can assure you, they did not." General Tak the Twelfth, leader of the Tabee clan declared as he walked over to the group. His shoulder cape snapped against his massive muscles as he abruptly stopped his brisk pace.

"General Tak." Tapito acknowledged, nodding in his direction.

"Chief." Tak responded, nodding his head in return.

"He's huge." Dusty whispered to Maxstrom as he noticed the size of General Tak's muscles.

Maxstrom simply raised his eyebrows and nodded in agreement.

"So what do you mean, General?" Akbu inquired.

"My defenses are airtight. There's no way anything got through without the Tabees killing as many as they could and sending a messenger to me."

"And you're sure of this?" Akbu questioned.

General Tak's deep blue eyes glared at Akbu. "You doubt the Tabees reputation?"

"Not at all." Akbu responded. "But things sometimes happen that one could not expect."

General Tak tensed his nose in frustration for a second and then released it. "I assure you, my defenses are so rock solid that my ancestors would be proud."

"Forgive Akbu, Tak. You should fall back to the great hall with the rest of the katlicans while we handle this threat." Tapito interjected.

General Tak's eyes opened wide as he stared at Tapito, aghast. "The Tabees have fought with and for the Shadicans for generations; ever since my ancestor, General Tak the First, and your former leader, Shadic the Third, formed an alliance. I would be remiss if I allowed you to fight while I hid in a fortress. In fact, my ancestors would grimace from heaven if I did so! It would be a disgrace to the Tabees; we never turn down a fight that's for a good cause."

Tapito and Akbu looked at each other.

"So what do you suggest?" Tapito inquired, returning her gaze to General Tak.

"I assume that your Shadicans need a few minutes to prepare for combat?"

"Yes. . .?" Akbu responded, not seeing where this was going.

"My Tabees are always ready to fight. We can meet the enemy head on and buy you the time you need."

"You have warriors, here?" Akbu inquired, confused.

"Indeed! I am surprised you have forgotten that each Tabee is a warrior. And most of those that are here are part of my elite unit. All we need is your permission, and we shall head to battle." Tak replied, looking at Tapito.

"Go. We'll join you as soon as we can." Tapito informed.

Tak nodded, and then ran out of the hut.

"I'm going to rally the troops." Tapito declared, and followed him out.

"At least you can test out the throwing stars I got you." Dusty interjected, trying to be positive.

"I don't think they'll work very well on rocks, bud. . ." Maxstrom responded.

"Good point." Dusty replied in a sad tone.

"So how tough are these things?" Akbu questioned.

"You remember my broken sword, right?" Maxstrom inquired in response.

"Oh. Well, this is going to be fun. . ." Akbu declared, as he looked out into the snowy night.

"Form up!" General Tak yelled as he stood behind his Tabee troops. The snow storm was almost a blizzard.

The Tabees, equipped with spears, fell fluidly into the standard Tabee formation of two Tabees deep.

"What's the troop report?" Tak asked, yelling down the line to his second in command, Kefa.

"We have four hundred and ten Tabees ready to fight and die for the katlicans!" Kefa called back.

"Good!" Tak responded.

Tak turned and looked over his troops in the direction of the enemy. He could see many faint red lights in the storm. The magmen were getting close.

"Formation five!" Tak barked, turning his attention back to his troops.

"You heard the general! First group, kneel!" Kefa yelled.

The command echoed down the line, and the first line of Tabees quickly knelt to the ground.

"Lower your spears!" Tak commanded.

"Lower spears!" Kefa repeated.

The Tabees quickly lowered their spears into combat position.

"Hold formation, and wait for them!" Tak hollered. "Prepare to execute strategy twenty-five!"

"Strategy twenty-five; prepare to pivot the charging opponents over the formation!" Kefa echoed.

General Tak picked up a spear and jumped into formation with his troops.

"Show no mercy!" General Tak yelled. "These creatures, whatever they may be, are attacking us on our brother's home turf! This is personal!"

The Tabees let out a war yell.

The magmen seemed to almost materialize out of the snow storm as they charged toward the Tabee formation. General Tak quickly looked around and guessed there had to be at least a thousand.

"Get ready!" Kefa hollered to the troops.

The magmen collided with the Tabees, and the Tabee's strategy was executed perfectly. The charging magmen impacted into the first line of Tabee's spears, and the first line thrust the back of their spears into the snow and used the magmen's momentum to throw the magmen over their heads. The second line used their spears to catch the magmen, and then slam the magmen into the ground behind them, head first. As the second line took the magmen, the first line rapidly leveled their spears again.

"Charge!" General Tak commanded his troops in a loud, authoritative voice.

The first line of Tabees quickly stood up and charged into the horde of magmen.

"Come on Dusty!" Maxstrom yelled, sprinting toward the ongoing battle.

"Remember Max. Your legs. Are bigger than mine!" Dusty yelled back as he struggled to breathe in the cold, snowy air.

The two were sprinting towards the fight, and as they were getting close to the sound of battle, the snow storm slowed to a more gradual snowfall. With the increased view range, Maxstrom saw magmen beginning to surround both sides of the Tabee's formation.

"We have to protect the flanks! Take the right one; I'll go to the left!"

"Got it!" Dusty responded.

Maxstrom had picked the left side for a reason; there was a small brook nearby, and it had not yet frozen. As Maxstrom passed it, he grabbed two large streams of water. He then looked to the fight, and saw three magmen about to attack the Tabees from behind.

"No you don't!" Maxstrom yelled as he dropped down and slid on the fresh snow.

The three magmen turned to look at Maxstrom, but instead of seeing him, two were greeted by a stream of water splitting their faces open. The third looked and saw that both of his friends had fallen, and let out an evil shriek as he started running at Maxstrom.

Maxstrom quickly grabbed another stream of water and shot it at the magman. The magman tried to dodge the stream of water at the last second, but it was too late. The blow landed, and it decapitated the monster.

"What's the plan, chief?" Akbu inquired, looking over at Tapito. They had managed to rally three hundred Shadican warriors, and everyone had gathered in the trees above the fight.

"The Tabees are already fighting the enemy. So what we're going to do is drop in on top of the magmen from the trees and lend the Tabee tribe a helping hand. Have our troops form up into groups of five, and drop down in squads."

"Alright, you heard the chief, pass it along!" Akbu ordered.

The sound of Shadican yells through the tall trees would have been heard if not for the loud battle going on below.

"You know you can't go down, chief." Wachuna whispered, who was standing between Akbu and Tapito.

"What? Yes, I can!" Tapito snapped back.

"You can't use your right paw!" Akbu yelled. "No, Wachuna is right. You need to stay up here. Please chief, for once in your life, actually listen to me."

Tapito thought for a moment.

"Alright, fine. I'll stay."

"Get the ropes ready!" Akbu commanded, and the Shadican troops strung ropes up on the branches to slide down into the fight below.

"Go!" Akbu yelled, grabbing one of the ropes and sliding down."

General Tak ducked to the side with lightning speed to avoid a magman's mace, and then swung his heavy battle sword into the magman's neck. Magma splattered out and went over Tak's head and onto the ground behind him.

"Behind you, general!"

Tak turned and saw a magmen about to split his head open. Then, suddenly, a Shadican blade fell from the sky and dove straight into the magmen's head. Of course, a Shadican was attached to this sword, and as the magman fell to the ground, Tak saw that the Shadican was Akbu.

"Good to see you!" Tak hollered as he spun around and jammed his sword into the belly of another magman.

"How did you know that one was there?" Akbu asked about the magman General Tak had just killed. Akbu rolled to the side to dodge another magman's attack.

"I heard him." Tak fired back.

"You heard him? In this racket?!" Akbu questioned, cutting the magman's legs off, and splitting his blade in the process.

"Selective hearing." Tak responded, and smirked at Akbu. "You probably won't get far with those Shadican blades; they're too fine. You need something with more blunt force for these rock-heads."

"If you got a spare sword, I'll take it!" Akbu yelled back.

Tak reached down and grabbed one of his fallen Tabee's swords.

"Here, try this on for size." General Tak yelled as he tossed the sword to Akbu.

Akbu caught the sword just in time, and spun around to strike a magman in the head. The blow threw the magman to the side, and he collided into the base of a Brownwood tree.

"You know, for most situations I wouldn't like this sword. But I got to say, for giving these monsters a beating, they're quite effective!" Akbu exclaimed with a smile.

Dusty threw himself backwards onto the ground to dodge a strike from a magman. This one was using a stone sword hand instead of a mace hand.

"Ha!" Dusty taunted, and kicked a fire blast with his feet towards the magman's abdomen.

The blast threw the magman back a few feet and knocked him down, but the magman was on his feet just after Dusty was.

"Come on, really?" Dusty complained. "I thought I had this down!"

The magman charged at Dusty. Dusty threw two fire punches at the magman, and both landed right on its face. The blows didn't kill him; but rather just split its face open a little, and made him skid to a stop.

"Really? Makbu made this look too easy." Dusty moaned.

The magman started running at him again. This time, Dusty mustered all of his strength and blew a fire blast into the magman's face with both paws. The magman's head blew clean off, shooting magma everywhere.

"You should try a sword!" Shacbu yelled as she fell from the trees and drove her blade into a magman's head.

"Swords don't really work on these things." Dusty replied as he shot another consecrated fire blast.

"You mean like this?" Shacbu asked as she jammed her sword into a magman's abdomen.

"That works; just don't do a side strike, or you'll end up with a broken blade, like Max."

"Noted. Thanks!" Shacbu yelled back as she ran towards another magman.

Maxstrom looked over to his right and saw that some distance away a magman was about to kill one of the Tabees. Maxstrom quickly reacted. He grabbed a large batch of snow, turned it into water, and shot it straight for the magman's head. But at the last second, the monster saw the strike, and moved its head to the side. It then turned and glared at Maxstrom.

"Well, that sort of worked." Maxstrom mumbled to himself.

The magman started running towards him. Maxstrom grabbed another batch of snow, turned it into water, and launched it again. This time, since the magman was closer, he couldn't dodge the attack, and magman's head split wide open.

"There we go!" Maxstrom declared.

"Hey, thanks!" The Tabee yelled to Maxstrom; back on his feet.

"No problem!"

"That's a pretty sweet ability." The Tabee hollered back as he cleaved a magman in two.

General Tak drove his sword into the head of one of the magman still alive on the ground.

"What a headache." He muttered, twisting his sword in the magman's head and then pulling it out.

The battlefield fell silent; but snow was still falling.

"Tabees! Report!" General Tak hollered across the field.

"All clear on the western flank!"

"No enemies left on the east side!"

"I think we're clear." General Tak declared, turning to look at Akbu.

"Good, cause using this heavy sword is exhausting." Akbu responded as he was gasping for air.

"I guess the Tabee troops are better than our Elite Guard after all." Tapito commented, sliding down a nearby rope.

"Hey now, chief. I'm used to light swords, not heavy swords." Akbu replied in his defense.

"I'm sure you would beat me in a sword fight, Akbu." General Tak commented in consolation as he gently patted Akbu's shoulder.

"See? See? It's just because we're fighting these boulders, and the Tabees have better weapons for it."

Tapito simply chuckled. "I hated not being able to help."

"But it was good you didn't, with your injury." Tak added. "We would have had to work harder to protect you, and that could have got soldiers needlessly killed."

Shacbu and Dusty appeared out of the snowstorm.

"So how'd that fire training do for you?" Tapito inquired.

"Oh, it was fantastic!" Dusty answered, slightly winded.

"Help!" A voice in the distance called.

The group took off running. It took them a moment to find the source of the call for help, but once they did, they saw it was Wachuna.

"Oh no!" Akbu cried, and then ran over to his friend.

Wachuna lay on the ground against a tree. His gut was sliced open. It wasn't terribly deep, but it was bleeding badly.

"I'm getting light headed here, Akbu." Wachuna responded, bobbing his head.

"No! No. Stay with me Wachuna!" Akbu commanded, dropping to his knees. "I need some bandages! Now!"

Dusty and Shacbu both ran to go find something as Akbu put his paws on the wound to stop the bleeding.

"Max!" Tapito yelled. "Do you have any bandages?"

Akbu turned and saw Maxstrom emerging from the falling snow. Maxstrom ran over and saw Wachuna.

"I can do better than that." Maxstrom declared, and grabbed a large pile of snow. He quickly turned it into water, put it in Wachuna's wound, and turned it to ice.

"Ahh! Ooh! That feels good." Wachuna mumbled.

"What did you just do?" Akbu asked in confusion, turning to Maxstrom.

"Stopped the bleeding with ice. It won't last forever, but it should give us enough time to get him some real medical attention." Maxstrom responded.

"I probably have several wounded troops that are in need of your abilities." General Tak informed Maxstrom.

"Of course. Let's go check for wounded." Maxstrom replied, standing to his feet.

The final count on the magmen killed was one thousand, two hundred and three. The Shadicans lost only seventy troops, and the Tabees lost forty two; but many were wounded from the engagement. This attack lead Tapito to call a meeting of the katlicans, since all of the katlican tribe leaders, or at least one of their representatives, were already present.

"I can assure you these magmen didn't get through my defenses." Tak responded, getting slightly aggravated that this question kept coming up.

"Then how did they get here?!" Chooan questioned. Chooan was the representative of the Dolphinians in Shavi. "The magmen came from the south; so there's no way they came from the desert. So, logically they must have come through your defenses!"

"Listen, you Dolphinians are great sailors. You don't fear water or the sea. Do you think I would ever lecture you on how to sail a boat?" General Tak fired back.

"No! But this isn't about sailing a boat, this is about an attack that happened! If I ran the boat aground, don't you think that would warrant you to have concern about my ability to sail?" Chooan responded.

"This is accomplishing nothing!" Tapito yelled, slamming her left fist onto the floor.

"I agree." Gumabu responded, stroking the white Snowisean fur on his chin. Gumabu was in Shavi for the festival. "I think someone needs to rally troops and head to the Tabee border."

"But there is no breakthrough!" General Tak responded in frustration. "When will you listen? The problem is elsewhere!"

"How about once the snow storm stops, we try to trace the steps of the magmen back as best as we can?" Akbu suggested.

"That's actually a good idea, save the fact snow will have covered any trace of them by that point." Chooan commented.

"I can send some scouts out to track the magmen as far back as they are able." General Tak informed. "All I need is permission from the chief."

"Do it." Tapito ordered.

The General immediately got up and went outside to speak with his second in command, Kefa.

"This is a waste of time. We know the Tabees have a breach! How else could we have received this attack?" Chooan inquired.

"If you're right, then we'll end up on the Tabee border sooner or later." Tapito responded.

"Okay, I sent word to have ten scouts leave immediately." General Tak informed as he walked back into the hut.

"Good. Now we need to discuss the military defense policy." Tapito declared.

"The military defense policy?!" Chooan cried. "That's never been used in the history of the katlicans!"

"It was created by General Tak the First for emergencies such as this." Shadan added, sitting off to the side.

"Yeah, but won't that instill panic?" Chooan asked.

"Chooan, we were attack by an unknown enemy, and we don't know how they got into our territory. The civilians are already panicking." Akbu responded in a calm tone.

"I think I need to head back to Snowisea in that case." Gumabu declared. "Will you be needing any Snowisean assistance for anything down here, Tapito?"

"No, thank you, Gumabu. Tell the Snowiseans that the defense policy is only in place until we can stop these attacks."

"But having a curfew! Making all the katlicans sleep in the fortress! Having a guard keep an eye on the city and any who leave to work in the field or that go to fish!" Chooan yelled. "That will destroy moral."

"Better weak moral than lost lives." Shacbu, who had been sitting silently next to Tapito, remarked.

"Wise words." General Tak replied. "Who are you again?"

"Shacbu. I'm the next chief."

"An honor to make your acquaintance." General Tak responded, bowing his head in Shacbu's direction

"I'm going to leave first thing in the morning." Gumabu declared.

"Allow me to send a guard with you." Akbu interjected.

"No, no, I have my own protective detail. Thank you, though. You need all the troops you can get here with the Shadicans."

"I want to rally an army together to track down where the breakthrough occurred." Tapito said, furrowing her eyebrows.

"I'm with you." General Tak added. "You have my full support."

"The Dolphinians are too far away to be able to rally an army to support you immediately." Chooan informed.

"That's fine. I can muster up a thousand Shadicans by noon tomorrow." Akbu responded.

"Glad to hear it. Get on that, if you wouldn't mind." Tapito requested.

"Of course, chief." Akbu said as he got up and walked out of the room.

General Tak's scouts had more success than the leadership had expected, and found the entrance to the new tunnel the magmen had used only about a day's march south of the Kachuna Forest. The problem was that there were magmen tracks leading both north, to Shavi, and south, towards Duba. The Tabee scouts collapsed the tunnel, and then informed General Tak that there was still a large threat running around behind the Shadican borders to the south. The joint Shadican-Tabee Army decided to march south and hunt down the magmen Army, wherever they may be.

Chapter 8

The End of an Era

B.Y. 4013

"For those who follow Him, death is not the end.
Rather, it is a glorious new beginning in perfection."
—Shadican Proverb

"My feet hurt." Shacbu moaned. "I haven't ever had to walk this much."

The Shadican and Tabee Army had been marching for about two weeks now. Most of the snow in the southern part of Shadicore had melted at this point.

"Shacbu, you have to toughen up. You're going to be the next leader." Tapito declared sternly.

"Sorry, chief."

Maxstrom looked up and saw several Tabee soldiers approaching them. General Tak's Tabees were faster than the Shadican Army, so they were a about half a mile ahead.

"We have a report for you from General Tak, chief!"

"What's the news?"

"Our scouts are still on the trail of the magmen, although it's faint. It is still leading south."

"We have to be close to Duba by now." Dusty chimed in.

"Indeed, Dusty. We should reach Duba by the end of the day." Tapito declared.

Tapito then turned back to the Tabee messengers.

"Thank you for the update."

The messengers nodded and ran off to rejoin the Tabee formation.

"You'll get to meet Makbu, Shacbu!" Dusty exclaimed.

"Who's that, your fire teacher?" Shacbu questioned.

"Yeah! He's an amazing Shadican. The best teacher ever!"

"Ouch." Akbu interjected. "Guess I won't be teaching you to be an expert sword fighter after all."

"Oh no wait! I didn't mean it like that!"

All of the sudden, the group heard a loud trumpet.

"What's that?" Shacbu asked.

"The Tabee's battle horn. We need to get up there!" Akbu responded.

"Nikacha, have the troops move at double speed!" Tapito yelled back to the Shadican Army's formation commander.

"You've got to help us! Duba is under attack! We're lucky we even made it out!" A desperate female Shadican cried to General Tak.

"Don't worry, we'll do what we can. How far is Duba from here?" General Tak inquired.

"At least three miles."

"General!" Tapito called. The Shadican Army had caught up with the Tabees. "What's going on?"

"Duba is apparently under attack." The General responded.

"What?!" Dusty cried. "Again?!"

"We don't have any time to waste. I know you can't move your Shadican Army as fast as we can move; so we're going to run ahead and get to the fight." Tak declared.

"That's fine. We'll take care of these civilians as well. Take Max and Dusty with you; having a couple of aces wouldn't hurt." Tapito replied.

"Can you two keep a fast pace?" Tak asked Maxstrom and Dusty as he raised an eyebrow.

Dusty chuckled. "General, Makbu's favorite way to torture me was long and fast jogs. I can keep up."

"Good. Then let's go!" Tak cried.

Chuba ducked as a magman's mace swung for his head.

"Is that the best you got?" Chuba, a Shadican defending his town, taunted.

The magman swung his mace again. Chuba jumped back, and then swung his sword for the magman's head. The sword hit, but split in two; only denting the magman's head.

"Say what now? Well, I mean, I guess it does look like you've got a hard head. . ." Chuba remarked.

The magman slammed his mace down into the ground where Chuba had been standing a second before.

"See I could do this all day. You guys are so clumsy and. . ."

All of the sudden, Chuba got hit from his left side and he went flying. A second magman had snuck up on him.

"Ahh!" Chuba moaned as he gripped his side.

The two magmen walked over to him, and both raised their weapons.

"Oh come on." Chuba declared as he tried to move, and winced in pain.

Chuba then saw two metal spears impale the magmen's heads from behind. Both heads split open, and the magmen fell to the ground. Chuba looked to see two Tabee warriors standing heroically.

"Oh, hi guys!"

"Keep moving, secure the town!" General Tak yelled, appearing behind his troops. "You, Shadican warrior, what's the status of the rock monster's assault?"

"I have no clue, sir." Chuba responded, realizing that this Tabee was important. "I was out fishing, and only got back here a few minutes ago."

"Are you alright?" General Tak inquired.

"I'm good. It just hurts to move right now."

"Alright, you stay here. We'll secure the town." General Tak declared authoritatively, and then looked back at the group of Tabees behind him. "Let's go!"

"Not like I'm going anywhere." Chuba replied, and set his head on the pile of debris surrounding him.

Maxstrom jammed one of the Tabee spears he had picked up into a magman's abdomen. The magmen fell backwards with magma sputtering out.

"Dusty, behind you!"

Dusty turned to see a magman running towards him. He quickly launched a fire ball right for the magman's face and split it in two.

"Makbu taught you well!"

"Yeah, I finally got it down! But I wonder where he is."

"We need to finish cleaning these magmen up and rejoin the Tabees!" Maxstrom yelled as he swung the spear like a bat into the head of another magman.

"On it!" Dusty responded as he launched a fire blast with a left kick.

The magman that received this blow flew back and slammed into a Shadican house, knocking down the wall and revealing a bathroom. Water quickly started to shoot out of the house.

"You hit one of the plumbing lines, Dusty!"

"Oops."

"No, not oops! Thanks!" Maxstrom yelled as he grabbed a stream of water and shot it at a magman. The blow landed center mass and blew the magman open.

"Oh! You're welcome then."

Maxstrom grabbed another stream of water, and saw a magman charging him from behind.

"Hey, I'm going to try something." Maxstrom said to Dusty, who was preparing to launch a fire blast.

He quickly turned the stream of water he was holding into an ice spear, and launched it at the magman. The spear went directly into the magman's left eye.

"Nice hit!" Dusty yelled.

The magman stopped for a second, and bent its head down. But then the spear's point melted, and the end fell onto the ground in a small pile of snowy mush.

"Um, Max?"

"Well that didn't work! So much for using ice weapons against these monsters!" Maxstrom yelled as he grabbed another stream of water and shot it at the magman's head. Dusty also shot a blast of fire and at the magman's chest. Both blows landed at the same time, and the magman exploded into pieces.

"I like that tag team combo. Makbu would be proud of us." Dusty remarked.

"Yeah, he would be! I think we're clear on this end; let's go catch up with the Tabees!"

"General Tak!" Kefa yelled.

General Tak pulled his sword out of the head of a magman on the ground. "Yes, Kefa?"

"We've cleared the north part of the town; the magmen are boxed in to our south!"

"Fantastic!" General Tak yelled in response. "Let's have our troops keep pushing the magmen back. Send a messenger to Tapito, and have her swing her army behind the magmen. We'll squash these rock monsters to bits!"

"Sounds good sir!" Kefa responded.

"Let's keep up the pressure! Push to the south!" A Tabee warrior echoed the command down the line.

"We're really crushing these magmen; it seems so much easier than the battle for Shavi!" Dusty exclaimed as both him and Maxstrom were running towards what remained of the south part of Duba.

Maxstrom was about to answer Dusty, but then looked in front of him and saw a magman missing an arm jump out in front of his path. He wasted no time, and quickly dropped to the ground and started sliding towards the magman with the Tabee spear he was carrying poised to strike. The magman raised his good arm, which was turned into a sword, and got ready to swing at Maxstrom. But Maxstrom's spear had more reach, and he stuck the spear straight through the magman.

"Nice one!" Dusty yelled.

"Thanks!" Maxstrom responded. He tried to pull the spear out of the dead magman, but saw that it was stuck. So he abandoned it, jumped up, and ran after Dusty.

Dusty had suddenly stopped and was staring in front of him. Maxstrom turned to see what Dusty was looking at, and saw that the buildings around the narrow road they needed to get through were on fire.

"That's a lot of fire." Dusty declared.

"Well we have to get through; there's no easy way around. You ready for this?" Maxstrom inquired, looking around.

"You mean run through it?"

"Yeah, and push the fire out of the way as we go."

Dusty took a deep breath. "I guess."

"On three. One. Two. Three!"

Both took off into the blaze and threw the fire back as they went. After a several seconds, Dusty gave desperate a yell.

"You good Dusty?" Maxstrom cried.

"I'm losing it!" Dusty responded.

"We're almost through! Just keep going!"

Dusty closed his eyes and focused on the two tasks before him: running and pushing the fire out of his way.

"I can't hold it!" Dusty yelled.

Maxstrom looked up and saw that they were almost at the end of the street, which led to the part of Duba that had been burned down in the first attack. He then looked over at Dusty and saw the flames getting closer and closer, and that he was slowing down.

"You can do it!" Maxstrom yelled, masking his uncertainty.

He then looked to his left past Dusty and saw a house that was shooting out water. It was another broken plumbing line.

"Hold on!" Maxstrom yelled as he kept pushing the fire back with his right hand and then grabbed a stream of water with his left. He then swung the stream of water from behind Dusty and hit him in the back, throwing Dusty forward and out of the flame. But just as Maxstrom saved Dusty, he lost his grip on the fire around him. The flame engulfed him.

"Max!" Dusty yelled, looking back. Maxstrom emerged from the flame, diving through the air. He hit the ground in a roll, and then collapsed to the ground.

"Max, your pack is on fire!"

Maxstrom looked at the small pack which he was still wearing, and saw a small flame on the corner. He quickly grabbed it and stifled the flame.

"That was close." Maxstrom declared.

"You think?" Dusty retorted, breathing heavily.

Maxstrom looked back, and started laughing.

"What's so funny?" Dusty inquired, confused.

"That was easily four hundred feet. I thought it was a bit shorter."

Dusty ignored Maxstrom's comment, and began looking around.

"What? What's up?"

"Shh! I hear something."

Dusty looked around for another moment, ears attentive, and looked at Maxstrom.

"Magmen are running near us."

Maxstrom turned to his right, and saw three magmen smash through one of the burning houses several hundred feet away.

"Let's get them!" Maxstrom yelled, jumping to his feet.

"I'll. I'll catch up in a second." Dusty responded, still breathing hard.

Maxstrom looked back at Dusty. "You good, bud?"

"Yeah, yeah! I'm good. I am. I just need to catch my breath."

Maxstrom hesitated.

"Max, go! You can take them."

Maxstrom nodded and ran towards where the magmen were. The magmen seemed confused as to where they were going, but turned to face Maxstrom once they saw him. Suddenly, Maxstrom saw a Tabee come sprinting out of the tree line just south of Duba. The Tabee jumped the magmen from behind; decapitating two of them with one strike. The third magman turned in surprise, and raise his mace to strike the Tabee. But the Tabee was ready, and lunged his sword into the magman's chest; killing it.

"Good job!" Maxstrom called.

The Tabee glanced over at him and suddenly had a furious look on his face.

"What?" Maxstrom inquired.

The Tabee started running at him full speed, sword poised.

"What are you doing?!" Maxstrom exclaimed.

"Stopping the threat to my kind!" The Tabee responded, still sprinting at Maxstrom.

Maxstrom dove to the side at the last second, just barely avoiding the attack.

"What are you talking about?" Maxstrom questioned, confused.

The Tabee didn't bother to respond, but instead let out a Tabee war yell and charged at Maxstrom, sword first again.

Maxstrom, who was still crouched from his roll, decided to do an unconventional tactic. He dropped to his back, pulled his feet to his chest, and shot a blast of fire at his opponent. The Tabee threw himself backwards onto the ground to avoid the blast. Maxstrom quickly jumped to his feet.

"This is all a misunderstanding." Maxstrom informed, getting ready to explain.

The Tabee suddenly threw something at Maxstrom. Maxstrom responded by rapidly moving his body to the side to evade the object. But it was too little too late, and the small rock clipped Maxstrom's left cheekbone. He let out a small cry of pain.

The Tabee sprung to his feet and started running towards Maxstrom again. Maxstrom's mind raced. He had to find a way to stop, but not kill, this Tabee. So he grabbed some water residue from a nearby plumbing line, consolidated it into a small ball, and quickly turned it to thin ice. He then threw this ice ball at his opponent's face. The Tabee, who was not expecting this kind of attack, couldn't react quickly enough to avoid the projectile. Maxstrom's ice ball landed dead on, and his opponent fell to the ground.

Maxstrom then grabbed some more water, but this time he turned it into an ice sword. He then walked over to the Tabee.

"What's your name?" Maxstrom questioned in a loud voice.

The Tabee rubbed his forehead were the ice ball had impacted him.

"Bezka." The Tabee responded.

"Look, I'm on your side. I'm. . ."

The Tabee reached out, grabbed Maxstrom's foot, and pulled. The attack worked, and Maxstrom fell to the ground. Bezka then grabbed his sword, rolled over, and swung it towards Maxstrom's face. Maxstrom moved out of the way of the blade just in time, and then rolled backwards to get away from Bezka.

"So who are you? Some paid mercenary to assist these monsters?" Bezka questioned.

"What? No. My name's Maxstrom. I live with the Shadicans."

"Liar!" Bezka yelled.

"Why does this keep happening to me?" Maxstrom muttered to himself.

Bezka glared at the human as he plotted his next attack.

"Come on, haven't you at least heard of me? The human Tapito took in?"

"Nope. Never."

Their conversation was interrupted by a loud yell from the side. Bezka looked up to see an infuriated Dusty flying through the air, fist raised. Bezka tried to raise his sword to defend himself, but was too late. Dusty's fist landed right on Bezka's jaw, and Bezka flew to the side.

"Get away from Max!" Dusty commanded.

"What are you doing, Shadican?!" Bezka asked in anger.

"I told you! I live the Shadicans. This is my friend, Dusty."

Bezka thought for a moment, and rubbed his jaw.

"In that case, you have my formal apology, human." Bezka responded, standing to his feet.

"But we've all been traveling together the last couple weeks. How did you not recognize Max?" Dusty inquired.

"What? What are you talking about? I came straight up from the Tabee State once I discovered that the magmen were planning to invade Shadicore."

"Wait, so you're not with General Tak's forces?" Maxstrom questioned.

"No. Is my uncle here?!" Bezka asked, surprised.

"General Tak is your uncle?" Dusty queried.

"Indeed!"

"Well his forces are clearing out the rest of the magmen in Duba as we speak." Maxstrom informed.

Suddenly, a broken beam snapped behind Maxstrom, and he turned to see another Tabee aiming a sword at him.

181

"Fika! Stand down." Bezka ordered.

"But sir. . ."

"He's on our side." Bezka declared.

"Oh. Sorry human. I'm not used to seeing your kind here." Fika apologized as he lowered his sword, and then turned to Bezka. "The Tabees we brought up from Fort Tip are just about done fighting off the remaining magmen in the forest."

"Well let's rally the Tabee soldiers and go greet my uncle then."

"Tak is here?" Fika inquired.

"Apparently. Human, could you lead the way?" Bezka inquired.

"Sure. And it's Max."

"Max. A pleasure to make your acquaintance." Bezka responded with a quick head bow.

The Shadican Army was at the base of a mountain just north of Duba, and had almost arrived at the fight in Duba. Once they passed this mountain, they planned to go past Duba, and attack the remaining magmen from behind.

"What's that noise?" Tapito inquired as she gasped for air.

"What noise?" Akbu inquired, who was focusing on running.

"It's an avalanche! Take cover!" Shacbu yelled, looking up.

The Shadicans tried to spread out, but because they were already slightly winded from the jog, many couldn't move fast enough.

Shacbu quickly ducked under a small cliff and curled up into a ball. The rumble of rocks grew louder, and she heard rocks falling all around her. The sound was deafening. But after a moment, all was quiet.

"Akbu? Tapito? Nikacha?" Shacbu called.

None of the rocks had hit her; but there were a couple of boulders nearby. She could see through a cloud of grey dust that many Shadicans had managed to avoid the rockslide.

"Magmen! Up on the cliffs!" A Shadican yelled, pointing with his claw.

Shacbu, still slightly dazed, turned her attention to the small mountain that had just launched a slew of rocks at them. She saw thousands of magmen running and sliding down the steep slope.

"Ambush! We need to fall back, now!" Shacbu yelled at the Shadican troops.

With Tapito, Akbu and Nikacha nowhere to be found, she was in command.

"What was that?" General Tak yelled to Kefa.

"What was what?" Kefa inquired, splitting a magman's legs off as he tried to run away.

General Tak looked around, and his eyes saw a giant cloud of dust to the north.

"I see magmen! Running on the hills!"

"What?! Impossible!" Kefa responded.

"No! We've been tricked; the majority of the magmen must have gone up into the mountains for some reason."

"No wonder why this battle seemed so easy; we've only been fighting a small force! How many are there?" Kefa inquired, trying to see what his commander was reporting.

"Thousands. We need to rally and get over there, now! Tapito has to be still there; she'll need our help."

Kefa let out a yell to let the Tabees know they were to rally on the commander, and then both Tak and Kefa took off running towards the real fight.

Shacbu thrust her blade into a magman that jumped down at her, and threw him to the side.

"Fall back!" Shacbu cried at the top of her lungs. She was holding her ground in the avalanche debris to cover the retreat.

"We have to regroup outside of the avalanche zone!" She yelled to a nearby Shadican.

"You got it, Shacbu!" He responded, and ran off.

Suddenly another magman jumped over a nearby boulder, lunging for Shacbu. She rolled to the side, and stabbed the magman in the side of the head. She then quickly retracted her sword. Shacbu looked to her right and saw a Shadican that had been wounded in the avalanche.

"Hey, are you alright?" Shacbu inquired, running over.

"No. I. . . I think my leg is broken." The Shadican responded.

Shacbu reached the Shadican, and helped him up.

"Lean on me. We're getting out of here!" Shacbu declared, and started moving as quickly as she could for the rally point.

But just as they were about to clear the avalanche's remains, two mag-men jumped in front of their path, ready to strike. Shacbu dropped the Shadican she was carrying, and lunged for one. She stuck her sword straight into his head, but looked to her left and saw the second one was swinging his mace for her head, and there was no time to move. But just when all hope seemed lost, a Tabee blade impacted the magman's arm, splitting it in two. The magman's mace went soaring past Shacbu's head. She quickly recovered her blade, and stabbed the second magman in the face.

"Good moves, Shacbu." The Shadican, who had just saved Shacbu's life remarked.

"Akbu!" Shacbu cried in joy. "You're not dead!"

"Not yet. Where's Tapito?"

"You mean she's not with you?" Shacbu inquired, a look of shock crossing her face.

"No. I thought she gave the rally order."

"No, that was me."

"Really? Wow."

"What? Was it a bad choice?"

"No, not at all actually." Akbu declared in a surprised tone. "I'm just impressed you were able to think so quickly and with such accuracy as to what we should do."

"Thanks. Then let's join the group and fight off this attack!" Shacbu yelled, grabbing the wounded Shadican she had dropped a moment before.

"Alright, Shacbu. Nikacha is dead, so you're in charge of this fight. Get us out of this mess." Akbu responded, helping Shacbu with the wounded Shadican.

"Tabees! Form up!" General Tak yelled.

He was on the northern edge of Duba, and about a half a mile away from the avalanche's location. Tabees were still running out of Duba and into formation. General Tak looked back at his troops. If he had to guess, he figured he still had about three hundred and thirty, against a couple thousand magmen.

"Great." General Tak muttered to himself.

"What's wrong, sir?" Kefa inquired, who was still standing next to his general.

"Nothing, I just wish we had more. . ." General Tak trailed off, as he looked to the southwest of Duba.

Kefa turned to where his commander was looking, and saw about five hundred Tabees running in formation around the town of Duba towards them. Bezka, Maxstrom, Dusty were at the head.

"What is this?!" General Tak yelled, tears in his eyes.

"Uncle! We heard there may be trouble up here, so we decided to lend a hand." Bezka hollered back to the General.

"Perfect. Tabees! Merge formations!" General Tak barked.

The Tabees let out another war yell in unison, and the five hundred Tabees fell in position fluidly right next to General Tak's troops.

"You ready?" General Tak inquired, smirking at his nephew.

"Just give the word, sir!" Bezka responded.

"Charge!" General Tak yelled to the now over eight hundred Tabees.

"They're trying to get around our flank! Form a circle!" Shacbu cried.

The Shadicans were not doing well. They had lost nearly half of their force in the avalanche, and since they were both separated and disorganized, their ability to fight back was weak. Shacbu did a quick count, and guessed that they only had about four hundred warriors remaining; some of which had been dragged from the rockslide and were seriously injured.

Akbu suddenly jumped over Shacbu's head, sword first. Shacbu turned and saw that he had killed a magman only feet away from her.

"Thanks Akbu!" Shacbu declared. "I'm just so focused on trying to come up with a plan right now."

"Of course; you focus on the strategy, I'll focus on keeping you alive."

Suddenly Shacbu heard a faint Tabee war yell from behind her. She turned, and saw that the Tabees were about an eighth of a mile away.

"Shadicans! Face the north; relocate the wounded to the south. The Tabees are coming." Shacbu ordered.

"You heard the commander! Let's move!" Akbu echoed.

The Shadican troops quickly shifted formation, opening up the south end for the Tabees to protect.

Maxstrom, who was slightly in front and to the side of the Tabee formation, saw that the Shadican formation was shifting. But he saw that they had shifted just a little too soon; several magmen were swinging around the Shadican flank and about to reach the gap before the Tabees. He quickened his pace to beat the magmen.

"Hey!" Maxstrom yelled at the group of five magmen.

The group turned, and Maxstrom shot a fire blast at one of the magmen's faces, splitting it open. He then skidded to a stop, dropped on his back, pulled his knees to his chest, and shot a blast of fire at two of the others. Both of them split open at the chest. The remaining two charged Maxstrom; but he was ready. He quickly did a back roll, and shot two fire blasts at the last two magmen's heads. Both split open.

"Watch out behind you!" A voice behind Maxstrom called.

Maxstrom turned and looked up to see a magman jumping towards him, and then saw a Tabee spear impale the monster and throw it into the ground.

"Thanks Bezka!" Maxstrom called through the loud noise of the fight.

"You're welcome human, I mean Max." Bezka responded.

The Tabees quickly filled in the Shadican Army's rear flank, as well as continuing through the center to bolster the sections of the Shadican formation that were weakened. The group of over a thousand katlicans was in a circle, facing the enemy on all sides.

"Dusty, watch your flank!" Akbu yelled, seeing the young Shadican was filling in an open spot in the formation.

Dusty quickly turned to his left and saw a magman charging him. In response, Dusty launched a powerful fire kick to stop the foe. The strike landed, but only knocked the magman back.

"Really?!" Dusty yelled in distress.

He then entrenched his stance and launched another fire kick at the downed magman, this time splitting him open.

"That's better." Dusty muttered.

Dusty heard a loud yell come from behind him, and then looked up to see a Shadican flying through the air; it was Akbu, sword first again. His blade landed right in the face of a magman about fifteen feet to Dusty's right.

"You're other flank." Akbu informed.

"Oh. Whoops. Thanks Akbu."

"No problem!" Akbu responded as he quickly retrieved his sword, and prepared to kill another magman running at him.

Maxstrom had decided to climb up on a large nearby boulder and launch fire attacks from a distance instead of joining the formation. Doing so gave him plenty of clear shots at the backs of unsuspecting magmen. He even found that he could get two or three with one shot if they were lined up right.

"Ha!" Maxstrom yelled as he split three magmen open with one strike.

"Max, to your left!" Dusty called from below.

Maxstrom turned to see a magman had just finished climbing up the massive boulder, and was charging at him. He quickly stepped to the side, and the magman charged headfirst off the boulder, and split his head on a rock.

But then Maxstrom heard a noise behind him, and saw another magman had just climbed up. This time, instead of trying to charge him, the monster aimed his rock sword at Maxstrom. The magman then swung for

Maxstrom's head, and Maxstrom ducked under the blade, shooting a fire blast at the magman's gut. The blow hit, but because Maxstrom had been so rushed in dodging the strike, his blow was not powerful enough to split the magman open. Instead, the monster simply staggered back.

"Woops." Maxstrom exclaimed in a flustered tone.

The monster then swung for Maxstrom's chest, and Maxstrom stepped backwards. There was a ripping sound as the magman's sword sliced the metal plate of Maxstrom's armor open, but Maxstrom was unharmed. Maxstrom then pulled his fist back and shot a large fire blast at the magman's body. The strike split the monster open, sending debris into hundreds of pieces over the magmen below.

Maxstrom paused for a moment to catch his breath, and then rejoined the fight.

"The east side is collapsing! Fill the gap!" Shacbu cried.

She then looked around and saw that no one was able to respond. The line was barely holding as it was. So she quickly jumped over from her position in the line, and ran at three magmen that had just broken through.

The three magmen, who were unsure of where to go after getting behind the katlican formation, saw Shacbu, and quickly redirected their attention to her; charging at their newfound target. Shacbu started running at them, and just as they were in range, she dropped to a slide, and stabbed the first magman in the chest. But due to the momentum, she had to let go of her sword while it was still in the magman's body. He staggered to a halt and collapsed, but the other two spun around to face their weaponless foe.

"Great." Shacbu mumbled under hear breath.

She then looked around to see if there were any weapons nearby. To her relief, she saw a Tabee spear; but it was halfway between her and the other two magman.

Her mind raced. She had to get the magmen away from the spear so she could get to it.

"Come on, boys! Come and get me if you dare!" She taunted.

The two magmen looked at each other, and then both simultaneous started charging at her. She started running away from them for a moment, and then stopped. The magmen were still charging. She then started running towards them; still weaponless. The magmen didn't hesitate, and were poised to strike. But just as they were about to close their range, Shacbu leapt into the air and dove between the two monsters, throwing herself into a roll on the other side of them while grabbing the Tabee spear. She then looked up to see her two foes grinding to a halt, and turning to face her again.

"Round three?" She inquired with a smirk.

The two monsters began charging her yet again. This time, she simply held her ground, and thrust her spear into the magmen on her right once he was within range. She then threw herself to the right to avoid the strike of the magman on the left, while still gripping her spear. She then ripped the spear out of the magman she had just killed, and threw the heavy spear straight into the head of the other magman; splitting it into pieces.

Shacbu let out a labored breath. She felt exhausted after that match.

"Shacbu, watch out!" Dusty called.

Shacbu looked up to see Dusty launch a fire blast past her and into a magman that had broken through to her left.

"Thanks Dusty!" Shacbu yelled.

"You good?" Dusty inquired, running over to her.

"Yeah. I'm fine. Just a bit worn out." She responded as she picked up the Tabee spear. "Let's get back to work."

Maxstrom looked around. The magmen were climbing up the boulder he was on from all sides, and he couldn't keep them back any longer. His eyes darted around the immediate terrain to see if there was a route for him to escape, and his gaze found a smaller nearby boulder about ten feet away in the opposite direction of the katlican formation. He wasted no time, and started running towards it. Just as he was about to leap, he saw a magman's head appear in his path; so he took an extra step and used the monster's face to leap towards the smaller boulder. Within seconds, he had landed; both of his feet hitting the boulder at the same time. He then quickly dropped on his back, pulled his feet to his chest, and launched a massive fire blast at the boulder he had just left. But instead of shooting a short burst, he kept the blast up for about fifteen seconds.

Suddenly, there was a giant cracking sound from where he had just been. Maxstrom looked past his feet and realized that part of the boulder had exploded! His eyes searched for any remaining magmen in the vicinity, but saw that they all had been destroyed.

Maxstrom gasped for breath. That strike had taken a good deal of his energy. His respite was short lived, however, as he saw a magman's head appear to his right; the monster was climbing up and about to attack him.

"Oh no you don't." Maxstrom declared, and shot a fire blast at the magman's head.

Bezka dropped to the ground and cut both of the magman's legs off. He then swung his sword up and drove it into the falling magman's face.

"Nice one!" Zepak yelled to his commander.

"Thanks!" Bezka responded, jumping to his feet.

He looked around the battlefield. While there were still plenty of magmen to kill; none were in his vicinity. So he decided to break formation and go hunt the magmen that were still running amongst the boulders.

"Where are you going?" Fika exclaimed.

Bezka gave no reply. He was grinning; ready to give more magmen a taste of his blade.

Suddenly, a magman stepped out from behind the boulder he was running past. Bezka tried to bring his sword up, but he was just too close. He impacted into the magman, throwing both him and the monster to the ground.

Bezka was on his feet in an instant; but he had lost his sword. It had flown out of his hand, and was lying about ten feet to his right. But standing next to his sword was another magman. Furthermore, the magman Bezka had just thrown to the ground let out an evil shriek, and stood to his feet. The monster then started running at Bezka with its mace ready. Bezka realized he would have to fight these magmen without his weapon; there was no other way. So he waited for the magman charging him to swing, and then ducked the strike. He then grabbed the magman's mace with his right hand to block its use, and swung the claws of his left hand against the monster's face. A nasty, high pitched scratching sound followed, and the magman's head snapped to the side from the force of this strike. Bezka then put his leg behind the magman's leg, and threw the creature to the ground. There happened to be a small rock directly where Bezka threw the magman's head, which split the creature's head open upon impact. Bezka smirked. He didn't even need a sword to beat these monsters.

But then he heard running behind him, and realized he had forgotten the other magman. He instinctively ducked, and dodged the magman's apparent sword strike. The creature staggered past Bezka, and then turned to face him.

"Come on!" Bezka yelled.

But then, two more magmen ran over to join their friend. The first magman looked back at his friends, glared at Bezka, and then gave an evil grin. Bezka turned to go for his sword, but saw another magman step out directly behind it. He then spun around to try and escape; but it was no good. Two more magmen stood blocking the remaining exit, all grinning. He was boxed in, with no weapon to defend himself.

"I guess I'm not that good after all." Bezka muttered.

Suddenly, he saw a flash of flame come from one of the boulders above, and split the magman open next to his sword. Maxstrom, who had launched this attack, dropped down next to the slain creature, grabbed Bezka's sword, and tossed it to him.

"Thanks!" Bezka exclaimed, and then spun around to face the other five magmen.

"Don't mention it." Maxstrom responded, and shot two quick blasts of fire around Bezka, lowering the number of magmen to three.

The three remaining creatures were shocked, and decided to push what little advantage they still had. All three started running for Bezka.

"Come on boys!" Bezka exclaimed as he swung his sword.

Maxstrom, who was ready to help the Tabee more, saw that Bezka had this fight well in hand. So he quickly climbed back up onto the boulder he had jumped from.

"The enemy is weak! Push the advantage!" General Tak cried above the noise of the battle.

He then took his spear and threw it into a magman's head.

"We can beat them! Come on!" He yelled as he drew his sword and ran at another magman near him.

The magman simply stared at Tak in surprise as his foe closed in. Within seconds, Tak had cleaved the monster in half at the waist, and then decapitated him.

The Tabees then let out a war yell, and started pushing the circumference of the formation; fighting viciously the whole way.

"There's not many left!" Maxstrom, who had just reclaimed his view of the battle, yelled down to General Tak.

"We've almost got them all; come on!" General Tak hollered as he impaled yet another magman.

Shacbu looked up. The battlefield now felt uncomfortably quiet. Her eyes scanned the surrounding area for the enemy, but only saw Tabees and Shadicans remaining.

"Finally." She whispered to herself.

She tried to let go of the Tabee sword she had picked up; but her paw wouldn't open. She tried to shake it violently, but still her grip remained frozen to the handle of the sword.

"Gah!" She yelled.

"You okay?" Akbu inquired, running over to her.

"I'm fine." Shacbu responded, embarrassed. "I just can't drop the sword."

"Oh. That's normal after a long fight. Here, let me help you." Akbu informed, reaching for Shacbu's paw.

He then gently peeled her fingers back one at a time.

"Thanks." Shacbu responded once the Tabee blade had clattered to the ground.

"Of course."

Shacbu then took in a deep breath.

"That was terrible." She declared, looking around the battlefield at all of the dead.

Suddenly Akbu had a look of horror cross his face.

"What?" Shacbu asked, surprised at his expression.

"Tapito! We have to find her!" Akbu cried, and ran off into the rubble."

Tapito gasped for air. It was getting hard to breath; the boulder that had knocked her down was still on top of her waist.

"Tapito!" A voice called out of the quiet.

"Here!" She gasped, hardly able to yell.

"I heard something. Over there! Come on!" A voice yelled from a distance.

After a moment, Tapito could hear the patter of several pairs of feet.

"No!" Akbu cried, dropping to his knees next to his chief.

"We need help over here!" Shacbu yelled.

"It's no use." Tapito declared. "You're not going to be able to move the boulder. Even if you could; we both know I don't have much time left."

Maxstrom, who had heard Shacbu's cry for help, came running over.

"Tapito!" Maxstrom yelled.

"Hey, Max." Tapito whispered.

"Let's get this boulder off of her! Give me a hand, Akbu."

"No Max. It's too heavy." Akbu responded.

"No! Tapito!" Maxstrom yelled, falling to his knees.

"It's okay Max. It's my time. Did we win?" Tapito inquired with another whisper.

"Yes; Shacbu led the army to a glorious victory." Akbu responded.

"Good. She will do well as the next chief. Max?"

"Yes, chief?"

"I've. Always considered you. As a son."

"And I've always considered you as a mother." Maxstrom responded as he wiped a tear from his cheek.

"I'm. Sorry."

"For what, chief?"

Tapito raised her paw, and beckoned for Maxstrom to come closer. He quickly leaned his ear towards her mouth.

"I'm sorry I didn't tell you sooner." She whispered quietly.

"Tell me what?"

"There's. A scroll. From your father." Tapito could barely speak now.

"What?" Maxstrom inquired through both grief and shock.

"It's in my. Pouch." Tapito declared, looking towards the satchel a couple of feet from her and trying to reach for it with her one good paw.

"Hey, I got it. I got it." Maxstrom said, stopping her paw. He then reached into her pack and pulled out a large scroll.

"I'm. Sorry. Max." And with that, Tapito let out her last breath.

"No. No! Tapito! Tapito!" Maxstrom cried.

He then sat back on the ground and wept. Shacbu simply looked around in shock; she wasn't able to cry. She didn't know what to think or what to do.

Maxstrom felt a paw on his shoulder. He looked up to see it was Akbu, and then realized that several Tabees had gathered around and were standing a short distance away.

"It'll all be okay, Max." Akbu informed through tears of his own.

"Will it?" Maxstrom questioned.

"Yes. It's hard, and we'll miss her. But there's a beautiful Shadican proverb that is appropriate for times like this. It says that 'For those who follow Him, death is not the end. Rather, it is a glorious new beginning in perfection.' She was a follower of Yasha, Max. We'll see her again."

Maxstrom reached over and gave Akbu a hug. Akbu quickly returned the hug. Maxstrom then reached over and pulled Shacbu in for a hug as well.

"It'll all be okay, Max. It'll all be okay." Akbu assured.

"The Tabees will provide an escort for Tapito as she makes her final journey back to Shavi." General Tak declared as he was having his arm wrapped. He had taken a minor cut from a magman's sword.

"Good. She deserves that." Akbu responded, as he wiped a tear from his eye. He then looked at General Tak, and saw his eyes looked moist.

"Tak, are you okay?"

"Yes. It's just that Tapito was a great leader. She will be missed." Tak replied, stifling his emotions to appear strong.

"Sir!" A Shadican yelled, running up to Akbu.

"What is it?" Akbu inquired, spinning around.

"It's Makbu. Our scouts found him in the mountains; the magmen got him."

"So that's why there were so many magmen in the mountains." Akbu mumbled.

"Dusty is going to be heartbroken. . ." Shacbu interjected.

"The other Tabee leader that came with us also found a weird creature, some kind of tunnel mole or something. Apparently the creature was forced to dig the tunnels for the magmen."

"That's how they created that tunnel." Akbu thought aloud.

"Do we have a count on the dead yet?" General Tak inquired after a moment of silence.

"Not yet." Akbu responded.

General Tak stood to his feet and dismissed the Shadican that had been wrapping his arm.

"I do not look forward to those numbers. Today has been a day of great loss." The General said in a somber tone.

"Indeed. Hey, did you see where Max went?" Akbu inquired.

"He went that way." General Tak said as he pointed north.

"Thanks." Akbu responded as he started walking.

"I suppose I should go find Dusty. . ." Shacbu sighed as she stepped towards where Dusty had last been seen.

Akbu navigated his way around several massive boulders before reaching a grouping of pine trees. He then pushed through the branches, and saw a clearing in the middle. Maxstrom had found a rock from the avalanche in the clearing, and was sitting on it. He had the scroll open in his hands with his back facing Akbu.

"Max. Are you okay?"

"Not really." Maxstrom responded, not looking back.

"I know this is hard. . ."

"I'm going back, Akbu."

"What?" Akbu questioned, confused. "Max, of course we're going back to Shavi."

"No. I mean I'm going back to Dauchenland."

"Max. I know you're upset, but you can't make that big of a decision right now, especially since Ottokar told you not to go back in spite of the news."

"You knew?" Maxstrom inquired angrily as he spun around.

Akbu paused.

"Yes, Max. I knew Tapito had the letter. She let me read it."

"Then why didn't you tell me!" Maxstrom yelled as he stood up and towered above Akbu.

"She ordered me not to say anything. Tapito didn't want to ruin your hope of being reunited with your family."

Maxstrom sat back down and stared at the ground.

"She wanted to tell you; she just couldn't bring herself to do it."

"How long have you had this?" Maxstrom asked.

"Since about two month before you and Dusty left for Duba."

"You've had this message for seven months!?" Maxstrom yelled as looked up at Akbu.

"I know, Max. I thought she should have told you sooner."

Maxstrom looked off into the distance.

"Max. . ."

"Akbu, I need to find out what happened to my father."

"Max. I hate to say this, but what if he's dead?"

"Then I need to find out for sure!" Maxstrom yelled. "I need to know! This scroll from him just leaves me with uncertainty!"

Both fell silent for a moment.

"I'm leaving, Akbu." Maxstrom declared, looking up into Akbu's eyes. "I'm going back to Dauchenland, and I'm going to find out what happened to my father."

"And nothing I say or do will stop you?"

"No."

"Then you are free to go. But let's just take one day at a time. Today was a hard day; let's just focus on recovering from that first, okay?"

Maxstrom took a deep breath.

"Okay."

Conclusion

Fess was growing impatient. The denac were never good at waiting. But then Fess thought he saw something in the distance traveling with rapid speed.

"Finally." Fess whispered to himself sinisterly in a serpentine voice.

After a moment, Sess, a twin denac to Fess, arrived.

"What took you so long?" Fess muttered in an angry tone.

"Shut up, Fess! I had to fight a luminous being Yasha sent after me. And then I ended up having to go past one of the dragon's lairs near the Salt Lake. You're lucky I even made it." Sess snapped back.

"Excuses, excuses. So tell me, how did the test run go?" Fess inquired, curious.

"The magmen performed quite well. But they're all dead now."

"Shame." Fess declared. "But nothing that wasn't expected. If the katlicans had fallen to that small amount of magmen, they wouldn't be worthy of the reputation they have."

"We'll have to get him to make more for us; many more. But I think we have perfected the design that Upa once had." Sess informed with a smirk.

"Good!"

"But, I don't think we will have as much luck attacking the katlicans again. Those Tabees are fast learners, and enlisted the help of the tunnel moles to ward off any further tunneling towards the katlican home that we may try. They also collapsed all of the tunnels that we had."

"Oh well, that's quite alright. Once the human makes enough magmen for us with the Tradjan Jewel, we'll just conquer the rest of the world first."

Both of the denac began laughing manically at this declaration.

"And do the katlicans have any idea where the magmen came from?"

"No. They think we're in the mountains east of the Dactalyon Wasteland."

"Fess! Sess! What's the report?" A voice called from deeper in the tunnel.

"Guess we should update the human." Fess muttered with a scowl.

"Indeed, indeed. Lead the way; I'm right behind you." Sess hissed in reply.

Character Index

It is important to note, dear reader, that not all of these characters are humans. Most, in fact, are not. As such, the ages of non-human characters listed is not to be understood in human terms, but rather within the terms of each kind. All katlicans come of age at 13 years old, while fire phoenixes come of age at 3 years old.

Also, bear in mind that there is a gap of 8 years of time between the first two chapters of this book. All ages, unless otherwise specified, are as of the second chapter of the book, which takes place in B.Y. 4013.

Abada. Abada is the God of Balyita, an all-powerful being that created everything. He is a good being; in fact, good and the God of Balyita are intertwined in nature. He also exists outside of time and the created realm; yet He chooses to try and have a relationship with His creation whenever possible.

Akbu. Akbu is a black furred katlican male who is a master of light, and thus is a Shadican. Akbu has blue eyes, and is distinguishable from most other Shadicans by the way he styles his fur; in a Mohawk at the top of his head. He is 21 years in age, and just over 3'6 in height. Akbu is the leader of the Elite Shadican Guard, and tasked with protecting the Shadican head chief. He fills the role of the Shadican's spiritual leader, and Akbu also bears the title of best swordsman in Shadicore. He's easy-going and fun loving, but also willing to kill anyone who may threaten the head chief. Akbu is the husband to Niba.

Alenard. Alenard is a male human, and a citizen of Dauchenland. He is on the Aceic Council, and thus is an ace. He has short brown hair, a jawline beard, and blue eyes. Alenard is 33 years old in the first chapter of this book (B.Y. 4005), has a muscular build, and is 5'10. He can control anything made out of stone, and his preferred move is to create armor for himself out of rock; assuming he doesn't need to get anywhere fast.

Aliofi. Aliofi is a male human, and a citizen of Dauchenland. He has blonde hair with a bald spot on the top back of his head, a goatee, dark eyebrows, and has brown eyes. Aliofi is 37 years old, has a scrawny build, and is 5'7. He is in charge of a large trading business in Dauchenland, and good friends with Ottokar, because Ottokar saved his life once.

Arkana. Arkana is a white furred katlican male, and thus is a Snowisean. He is 14 years of age, has yellow eyes and is approximately 3 feet in height. He is a member of the Snowisean Army stationed in Feshback, which is located in the southern part of Snowisea. Arkana is a new recruit to the army, so even though he is skilled, he is the lowest rank.

Bacham. Bacham is a male human, and a citizen of Dauchenland. He is a baker who agrees with how the Aceic Order has handled difficult matters over the years. Bacham has a balding head with a short black beard, and blue eyes. He is 35 years old as of the first chapter of this book (B.Y. 4005), has a big belly, and is 5'9. Bacham owns the best bakery in Haiedenburg.

Barz. Barz is a male human, and a citizen of Dauchenland. He has the ability to control fire, making him an ace. He has blonde hair, blue eyes, and is 12 years old as of the first chapter of this book (B.Y. 4005). He is only mentioned in passing between Ottokar and Maskima; they decided to keep his identity secret, and had initially planned on bringing him in to the order two years early for both training and protection.

Bezka. Bezka is a katlican male with black stripes, light grey fur, and a stubby tail, and is thus a Tabee. He is 3'8, has blue eyes, and a muscular build. Bezka is nephew to General Tak, and one of the top warriors of the Tabee tribe. He is determined, and loves a good fight. Bezka is the commander of a Tabee squad of warriors, although he has the authority to take charge of a large unit when he wants.

Chipo. Chipo is a black furred katlican male who has the potential to control light, and thus is a Shadican. He has yellow eyes, and is approximately 2 feet in height. Chipo also has a pink nose; a rare feature amongst the Shadicans. He is also a kit, being only 8 years of age. Chipo is the nephew of Makbu.

Chooan. Chooan is a grey furred katlican male, and thus is a Dolphinian. He has light brown eyes, is 23 years of age, and is just under 3 feet in height. He is the representative of the Dolphinian tribe in Shavi, and thus is the spokesperson for his tribe to the Shadicans.

Chuba. Chuba is a black furred katlican male, and thus is a Shadican. He has yellow eyes, is 15 years in age, and is 3'4. He also has a particularly long goatee for a Shadican, especially for his age. Chuba is a part time warrior stationed at Duba, and also works for a fishing business. Chuba is a goofy and fun loving Shadican.

Dega. Dega is a male human. He is a blond citizen of Dauchenland, has hazel eyes, and is 5'9. Dega is a trading companion to Aliofi, and accompanies his partner on their journey to the Shadic River with Maxstrom in B.Y. 4005.

Dubger. Dubger is a tunnel mole kidnapped by the magmen and forced to dig tunnels for them to attack Shadicore. Tunnel moles come from near the Dactalyon Wasteland, which is where Dubger is from. Dubger has the typical tunnel mole appearance; harry, has the facial appearance of a mole, has shovel-like hands, and is about ten feet in length.

Dudanca. Dudanca is a male human that has a fairly short haircut, a trim beard, and dark brown eyes. He is a citizen of Parcha, approximately 6 foot, and quite muscular with a few extra pounds. He is a trapper; which means his primary occupation is sneaking across the katlican border and taking prisoners back to sell to the highest bidder.

Dusca. Dusca is a black furred katlican female who has the potential to control light, and thus is a Shadican. 9 years of age, has orange eyes, and is approximately 2 ½ feet in height. She is the younger sister of Dusty, and as a result, she naturally enjoys annoying him. But secretly, Dusca looks up to him and has great respect for her older brother.

Dusty. Dusty is a black furred katlican male who has the potential to control light, and thus is a Shadican. He is 13 years of age, has green eyes, and is 3'5. Since he has the ability to control fire, Dusty is recognized as a fire ace by his fellow Shadicans. He is best friends and housemate to Maxstrom. Although sometimes Dusty might have his moments where he doesn't pay enough attention to the situation at hand, his problem solving skills are fantastic, and he is an incredibly loyal friend. He loves swords, weapons, and anything to do with fighting. Dusty also has incredibly soft fur in comparison to most other Shadicans, but this feature comes with the downside of his fur attracting dirt or other debris; and that's how he received his name.

Feftan. Feftan is a 5 year old male fire phoenix, and about 5 feet in length. He is clumsy and awkward, but has a good heart. As all fire phoenixes, he has the ability to talk, and he has red, orange, and yellow feathers, along with a long and slightly curved beak. He also has the ability to burst into flame without burning up, making him not an ace, but a gifted creature.

Fesha. Fesha is a black furred katlican male who has the potential to control light, and thus is a Shadican. He is 15 years of age, has yellow eyes, and is 3'5. He is a young Shadican who gets caught up in rumors and lies about Tapito, and ends up taking rash action against the Shadican leadership as a result.

Fess. Fess is an evil spirit, also known as a denac. Being an evil spirit, he is not always visible. But when Fess is visible, he is somewhat see-through, yet also dark in appearance. He resembles a serpent. Fess is one of the highest ranking denac remaining after the fall of Upa. He is a 'twin' to Sess.

Fika. Fika is a katlican male with black stripes, light grey fur, and a stubby tail, and is thus a Tabee. He is 3'6, has orange eyes, and has a muscular build. He is an outgoing, goofy, and sometimes careless Tabee. But Fika is a great warrior, and a loyal companion. He is most loyal to Bezka, the commander of his Tabee squadron.

Gumabu. Gumabu is a white furred katlican male, and thus is a Snowisean. He is 42 years of age, has blue eyes, and is approximately 3 feet in height. He is the elder that governs Feshback, and he is also the recognized leader of the Snowiseans. However, the Snowiseans have a more lax form of government than the other katlican tribes do, so Gumabu is usually not overwhelmingly busy. A bit hard of hearing, and is a caring soul. Gumabu is also a bit hunched over.

Habu. Habu is a white furred katlican male, and thus is a Snowisean. He is 30 years of age, has yellow eyes, and is 3'1. Habu is the captain of the

Snowisean forces stationed in Feshback, which also makes him head of the small Snowisean Army. He is a feisty commander who strives to inspire his troops by example, and is willing to lead his troops from the front lines.

Hiffa. Hiffa is a male human who can control both metal and the acidic sap from the ayoxium flower, and is thus an ace. Being an ace in Dauchenland, Hiffa had the potential to join the Aceic Order, but Kafahr claims that he refused this opportunity. Hiffa is 24 years old as of the first chapter of this book (B.Y. 4005), has brown eyes, a muscular build, a shaven face, thin eyebrows, and is barely 6 feet in height.

Ipachoo. Ipachoo is a grey furred katlican male, and thus is a Dolphinian. He is 10 years of age, has yellow eyes, and is 3'2. Although he is a Dolphinian, he was adopted by Dusty's family, and thus is Dusty's brother.

Javon. Javon is a male human who can control both stone and dirt, and is thus an ace. He is also on the Aceic Council. He is 30 years old as of the first chapter of this book (B.Y. 4005), has green eyes, a lean muscular build, a squared goatee, and is 6 feet in height. Technically, Javon is from Parcha, but since he was adopted by the Aceic Order, he is also recognized as a citizen of Dauchenland.

Kafahr. Kafahr is a male human, heir to the throne of Dauchenland, and nephew to Lustan. He is 47 years old as of the first chapter of the book (B.Y. 4005), has light blue eyes, is somewhat athletic, and is 5'5. He has average length black hair in a bowl-cut style, as well as a thin moustache that is accompanied by a goatee. He is the evil leader of the Purman Order, which takes over Dauchenland after Lustan's death. Kafahr sets out to destroy the Aceic Order, and publicly blames them for Lustan's difficult rule.

Kefa. Kefa is a katlican male with black stripes, light grey fur, and a stubby tail, and is thus a Tabee. He is 26 years in age, has the usual muscular build of the Tabees, has light brown eyes, and is 3'7. He is 2nd in command of the Tabee troops that accompany General Tak.

Klanab. Klanab is a male human, citizen of Parcha, and a trapper of katlicans. He is somewhat new to the business, is only 28 years old, has a muscular build, has light blue eyes, and is 6'5 in height. He keeps his hair and beard short. Klanab is a bit of a meathead, and doesn't always think about what's going on.

Kusan. Kusan is a male human, and citizen of Dauchenland. He is the father of the Kafahr, and brother to Lustan, making Kusan royalty. He died before this book begins at the age of 60. He had thick, black hair along with a thick beard, and was 5'9 in height. Kusan also had blue eyes. He hated the Aces, and instilled in his son the same hatred. In fact, Kusan started the underground organization of the "ghosts," or assassins, also known as the Purman Order, to begin weakening the Aceic Order. Overall, the mission was an incredible success.

Lazda. Lazda is a black furred katlican male that has the potential to control light, and is thus a Shadican. He has yellow eyes, is 3'5, 40 years of age, and has a frail build. Lazda is the elder of Duba. He is quite energetic and expressive.

Lubu. Lubu is a black furred katlican male that has the potential to control light, and is thus a Shadican. He has orange eyes, is 3'2, 12 years of age, and has a normal build. Lubu is a bully, and enjoys picking on katlicans around his age.

Lustan. Lustan is male human, and the King of Dauchenland that dies in the first chapter of this book (B.Y. 4005); in fact, his death starts the story. Lustan died at 75 years old, and naturally had white, thinning hair along with a white beard. He had brown eyes, and was quite frail in his final years due to sickness. He was 5'10 in height. Lustan was a bad king, and abused his authority by forcing the people of Dauchenland to find him gold. In other words, he allowed his desire for material wealth to come before other people.

Makbu. Makbu is a black furred katlican male that can control both light and fire, and is thus a Shadican. He is 2'11 in height, has yellow eyes, and has moderate muscle due to his heavy focus on cardio. He also has longer fur on the sides of his face, giving the appearance of having sideburns. Makbu acts a bit crazy at times, although in reality he is entirely in control of his actions. He prefers to be withdrawn from society; and dislikes too much social interaction. He prefers to spend much of his time in the mountains drawing closer to Abada. In other words, Makbu is an introvert. He is one of the few Shadicans that can control more than just light; he is a master at both light and fire. Makbu is also known amongst the southern part of Shadicore for having great wisdom.

Maskima. Maskima is a male human citizen of Dauchenland who can control sound and water, and is thus an ace. He is also the head of the Aceic Order's council; making him the commander of the Aces. He has grey hair along with a greyish-silver beard, is 6 feet in height, and has blue, kind eyes. He is 61 years old as of the first chapter of this book (B.Y. 4005), but is quite muscular for his age. He is also known for having wrinkles on his face from smiling so much in his life, even in darker days. He is also the father of Matakar.

Matakar. Matakar is a male human citizen of Dauchenland, and the son of Maskima. He is 6'1, has brown hair and a beard, brown eyes, and is 24 as of the first chapter of this book (B.Y. 4005). Matakar can control rock and has the rare ability of being able to turn rock into lava, and is thus an ace. He is also an Aceic soldier, and is stationed in the southern part of Dauchenland before the Purman Order came to power.

Maxstrom. Maxstrom is a male human who can control both fire and water, and is thus an ace. He is 8 years old when the book begins (B.Y. 4005), and is 16 as of the second chapter (B.Y. 4013). Maxstrom has dark green eyes, dirty blonde hair, and is 6'3 in B.Y. 4013. He is a citizen of Dauchenland, but a resident of Shadicore due to the takeover of the Purman Order. He is the main character in this book.

Meeka. Meeka is a black furred katlican female who has the potential to control light, and is thus a Shadican. She is 3'4, has yellow eyes, is 30 years old, and has a lean build. She also has a pink nose; one of the few Shadicans to own such a feature. Meeka is Dusty, Dusca, and Ipachoo's mother.

Nacha. Nacha is a white furred katlican female, and is thus a Snowisean. She is 3'5, has blue eyes, is 16 years old, and has a slightly muscular body. She is a Snowisean warrior stationed at Feshback. Nacha doesn't like humans because her sister, Sancha, was kidnapped by trappers a couple years ago.

Nakbu. Nakbu is a black furred katlican male that has the potential to control light, and is thus a Shadican. He is 3'3, has yellow eyes, and is 25 years of age with a normal body build. Nakbu is a member of the Elite Guard that is responsible for keeping Tapito safe.

Nandu. Nandu is a black furred katlican male that has the potential to control light, and is thus a Shadican. He is 3'7, has orange eyes, is 22 years of age, and has a normal body build. Nandu is one of Tapito's lower ranking advisors appointed by the Shadicans, and as a result only shows up for major decisions.

Nathar. Nathar is a male human Saoland tribesman. He is 17 years old, is 5'11, has brown eyes, and has light brown hair that is about 3 inches in length. Nathar is quite ambitious, and does not easily trust those around him.

Niba. Niba is a black furred katlican female that has the potential to control light, and is thus a Shadican. She is 3'4, has green eyes, is 19 years of age, and has a normal build. Niba is a soldier in the Shadican Army, and she is married to Akbu.

Nikacha. Nikacha is a black furred katlican male that has the potential to control light, and is thus a Shadican. He is 3'6, has yellow eyes, is 28 years of age, and has a muscular build. Nikacha is a Shadican soldier who is particularly good at directing the Shadicans in formation.

Ofpila. Ofpila is a female human citizen of Parcha. She is 30 years old, is 5'6, has hazel eyes, and black hair. She is a trapper that attempts to capture katlicans and sell them to circuses or the highest bidder. Ofpila is quite vain; taking an obsessive interest in diamonds, gold, and the like.

Ottokar. Ottokar is a male human citizen of Dauchenland that can control fire, and is thus an ace. He is 38 years old as of the first chapter of this book (B.Y. 4005), is 6'2, has brown eyes, and short black hair with a trim moustache and goatee. He is a citizen of Dauchenland, and is a member of the Aceic Council. Ottokar is an espionage and intelligence expert within the Aceic Order, and he is also quite familiar with celestial navigation. One of his favorite attacks in a fight is to use blue fire. Ottokar is also Maxstrom's father, and the husband of Retta.

Puka. Puka is a black furred katlican male that has the potential to control light, and thus is a Shadican. He has yellow eyes, is 3'4, 20 years of age, and has a normal build. Puka is a warrior stationed in Duba.

Putkan. Putkan is a male human that can control electricity, and is thus an ace. He is 35 years old as of the first chapter of this book (B.Y. 4005), is 6 feet in height, has blue eyes, and has brown hair that is almost styled into a mullet. He also has a pointy goatee on his chin. Putkan is a member of the Aceic Council, and is normally a kind individual.

However, his wife was recently killed, and Putkan still has rage pent up from the incident, making him a very unpleasant person.

Rayduan. Rayduan is a male human Saoland tribesman that can control water, and is thus an ace. He is 43 years old, is 5'11, has hazel eyes, and has light blonde hair. Rayduan is an experienced water ace that lives a life of solitude. He is not a member of the Aceic Order.

Retta. Retta is a female human Saoland tribeswoman, but since she married Ottokar, she also has a Dauchenland citizenship. She 39 years of age as of the first chapter of this book (B.Y. 4005), is 5'8, has hazel eyes, and has brown hair. She is also the mother of Maxstrom.

Rina. Rina is a female human tribeswoman of Saoland. She is 36 years of age, has blue eyes, and has brown hair. She is a resident of the town of Glas. Rina is a natural host and caretaker to anyone that she comes in contact with. Rina is also the mother of Nathar.

Sancha. Sancha is a white furred katlican female, and is thus a Snowisean. Her appearance is unknown, as she is only mentioned once in passing to Maxstrom. Sancha is the sister of Nacha that was captured by trappers.

Sess. Sess is an evil spirit, or a denac. Being an evil spirit, he is not always visible. But when Sess is visible, he is somewhat see-through, yet also dark in appearance. He resembles a serpent. Sess is one of the highest ranking denac remaining after the fall of Upa, and 'twin' to Fess.

Shacbu. Shacbu is a black furred katlican female who can control light, and thus is a Shadican. She is 14 years of age, has deep green eyes, and is 3'5. Shacbu also has deep green eyes, and a small spot of fur on the top of her head next to her left ear that is red. She is the heir to the Shadican chief; meaning that she is to succeed Tapito when Tapito dies. This responsibility puts a lot of pressure on this young katlican, as her fighting has to be top notch to be able to inherit the position. If she fails, she runs the risk of being outcast by all Shadicans forever.

Shadan. Shadan is a black furred katlican male who has the potential to control light, and is thus a Shadican. He is 39 years of age, has sunken blue eyes, and is only 3'3 in height, not factoring in that he is somewhat hunched over. He is an older Shadican, and is Tapito's advisor from when she took over the position of head chief. He often has wise insights about troubling issues, but he usually has trouble staying awake during meetings and other pleasantries.

Sheni. Sheni is a black furred katlican female who has the potential to control light, and is thus a Shadican. She is 3'5, has yellow eyes, and an average build. During the day, Sheni is a teacher. She explains various farming techniques and how and why stuff grows to Shadican kits, as well as teaching tricks for growing plants more efficiently. Sheni also serves the role of night guard in the Shadican capital of Shavi on a rotational basis, meaning she only fills the role once or twice a week, and usually only takes a shift if it fits her teaching schedule.

Tak. General Tak the twelfth is a katlican male with black stripes, light grey fur, and a stubby tail, and is thus a Tabee. He is 3'9, has deep blue eyes, and is incredibly muscular, even for a Tabee; and the Tabees are known for being naturally strong. Tak is the commander of all of the Tabees, and thus is recognized as General Tak. He is a vicious and determined warrior, ready to crush those who stand in the way of safety for his tribe, or for any of the surrounding katlican tribes.

Talican. Talican is a black furred katlican male who has the potential to control light, and thus is a Shadican. He is 23 years of age, has green eyes, is 3'5 in height, and has a normal build. Talican is one of Tapito's lower ranking advisors elected by the Shadicans, and thus only occasionally shows up to meetings with the chief. He is also a soldier in the Shadican Army. Talican despises Akbu.

Tapito. Tapito is a black furred katlican female who is a master of controlling light, and thus is a Shadican. She is 30 years of age, has yellow eyes and spot of white fur at the base of her neck, is missing a piece of her right ear, and is 3 feet in height. She has a slim, but fit body build. Tapito is the current head chief of the Shadican tribe, and as a result is recognized as the 'leader' of all the katlicans. She is also a friend of Ottokar, although at a distance, since they live half a continent away.

Turibu. Turibu is a black furred katlican male who has the potential to control light, and thus is a Shadican. He is 25 years of age, has yellow eyes, is 3'7 in height, and has a moderately muscular build. He also has a patch of white fur that surrounds his left eye, which makes him stand out from most Shadicans. Turibu is a highly respected individual within Shadican society, and thus will show up to speak with the chief from time to time. He is a retired member of the Shadican Army with mostly honorable service. Turibu also has a bit of a temper.

Wachuna. Wachuna is a black furred katlican male who has the potential to control light, and thus is a Shadican. He is 20 years of age, has green eyes, is 3'7, and has a somewhat muscular build. Wachuna is a member of the Elite Guard tasked with keeping the chief safe. Wachuna can be cranky at times, and will sometimes snap at those around him as a result. He also has hearing damage from an accident when he was a kit.

Yasha. Yasha is the son of Abada, known as the God of Balyita. He has deep blue eyes, dark brown curly hair, and a short beard. He is around 6 feet in height. He is fully God and man, and sacrificed His life to save His creation well before this book takes place. Since He was a perfect sacrifice, He rose again with eternal life, and gives that gift to any who would ask Him and strive to do what is right. He sometimes walks amongst His creation on Balyita, lending aide to those in dire need.

Zepak. Zepak is a katlican male black stripes, light grey fur, and a stubby tail, and is thus a Tabee. He is 17 years of age, has orange eyes, is 3'7, and has the normal Tabee muscular build. Zepak is a quieter Tabee, but loyal to the death. He is one of Bezka's top soldiers and friends.

Location Index

Braxland. Braxland is one of the Northern Kingdoms that fragmented from the Kaben Empire. Braxland is North-East of Dauchenland. This kingdom does not hold any relevance for this particular book. The key feature of this kingdom is that it controls a massive lake with several outlets, which allows for rapid transportation and trade throughout its territory.

Chahami. The Empire of Chahami is not one of the fragments of the Kaben Empire; in fact, the Empire of Chahami was created only about two hundred years after the Kaben Empire was created. Consequently, Chahami is the oldest country present in the northern part of modern Balyita. Chahami is known for the massive wall that was constructed on its border. This wall was made to keep out the expanding Kaben Empire, and the wall succeeded in its mission; the wall has managed to keep the modern kingdom of Crugia at bay. Chahami is also known for crafting incredibly strong swords. The Empire of Chahami is not relevant for this particular book.

Crugia. Crugia is one of the Northern Kingdoms that fragmented from the Kaben Empire. Crugia is east and slightly south of Dauchenland. This kingdom does not hold any relevance for this particular book.

Dactalyon Wasteland. The Dactalyon Wasteland is a rough and incredibly rocky plane surrounded on three sides by mountain chains. No humans reside in the Dactalyon Wasteland, due to its inhospitable nature, and because of the dragons that make their homes in the vicinity. The tunnel moles also reside around this area, however, they usually stay underground. The Dactalyon Wasteland is to the south of Dauchenland, and borders Istria to the west.

Dauchenland. Dauchenland is the largest of the Northern Kingdoms that fragmented from the Kaben Empire. The Dauchenland Army is also the most powerful in comparison to all the other surrounding nations. Since Dauchenland is central amongst the Northern Kingdoms, they dominate most of the trading industry within the Northern Kingdoms of Balyita.

Chatburg. Chatburg is a small border fort. The primary feature of this fort is that there is a town, but most of the town is within the walls of the fort, and as a result, the town is quite small. This fort is left over from the second Dauchenland and Parchan war several hundred years before this book.

Haiedenburg. Haiedenburg is the capitol of Dauchenland, and is the largest city in the Northern Kingdom of Balyita. Directly to the east of this city is the Rhen River, although this section of the Rhen does not have its maximum width; the Rhen becomes much wider shortly after passing Haiedenburg, where it is fed by several other small streams. Across the smaller portion of the Rhen to the northeast of Haiedenburg lies the central command of the Aces; a small castle in the mountains. Besides having a river and mountains protecting it, Haiedenburg also has several small canyons dug outside of the walls to make an invasion even more difficult.

Nect River. The Nect River is a moderate sized river that passes through the west and southwestern part of Dauchenland. On either side of the Nect, numerous castles can be found serving both the purpose of protection, and tolls. The Nect feeds into the Bugden Marsh.

Rhen River. The Rhen River is a massive river that serves as the southern border of Dauchenland and Crugia. This border is the result of neither nation being able to successfully mount an invasion across it in past wars. The Rhen winds down to the south of Crugia, creating its southern most border, and then spills out into the Trak Sea, which is the expanse of water between Crugia and Chahami.

Strom Forest. The Strom Forest is a forest in the southern part of Dauchenland, and is between Haiedenburg and Sudberg. The forest also touches a section of the Rhen River.

Sudberg. Sudberg is a small castle with a town in the far south east-ern corner of Dauchenland against the Rhen River and the southern mountains. Considerable unrest against the Aceic Order has been seen in this town as of the beginning of this book.

Tharin. Tharin is a large city in Dauchenland. It has great control over those journeying to Parcha and Istria, and is central amongst these trading routes.

Denga Desert. The Denga Desert is a large desert between Parcha and the Shadic River. This desert serves as a natural deterrent against invasion to the katlican homeland. Also, there are legends of sand monsters that live in the desert, and these stories adds to the psychological effect of this desert being an impassible boundary.

Dolphinian States. The Dolphinian States are several sections of land owned by the Dolphinians, both on the main continent and off on several small islands in the Western Ocean. These states are largely irrelevant for this book.

Istria. Istria is the remains of the reformed Kaben Empire after its fall. Istria is nothing like the former Empire in glory, size, or might; in fact, Istria is the smallest of all of the Northern Kingdoms.

Parcha. Parcha is one of the Northern Kingdoms that fragmented from the Kaben Empire, and lies to the west of Dauchenland. Although Parcha is not a massive country, the Parchan people are quite hardy.

Chateau Lance. Chateau Lance is a small fort. The primary purpose of Chateau Lance is to serve as a border fort against the kingdom of Dauchenland. It is a remnant of the second Dauchenland Parchan war from several hundred years before.

Chatel Crete. Chatel Crete is a town used as a base of operation for those looking to cross the Denga Desert and to trade with the Shadicans.

Chatel Mill. Chatel Mill is a large town that is in the middle of the kingdom of Parcha, and serves as a central trade town. Most roads throughout the country converge at Mill, making it an inevitable stop in almost any journey throughout the country.

Saoland. Saoland is a small country, primarily inhabited by tribesmen that are separated into various clans in the mountains and highlands north of Snowisea.

Glas. Glas is a small town just north of the Snowisean border, and not far from the foot of the mountains.

Skye. Skye is the capital of Saoland, and the center of the largest tribe. It is also the only "city" in Saoland.

Shadicore. Shadicore is the largest of the katlican states, and the home of the Shadicans. This place is where Maxstrom is sent by his father, Ottokar, for safe keeping.

Baki. Baki is an incredibly small town just east of the town of Shavi. Baki is a port and fishing town resting on the Shadic River.

Chey Forest. The Chey Forest is a forest consisting of normal sized trees, such as pine, and serves as the southwestern border of Shadicore.

Duba. Duba is the largest 'city' in Shadicore besides Shavi, although it is closer to a large town in its size. The primary occupation of those that live in Duba is fishing because Duba is directly next to the Shadic River and south of Tuba Lake.

Kachuna Forest. Kachuna Forest is one of two forests with Brownwood pine trees in Shadicore. Shavi, the Shadican capitol, is located in this forest.

Lina. Lina is a small Shadican town just north of the Chey Forest.

Shadic River. The Shadic River is the river that starts at the border of Saoland and ends in the Tabee Swamp. It is one of the largest rivers in Balyita, and provides a formidable boundary against invasion from the east.

Shavi. Shavi is the capital of Shadicore, and is located in the Kachuna Forest. This city consists of thousands of treehouses constructed in the massive Brownwood pine trees of the south eastern corner of the Kachuna Forest.

Tuba Lake. Tuba Lake is the part of the Shadic River that bulges into a lake just north of Duba.

Ubu Forest. The Ubu Forest is a grouping of normal sized tree that serves as the southern border of Shadicore.

Snowisea. Snowisea is the home of the white furred katlicans, known as the Snowiseans. It is a single state that can be found north of Shadicore. This state primarily consists of various mountain ranges.

Feshback. Feshback is the capital of Snowisea. This particular city is spread out over a large area, while also being somewhat moderate in size.

Nuna Peak. Nuna Peak is the northern home of the fire phoenix tribe that Feftan is a member of. It resides somewhere in the mountain chain north of Feshback

Tabee State. The Tabee State is home to the katlicans that have black stripes, light grey fur, and a stubby tail; otherwise known as the Tabees. The Tabee State largely consists of both mountainous and swampy terrain; the Tabees are not creatures of comfort. They prefer the tactically critical ground to help keep their kind safe.

Fort Bek. Fort Bek is the Tabee fort just north of the Bugden Marsh. All of the Tabee's places of residence are forts; designed to ward off any impending threat. Fort Bek is a fairly large "town" with a system of walls surrounding it.

Fort Tip. Fort Tip is the Tabee fort on the western side of the state, and is located on a peninsula. This fort serves as a watch tower to fend off any invasion that could come from the ocean that poses a threat to the Tabees and the other katlican tribes. Fort Tip is a large port with a system of walls for protection.

Southern Peak. Southern Peak is a mountain that the fire phoenixes migrate to and from, and is located in the mountain just to the north of Fort Bek and across the Shadic River. The specific location is not verified, since this mountain is only known by this name to the fire phoenixes, and they usually keep to their own kind.

Tabee Swamp. The Tabee Swamp is a section of the Bugden Marsh that the Tabees claimed as their own to keep the southernmost katlican border safe. They rotate different units of their army through this area to keep a constant eye on a potential weak spot in their borders.

Dictionary

Abada. Another name for God in Balyita, most commonly used by the katlicans.

Ace. Any creature that can control one or more of any element or has some other form of gifted ability to control something within Balyita. All Shadicans can control light, but they rarely refer to themselves as "light aces" since the ability is common to them all, although not many master it in the modern era. Generally, Shadicans only call one of their kind an ace if he or she can control something beyond light.

Aceic Council. The council that leads the Aceic Order.

Aceic Order. A collection of Aces that adhere to the doctrine that all creatures are made equal by God, and as such deserve protection from evil, whether that evil appear in the form of man, beast, or spirit. The Aceic Order only consists of human aces, and aces are usually recruited at the age of fourteen to begin their training, which usually lasts for between two to four years.

Aceic Troop. A soldier within the Aceic Order.

Ayoxium Flower. A vibrant flower with deep purple outlined by neon green. It can be found in Parcha and the eastern border of Dauchenland, although it is not an incredibly common flower. The flower itself is usually less than a foot in height, and there are never more than three flowers that grow together at a time. The taproot, which extends deep into the ground, harbors a large amount of acidic sap that burns almost anything it touches. However, the stem and taproot covering this sap contains a neutralizing agent that renders the sap inert should there ever be a break or cut in the flower. The only way the sap can be removed while retaining its acidic form is by having an ace that can control the sap extract it through the flower head. Aces that can control the ayoxium flower sap can also control several other types of sap found in various plants throughout Balyita; while a couple are medicinal, most of them are completely useless for either medical or combative use.

Balyita. The name of the world that this story is told upon. It is pronounced Bal-Yita; the Y is not said as a vowel, but as a consonant.

Brownwood Pine Tree. The types of massive trees some Shadicans have used to hold their treehouses. Shavi, which is located in the Kachuna Forest, consists solely of Brownwood pine trees. These trees are also incredibly resilient; they can survive, and even thrive, after up to three quarters of the tree has been drilled out. They also can easily bear weight and structures built on the sides that other trees cannot.

Dolphinian. Any grey furred katlican. Dolphinians also have a gift; they can absorb oxygen from water around them, allowing them to hold their breath for longer periods of time underwater. Since this is not an ability to control an aspect of Balyita, this does not make them aces, but simply a gifted creature.

Fire Phoenix. A large bird with bright red, orange, and yellow feathers that is about five feet in length. The fire phoenixes can talk, and they also have the ability to burst into flame without burning up. This ability does not make them fire aces, but rather qualifies them as a gifted creature. The fire phoenixes have a long and slightly curved beak.

Katlican. A creature that stands between three to four feet in height when fully grown, and resembles both a cat and a human. Katlicans have many facial features in common with a cat, but most of their biological body resembles a human's. They can run on all fours; but since they often carry weapons and other items, they usually prefer to walk on their hind two feet, almost identical to a human. They also only have four fingers; they can use either the top or bottom finger, or both, as a thumb, allowing them the same ability of grip that a human has. Katlicans also have claws, fur all over their body, and a tail.

Kit. Katlican child.

Logas. Logas is Abada's Law given to creation. It contains a set of rules for optimal living on His creation, and if followed, grants the follower eternal life on the new earth yet to come. Failure to follow the law, even the smallest portion of it, results in eternal punishment. And everyone is guilty of failing the law on Balyita. But Abada did not leave all hopeless. He his son Yasha to pay the price for those who fail to keep the law, and those who accept His gift are given eternal life on the new earth.

Luminous Being. Heavenly beings that serve Abada.

Magman. A rock monster, resembling a human in shape, with magma flowing inside of its head, body, and limbs. It is possessed by an evil spirit minion, and that is how it can move and has 'life'.

Purman Order. The Purman Order is an organization set up by Kafahr, the King of Dauchenland. The supposed goal of this organization is to protect Dauchenland and purge itself of those who have 'harmed' the kingdom, and Kafahr purposefully incorrectly identifies these people as the Aceic Order, which is his means of revenge against the Aceic Order. Kafahr is also subtly using this order as a way to identify a common 'enemy' amongst the Dauchenland people and keep their focus elsewhere to help him institute a police state, which he believes is the best way to rule Dauchenland.

Shadican. A black furred katlican that has the potential to control light.

Snowisean. A white furred katlican. Snowiseans also have the ability to adjust their body temperature slightly to fit the environment they are in, which allows them to be able to thrive in colder climates.

Tabees. A katlican with black stripes, light grey fur, and a stubby tail. This species of katlican is naturally muscular and strong boned. The Tabees are also incredibly tough. They guard the southern part of the katlican states, and help fend off some of the more dangerous threats to their neighboring tribes.

Tunnel Mole. A tunnel mole is a large mole, measuring at about ten feet in length. They have shovel like feet, are harry, and have a face similar to that of a regular mole. These creatures hate being on the surface, and prefer to be deep underground, tunneling below Balyita. They can usually only be found underneath certain locations within the Dactalyon Wasteland. They are a rare kind of animal.

Year. The years on Balyita do operate on a three hundred and sixty-five day basis. However, those on Balyita do mark the months differently, and each year begins when winter is near an end, which means each New Year is rapidly followed by spring.